To Judy

God Bless you

[signature]

Pretty Bird

PHILIP JEFFRESS

LifeRich Publishing is a registered trademark of The Reader's Digest Association, Inc.

LifeRich Publishing books may be ordered through booksellers or by contacting:

LifeRich Publishing
1663 Liberty Drive
Bloomington, IN 47403
www.liferichpublishing.com
1 (888) 238-8637

ISBN: 978-1-4897-2383-3 (sc)
ISBN: 978-1-4897-2384-0 (hc)
ISBN: 978-1-4897-2382-6 (e)

Library of Congress Control Number: 2019909496

Printed in the United States of America.

LifeRich Publishing rev. date: 09/26/2019

1
CHAPTER

AWAKENED BY A PESKY horsefly and the urge to pee, Joshua knew to move quietly. Lonnie had warned him, "If you wake me up, I'll beat the snot out'a ya!" In his eleven years of existence, Joshua had never lost his snot to a beating, but he didn't like the sound of it. He slid out of bed quietly, tiptoed over to an open window, and peed on the ground below.

The air was dank and musty with the smell of common ragweed still wet from an early morning rain. A bantam rooster crowed his dutiful announcement of another new day, and a choir of cows in the neighboring pasture mooed their morning anthem in harmonic tones of deep bass, rich baritone, and high tenor. *The neighbor down the road has not yet fed his herd,* Joshua thought.

Early morning sunlight crept into the tiny cabin Joshua Jennings shared with his younger brother, Matthew, and their older stepbrother, Lonnie Crandall. Lonnie occupied the ground-level room, and the brothers shared a bed in an open loft accessible only by a narrow ladder.

Joshua slid back into bed to wait for his father's call to help feed livestock and milk their two cows in time to eat breakfast and get on to other chores.

He had been apprehensive since the day Lonnie arrived with his mother and two sisters following the merger of the Jennings and Crandall families. A burly lad of seventeen, Lonnie fit Joshua's image of an ogre in one of the make-believe stories his mother had told. He had splotches of unshaven beard that could not hide deep pockmarks etched in his face and neck. His disheveled hair never looked clean, even after he said he had bathed. His deep-set eyes seemed too far apart, or perhaps his nose was too small for the rest of his face. Words were scarce. Pleasantries and conversations were nonexistent.

Joshua grabbed at dust particles that seemed to shimmy up and down a shaft of sunlight that squeezed its way through a crack in the wall just above his head. He thought about how his life had changed since his mother's premature death almost three years earlier. Both he and his mother, Hannah Potter Jennings, had contracted pneumonia and were gravely ill for several days. He had trouble coming to terms with why he had been spared and his mother taken away. And now, he was even more resentful that his father had remarried and brought Lonnie into his life.

He rested on his back with his head cradled in his hands, his skinny and tanned but hairless legs extending out from under the sheet. His father's abrupt announcement rang in his memory.

"You boys will be just fine out here," Franklin said. "We need room in the house for me an' Maggie, an' the girls. Besides, Lonnie's older, an' he can help take care of you. It'll be the first time you've ever had an older brother."

That was that. It didn't matter that Joshua didn't want Lonnie for an older brother, nor was it comforting to know that Lonnie didn't want to be his older brother. Franklin was a man of intractable authority, and he had a volatile temper. So Joshua remained silent. But as he saw it, he and Matt had been kicked out—evicted, even—banished to the confines of a dirty, dilapidated cabin that still smelled of its prior contents: hoes, rakes, shovels and other hand tools, old bags of seed, rusty parts of farm implements, and rat droppings.

The family's main house was typical for rural west Kentucky in 1921. It was a simple, raised structure Franklin's father had built of oak and maple lumber about thirty years earlier. In addition to an eat-in kitchen and a parlor, there were three bedrooms. Franklin and Maggie slept in the main bedroom. With space for a potbellied stove and two chairs, it was the gathering place for family time, especially on cold winter evenings.

Prior to the merger of the two families, the second bedroom had been occupied by the Jennings children: Joshua; Jessie, his sister, two years older; and Matthew, two years younger. After Franklin and Maggie were married, the Jennings boys were moved to the cabin with Lonnie to make room for Jessie and Maggie's two daughters. Reba was a year or so older than Jessie, and Naomi was Joshua's age. The third bedroom was added to provide living quarters for Gerthy Jennings, Franklin's bachelor brother.

Joshua rubbed his eyes and rolled over onto his side. There, not more than six inches from his face, was Matt, making his "monster" face—staring bug-eyed and baring his lower teeth. On eye contact with Joshua, he stuck out his tongue and laughed.

"What are you doin'?" whispered Joshua. "You're gonna wake up Lonnie."

"Did I scare ya?" Matt stuck out his tongue again, and then repeatedly, like a snake, and he laughed even louder.

Joshua grabbed him, squeezed the back of his neck with one hand, and tried to cover his mouth with the other. "I said quit it! If you wake up Lonnie, we'll both be in trouble."

"I'm not scared of Lonnie," insisted Matt. "Besides, it's time he woke up."

"You're not scared of Lonnie 'cause he doesn't bother you like he does me."

"Aw, he won't do nothin'. He might yell an' holler some, but he won't hurt us. I'll show you."

Matt jumped out of bed, grabbed a shoe, and tiptoed to the edge of the loft overlooking Lonnie's bed. He held it by the laces and dangled it over the banister.

"Don't you dare!" insisted Joshua through clenched teeth.

Matt swung the shoe in circles above Lonnie's head. "I'm gonna drop it on the count of ten," he warned. "One … two … three."

Joshua rolled out of bed and approached slowly, thrusting his clenched fist in Matt's direction.

"Four … five … six."

With both fists clenched, Joshua inched carefully toward Matt. Just as he was ready to spring to snatch the shoe away, the cabin door swung open, and Franklin stepped inside. Matt pulled the shoe back over the railing, and both boys scurried to get dressed.

"Time to do your chores," Franklin announced. "You boys come on. We got lots to do today."

"Don't call me a boy," mumbled Lonnie. "An' even if I was a boy, I ain't never gonna be *your* boy."

"Well, whether you're mine or not, you need to help out around here just like the rest of us," continued Franklin. "Y'all get your clothes on an' meet me at the barn. After we do the milkin' an' eat breakfast, I need you to help me clean out that fence row between us an' Vernon's place."

As Franklin turned to leave, Matt and Joshua were already busy getting dressed.

"I don't feel like workin' today," yelled Lonnie. "You an' yer little boys can do it without me. I aim to get some more sleep."

Franklin turned and bolted back into the cabin. He slammed the door and stood at the foot of Lonnie's bed. "As long as you're eatin' my food an' sleepin' in my bed, I reckon you'll do what I say. Now get out'a that bed an' help, or leave and don't come back."

"All right. I s'pose I'll help with the feedin' an' milkin', but I won't be cleanin' out no fence rows."

Franklin turned and left the cabin, grabbed his pails, and headed for the barn, where his two mixed-breed cows waited in a single stall to be fed and milked. From a wooden bin, Joshua and Matt got the cows' feed, a mixture of ground corn and hay with molasses as a sweetener. They poured it from their buckets into a common trough to let the cows fill their bellies and remain content while Franklin filled his two large pails with their milk.

"Let Lonnie slop the hogs and feed the horses," Franklin instructed.

Maggie always made biscuits for breakfast. Before Franklin left the house to get the boys, he helped her kindle a fire in the firebox of her oven using small pieces of cured oak.

"Go to the smokehouse an' get me some lard," she told Reba, whom she was teaching to cook. Lard rendered from hogs killed in the winter was kept in a crock jar in the smokehouse and used for all her baked goods.

Maggie measured out the amount of flour she needed by counting handfuls as she transferred it from her flour tin to her oval wooden biscuit bowl. She pushed the flour up the sides of the bowl to leave a little pond to hold the other ingredients. When Reba returned with the lard, Maggie scooped out a handful and plopped it in with the flour. She added some buttermilk and soda and then squashed it all together repeatedly with her fingers until she had a ball of dough. After placing the dough on a floured cloth, she used her wooden rolling pin to flatten the dough and then stamped out her biscuits with a metal biscuit cutter. She knew the exact time to put them in the oven, and they were brown and piping hot just as the family sat down to eat.

Franklin sat at the head of the table, and from her chair closest to the stove, Maggie served the hot biscuits to be eaten with plenty of freshly churned butter and molasses produced from sorghum grown on the Jennings farm. They drank tall glasses of sweet milk from their cows.

The sounds of idle chatter and youthful bickering were mixed with jangling of eating utensils to create the Jennings family's typical mealtime racket.

"Papa, please make Matt quit smackin' his lips when he chews."

"That ain't smackin'—that's eatin'!"

"Ooo! Quit showin' your food."

"Don't say *ain't,* Matt. Say *isn't.*"

"There's more biscuits in the oven. Anybody need more to eat?"

When it appeared that all had eaten their fill, Franklin rose from his chair. "Well, if everyone is done, I'm gonna take the boys with me to get started cleanin' out the fence row between us an' Vernon's place. Lonnie, I'll need you to cut those big weeds an' bushes growin' down there between the fence and the barn. It'll only take us a couple a days if we work steady."

Lonnie gulped down his last swallow of milk, rose from his chair, reached over one of the younger children, and slammed his glass down hard on the table.

"I helped with the feedin', but I don't reckon I'll be cuttin' any weeds or bushes or anything else," he roared. He glared and pointed his finger at Franklin. "You can't make me do nothin'! You ain't my daddy, and I ain't your slave!"

"Well, I guess you will if I say so!" Franklin shoved his chair back from the table.

"Aw, you're nothin' but a drawed-up old man," taunted Lonnie. "An' I ain't scared of nothin' you can do."

In an instant, Franklin jumped to his feet. His right hand, though still at waist level, was balled up in a tight fist. Although he was a man of small stature, his temper had helped to create opportunities for a scrap on several occasions, and as he sometimes boasted, he had never backed down from a fight. What he lacked in height, he more than made up for in strength and quickness. His forearms were particularly strong; although he had never been trained as a fighter, he seemed to possess a natural ability to deliver sharp blows with his fists, and he was an experienced grappler.

Red-faced with anger, he moved toward Lonnie, and his words mixed with saliva as they spewed from his mouth.

"You will most certainly do what I tell you to do!" he blared.

Franklin raised his fists. Maggie pulled her apron up over her mouth and began to cry.

"Well, let's see if you can make me," challenged Lonnie.

In an instant, Franklin sprang like a large cat, landed a quick left hook to Lonnie's ear, and grabbed him around the neck with both arms. Somewhat caught off guard, Lonnie fell against a chair and then onto the floor with Franklin on top of him. He pushed against Franklin's chest, trying to free himself from his grasp, and then he kicked violently, like a long-legged young colt trying to free himself from hobbles.

The combination of Lonnie's size, youth, and rebelliousness was no match for Franklin's superior experience as a fighter. The two rolled on the floor as Lonnie tried in vain to break free of Franklin's grasp. As Lonnie tried to get up, Franklin whirled to reverse his chest-to-chest bear hug on Lonnie to a position behind him with his neck in a choke hold.

"Don't ever talk back to me like that again," he demanded. "Until you're ready to leave here for good and make it on your own, you'd better plan to work like the rest of us."

With that, Franklin released his hold on Lonnie's neck and stood up. Lonnie rubbed his neck and muttered, "I'll be out'a here sooner'n you think. I can't stand you or your damn kids!" He jumped to his feet, bolted to the door, and delivered a parting shot to the back of Joshua's head with the side of his elbow. Joshua flinched but said nothing. The pit of his stomach tightened into a sickening knot as it had on the other occasions when Lonnie and his father had fought.

With the slam of the screen door, Lonnie was gone to an unknown destination, but by nightfall, he was back in the cabin.

2
CHAPTER

PEOPLE WHO DIDN'T KNOW him well defined Gerthy Jennings by his lameness and his lack of a wife. Gerthy accepted those conditions as facts of life that he would neither fret nor talk about.

At the Mount of Olives Baptist Church, Gerthy's physical handicap and bachelorhood disappeared under the white cloak of his soul. He was a quiet and unassuming leader, devout in his religious beliefs in both thought and deed. Gerthy was a deacon and the congregational song leader by choice, not by obligation.

When the Jennings children were preschoolers, he was introduced as Uncle Gerthy, their father's older brother, who had come to occupy the extra room recently added to the house. They gawked at first at his strange gait—one foot wanted to walk, but the other foot insisted on going tippy-toe. They knew he had never had a wife, but there was no urge to ask why.

Joshua had come to know his uncle as a wise counselor and as his close friend, especially since the death of his mother. His instruction about life was ever unyielding, but never threatening. Joshua visited with his uncle frequently.

A short time after he had witnessed the fight between his father and Lonnie, Joshua went to the side entrance that allowed Gerthy private access to his part of the house. It was early afternoon, and Joshua knew that unless it was Gerthy's nap time, he would be a welcomed guest.

As he approached the side of the house, he heard Gerthy's solo to the world:

"Sweet hour of prayer,
Sweet hour of prayer
That calls us from a world of care
And bids me at my Father's throne
Makes all my wants and wishes known;
In seasons of distress and grief,
My soul has often found relief
And oft escaped the tempter's snare
By thy return, sweet hour of prayer."

Joshua hesitated to interrupt at midverse, but he was not surprised to hear his uncle continue. Gerthy hardly ever looked at a hymnal when he sang in church. He knew the words to every stanza of almost every hymn, and he seldom stopped after only one verse.

"Sweet hour of prayer,
Sweet hour of prayer,
The joys I feel ..."

Joshua knocked.

"The bliss I share ... Come in!
Of those whose anxious spirits burn ...

"Hey, look who's here! Come on in and talk to your old uncle."

Gerthy's room was just large enough to accommodate his featherbed that rested on a simple metal frame, a wooden ladder-back rocking chair, an old trunk, a pedestal table, and a large bookcase filled with books. On the table were Gerthy's daily essentials, a kerosene lamp, a small writing tablet, and his well-worn Bible.

As Joshua entered, Gerthy rocked forward in his chair and extended his hand to his nephew.

"Come on in here and sit a spell," he said, motioning to the trunk.

Joshua sat cross-legged on the trunk with his back against the wall, his elbows on his knees, and his chin in his hands. His black hair was parted on the left and combed just the way his mother had done it as far back as he could remember. His legs and torso were thin, but work on the farm had given him unusual strength for his age, particularly in his hands and forearms.

"Uncle Gerthy, I heard you singin'," he said, seeking a comfortable way to start a conversation. "Why do you sing so much? Is singin' what makes you so happy all the time?"

"Well, I never gave it much thought," replied Gerthy. "I don't know if I sing because I'm happy, or if it's the singin' that keeps me happy. Maybe it's a little'a both. But I always seem to have a song on my mind, and it just comes out without me thinking too much about it."

"Sometimes I do that, too," said Joshua, nodding. "I'll be workin' in the field or somethin', and then I just start singin'."

"Yep," continued Gerthy, "I think God gives us songs to sing to remind us that He's right there with us every step of the way. When you're out there in that west field plowin', He's there—or when I'm sittin' in my rocking chair, He's here, too. He sends his Holy Spirit in lots'a different ways—sometimes, maybe, in the songs He lays on our minds."

Then, after a brief pause, Gerthy asked, "What's your favorite hymn?"

"I dunno," replied Joshua. "I like a lot of 'em. What's yours?"

Gerthy rocked back, staring up at the ceiling for a moment, and then answered, "Oh, I reckon I don't have just one particular favorite. But I'm real fond of 'How Firm a Foundation,' and I like 'On Christ the Solid Rock I Stand,' and another one I really like to sing is 'When I Survey the Wondrous Cross.' Those would be some of my favorites, I guess."

Thinking of what his uncle had said about the Holy Spirit, Joshua asked, "Was the Holy Spirit there with you when the barn door hit you in the mouth?"

The incident he had recalled was one Gerthy would have preferred to forget. About a year and a half earlier, during the autumn, Franklin had agreed to sell a young bull he had raised as breeding stock. Not yet fully grown, the calf weighed six to seven hundred pounds, the offspring of a Jersey cow with a Brown Swiss sire.

The plan was to herd the young bull into a stall in Franklin's barn, where it could be restrained and haltered. The stall was narrow—just wide enough for the bull to enter, but not wide enough for him to turn around. There was an opening for the bull's head to pass through and a trough with feed to lure him in. Once the bull's head was through the opening, a heavy timber would be rotated over to secure it.

Franklin and the bull's purchaser had recruited Gerthy to man the barn doors. They were double doors, at least ten feet tall, hinged on the outside and coming together to meet in the middle when closed. First, Gerthy was to open both doors wide, pushing them back against the outside of the barn. Then, when the bull had been herded into the barn, he would close the doors and latch them while the others got him into the stall and applied the halter.

Ropes were attached to each side of the halter, allowing the two men to walk the bull out of the barn and tie him to the back of the wagon. The bull's new owner would drive home in his horse-drawn wagon, with his newly purchased bull following behind.

The second part of Gerthy's assignment was to open the barn doors on Franklin's signal that they were ready to bring the bull out of the barn.

Step one went according to design. Gerthy opened the barn doors, the young bull was herded in, and he closed and latched the doors as instructed. He stood back against the outside of the barn, seemingly out of harm's way. Inside the barn, the bull remained calm as the halter was placed on his head, the neck restraint was loosened, and he was allowed to back out of the stall.

Just as Franklin was about to call to Gerthy to open the barn doors, a bantam rooster began making amorous advances on a hen there in the barn. The hen flapped her wings, squawked, and raced under the bull, with the determined and equally raucous rooster in hot pursuit. The bull was completely spooked. He bolted and yanked both men to the ground as they tried to hold on. He butted the barn door with such force that its wooden latch was splintered into fragments, and the door flew open and hit Gerthy flush in the face.

Though knocked to the ground, he remained conscious. Blood covered his face and drenched his shirt and the top part of his trousers. His nose was broken and his lips were cut, and by the time Franklin, and Percy got to him, he was spitting out most of his front teeth.

Joshua and Matt, who had been watching from the back of the yard, climbed the barnyard fence and raced to see their uncle. Aghast at the sight of his bloody face, they wondered if he would survive. Survive he did. But he lived the rest of his happy, God-fearing life with a full set of dentures. It was the memory of that incident that prompted Joshua's question about the Holy Spirit.

Gerthy laughed. "Well, I try not to think about getting my teeth knocked out," he replied. "And now that you asked, I can't recall what I was thinkin' at the time. At first, I was sort'a addled, and I didn't know what had happened."

"Did God want you to get hit by that barn door?" Joshua asked.

"Boy! You're full of tough questions today, aren't you?" Gerthy adjusted himself in his rocking chair.

"Well, no, I don't think God made that bull bust through the door an' hit me. I think the bull did that on his own. I think what God did was to give healing power to my nose and mouth in order to keep me singin'. And maybe the Holy Spirit was there to keep it from being any worse than it was. I don't know for sure, but that's the way I've got it figured."

Joshua shifted his feet from the top of the trunk to the floor and began to shake his legs up and down nervously on his toes.

"Uncle Gerthy, why'd my daddy hafta get married again, anyway?"

Gerthy paused.

"I 'spect your father felt awful lonely after your mother died. And I think …"

"I felt lonely, too, but that doesn't mean I need a new mama!"

"You interrupted me before I was through."

"I'm sorry."

"That's okay. What I was sayin' is that Franklin had lots'a responsibility on him, and he felt like you kids needed a mother, and he needed a wife. Besides, seems to me like your daddy and Maggie love each other. And I know for a fact he wants what's best for you kids."

"I like Mommie okay," said Joshua, "but she'll never take the place of my real mother."

"Yeah, I'm sure you're right about that. And nobody expects her to—not even your father."

Joshua scratched an itch under the bib of his overalls. He got up from the trunk, ambled around the room, and then stopped at the window with his back to his uncle.

"Why do people hafta die?"

As Gerthy pondered his answer, Joshua continued. "I don't know why my mother had to die. Did God take her away from us on purpose?"

Gerthy prayed for the right words to answer such a deep question asked sincerely by such a good boy. His blue-green eyes smiled in concert with the rest of his countenance.

"I don't fully understand why people hafta die," he began. "What I do know is that God puts us here on earth for a time, and none of us knows how long that will be. We're just supposed to live like He wants us to for as long as we're here."

Then, rocking forward to rise from his chair, he patted down the remaining tufts of his thinning hair and then placed his hand on Joshua's shoulder.

"I can't tell you why God took your mother to be with Him when she was still so young. But I can tell you this. Your mother lived more in the time she was alive than most people could in two lifetimes."

"But why couldn't God leave her here a little longer?" asked Joshua.

"The promise He gives us is that our body may die, but our spirit lives on. And the way your mother lived and the way she took care of you while she was here will make her spirit be with you every day. It's just like God giving us His spirit in those songs. He gave us His spirit in your mother's life, and that will be with you forever."

"I'd still rather have her here than her spirit," insisted Joshua.

"Of course you would. That's natural. We all miss ..."

"Her spirit can't talk to me, and comb my hair, and read stories to me, and play pretty bird with us like she used to."

"I know," agreed Gerthy. "I know."

After a brief silence, Joshua's eyes drifted over to focus on Gerthy's crippled foot. In spite of his handicap, Uncle Gerthy was the strongest man knew. A smile crept across Joshua's face, and he broke the silence.

"Remember that time the bees got after you at the picnic?" he asked with a laugh.

"Naw!" Gerthy smiled broadly. "I don't recall any such thing!"

"Uh-huh," insisted Joshua, jumping to his feet and pointing. "It happened right out there in the front yard. I won't ever forget that!"

"There's some things you're not s'posed to remember."

Gerthy laughed and playfully jabbed at the boy with his cane.

3
CHAPTER

GERTHY'S STRENGTH OF MIND and spirit had not helped him overcome his fear of bees.

Before his death, Granddaddy Jennings had built and tended five large hives of honeybees located to the south of the house next to the fence that separated their property from the neighboring farm. Franklin continued to tend the hives after his father died. Each year he took the mild, sweet honey made from the blossoms of apple, pear, and cherry trees and white clover. With the honeycomb, it was stored in mason jars. As did the rest of the Jennings household, Gerthy enjoyed generous helpings of honey poured over hot buttered biscuits or corn bread. But he hated bees.

Typically, bees swarmed in August. And it was in August that Maggie's flower garden was in full bloom. Each year since her marriage to Franklin, she had planted a fine, large bed of flowers in the front yard at the southwest corner of the house. It contained roses, zinnias, marigolds, violets, peonies, sweet peas, and asters. The garden's bouquet was like a "free nectar" sign for bees. And they came.

The second Sunday in August was the date for the annual Jennings reunion and family picnic. Aunts, uncles, cousins and their families came from as far away as Missouri and Tennessee.

Long tables made of planks supported by sawhorses were covered with checkered tablecloths and laden with food. It was good ole country food— home-grown and home-cooked, but viewed as a blessing from on high. As they partook of this meal, they would forget their poverty.

There was fried chicken, country ham, roast beef, corn on the cob, coleslaw, green beans, lima beans, pickled beets, black-eyed peas, potato salad, fresh sliced tomatoes, cucumbers, onions, corn bread, and Aunt Bertha's green stuff that no one could identify.

The almanac had promised good weather. It was, indeed. The haze of previous hot summer days was blown away by a gentle breeze out of the north that brought temporary relief to the dog days.

Waiting for latecomers to arrive, most of the younger children ran helter-skelter through the yard playing noisy games of tag and hide-and-seek. A few of the older boys found shady spots for games of mumblety-peg and marbles. The boys wore bib overalls with no shirt underneath, and most of the girls had on simple print dresses made of cool cotton fabric from flour sacks.

Joshua's older sister, Jessie, tried to organize the playtime. "Do y'all wanna play pretty-bird-my-cup?" she yelled. She was lukewarm about the idea but knew of nothing else to suggest that they had not already done.

"Yeah, let's play pretty bird!" said Matt. "I love to play pretty bird."

Others weren't so sure.

"I never heard'a purty bird my cup."

"That sounds like a dumb game."

"Do we get to put a bird in a cup?"

"How do ya play?"

Organizing the game and instructing the players was a thorny task.

Pretty-bird-my-cup was a game Hannah Jennings had introduced to her children when they were much younger. They had not played since their father's remarriage and the arrival of new members of the household.

"Y'all shut up an' listen! It's easy," declared Jessie. "And it'll be fun if y'all play right."

"Want me to go get the rag?" asked Matt.

"No, it was my idea, an' I'll get the rag. Now let me tell y'all how to play. See we all get in a circle. But first we gotta get a wet rag, an' then we sit in a circle. I'll start. I'll hold the rag and think of some kind'a bird.

After I have a particular bird in my mind, I'll call out 'pretty bird in my cup, what sort's yours?' An' then we go around the circle an' let everybody take a guess. An' then when you guess the same thing I thought of, I throw the wet rag an' try to hit you with it. See?"

"That's a dumb game. It doesn't make sense," someone growled.

"I'll play," said Joshua, throwing a handful of acorns to the ground.

Joshua liked the game mainly because it was a vivid reminder of his mother. After all, she was the one who formed them in a circle when they were very small children, and she played along with them. She had used a small, soft pillow as the projectile. The wet rag idea was a revision of the rules he and Jessie had made to keep the game interesting even as they had grown older.

Pretty bird was more than a game to Joshua. As a game, it was a trivial memory of an earlier time in his childhood. As it reminded him of his mother, however, it was a treasure.

Amidst the confusion of other children preparing to play the game, Joshua thought about his mother. He was oblivious to stick-throwing, hair pulling, kicking, fussing, and the other commotion interlaced with repeated instructions and endless questions that preceded the start of the game.

He remembered the softness of his mother's skin and her dark brown hair that cascaded over her shoulders and reached the middle of her back when she wore it down. He remembered that when he sat beside her and she pulled him close, he could feel its silkiness next to his face. Usually, though, she wore her hair in a twist or a bun, exposing her slender, graceful neck, her high cheekbones, and her petite ears.

Even her hands were soft. How could hands that mopped, swept, washed clothes and dishes and floors, hoed, raked, pulled weeds, milked, gathered eggs, slopped hogs, and performed untold other chores around the farm be so soft?

He remembered her voice. He had felt calm and protected when she talked. Words from her lips were like a song—melodic, full of passion, and yet gentle, especially when they were words of assurance, praise, and love. He remembered the times she had sung,

"'I love you mother,' said little Fan,

'Today I'll help you all I can …'"

Then she had said, "Joshua, that song reminds me of you, because when I ask you to help me, you always do it willingly."

Joshua was sure that his mother had been the best mother in the whole world, and he couldn't stop missing her.

"Hey, Joshua! What's a matter with you? Are you gonna play pretty bird or not?"

"Yea, I'm gonna play. Who's got the rag?" he said.

Jessie held up the wet dishtowel wadded up in her right hand and shouted, "Pretty bird in my cup, what sort's yours?"

"Sparrow!" yelled Matt.

"No!"

"Jaybird," guessed Joshua.

"No!"

"Redbird," tried Reba.

"No!"

"Vulture," called Milton.

"What?"

"Vulture!" he yelled.

"That's not it," said Jessie.

"What's a vulture?" inquired Matt. "I never heard'a no vulture!"

"It's a buzzard, stupid! Are we gonna play or not?"

It was Matt's turn again.

"Chicken hawk!" he yelled, jumping up and down.

Jessie hurled the dishrag without saying a word. It hit Matt with a loud *splat*, right in his upper chest and neck. Totally startled, he yelled "Hey!" Then he looked down at the wet spot on the bib of his overalls, picked up the wet towel, and began to chase Jessie around the yard, trying to hit her back.

Jessie screamed for help, but Matt was too speedy. As he closed in on her, he hurled the rag southpaw style, and it caught her squarely in the back of the head. She screamed again, turned, and momentarily thought of chasing Matt to get revenge, but he was gone.

"That's the last time I play pretty bird with you, you little chicken," she yelled furiously.

"This is one of the better games of pretty-bird-my-cup we've ever had," muttered Joshua to no one in particular.

The food was now assembled and arranged in proper order on the longest table, and two of the women fanned away flies with leafy branches of a maple tree. Lemonade was poured and handed to each one who passed the table's end with a plate piled high with food. Finally, empty bellies were soon to be filled, and starving children would receive nourishment!

As the host of this banquet, Franklin tapped on a glass with a spoon and announced, "Now, before we eat, I'll ask Gerthy to say our blessing. Let's bow our heads."

Gerthy hopped up from the crate he had been using as a chair and stood on his good leg with the toe of his crippled leg resting on the ground. He began, "Dear Lord, we thank Thee for all the blessings of life, for we know they come from You. We are thankful for life itself and for the joy we have of being assembled here together on this beautiful day."

Gerthy's prayers were commensurate with the magnitude of the event. Since this was a large family gathering and a bountiful feast, all those in attendance knew the blessing would be equally long and glorious.

"We thank You for each home represented here, for the lives of each one, and for the lives of those of our family who have gone on to be with You. Let us never forget the blessings of their memory, and let us pattern our own lives more after the life of Your only Son, Jesus ..."

Now Gerthy was getting cranked up, and his dynamic words and his sincere delivery had captured even the youngsters' attention. Unbeknownst to anyone except for Gerthy, however, a bee was buzzing at the back of his head, and he was terrified as he continued to pray, not wanting to end the blessing without even giving thanks for the food.

"And now, merciful Father, we thank ... uh ..."

He waved his hat at the bee quietly.

"Uh ... we thank You for this food and ..."

The bee darted at him, hitting him in the back of the head but with its stinger retracted.

"Hey!" he shouted, and some of the folks began to peek out of one eye to see what was wrong. Others thought he had really gotten the spirit so deeply that it caused him to shout. But Gerthy was determined not to let his fear of the bee ruin his prayer.

"Uh … we thank Thee for this food and all those who have prepared it, and we pray that just as it nourishes our bodies, You will continue to nourish our … Oh, Lordy, Lordy!" he yelled as the bee found its way under his collar, stung him on the neck, and buzzed around under his shirt.

Gerthy jumped back and tripped over the crate behind him, but without falling completely to the ground. He regained his balance and went hobbling off through the yard, yelling and uttering strange noises that no one present had heard before.

With staccato steps, hops, and skips, as his withered limb would allow, he circled the table. He pulled to get his shirt out of the back of his trousers with one hand and tried to swat the bee with his hat with the other hand.

The abrupt ending to his beautiful blessing and the sight of him as he hop-skipped through the yard led most to believe that he had been totally overcome by the Holy Spirit.

"What happened to Gerthy?" someone whispered.

"Is he possessed? Somebody help him," another pleaded.

"Sounds like he's a-speakin' in tongues!"

Whispers among the crowd became murmurs, and finally, two men who realized what had happened chased after him. They freed the bee from his shirt and escorted him back to sit in the shade to recover.

"Can we eat now?" asked one of the children.

"God bless this food. Let's eat," said Gerthy.

4
CHAPTER

THE SUMMER OF 1921 was unseasonally oppressive in West Kentucky. By late August, the hot, dry weather had sucked the water out of the farm's cistern, and to make matters worse, Franklin had begun to see grit in his well water. A new, deeper well with a new screen was mandatory to supply the family with pure water. This was not a job for one man, and Franklin did not have the means to hire it done.

Fortunately, in the preceding spring, he had helped Vernon Starr dig a new well on his place, and by gentleman's agreement, it was understood that Vernon would help Franklin when he decided to put in his own well. Neither man knew it would be necessary so soon.

Another neighbor who "owed" him some work was Dossie Smith. Franklin was one of a crew of six men who had helped him build his new barn a year and a half earlier. Dossie, a man in his sixties, had agreed to pay off his debt to Franklin by doing odd jobs as needed. He was unable to do heavy work, but he was a willing hand to assist in the digging of Franklin's well.

No money changed hands, there was no strict accounting for hours worked, and there was no written contract. By oral agreement, friends and neighbors regularly assisted each other to accomplish what none of them could have done alone.

The work was to be done in the late afternoon hours and on weekends when Vernon was not in his classroom as a teacher at Lodgeston School. At a slow but unwavering pace, the task would take many weeks to finish. Finally, by late October, the tired but jubilant men had augered their way through topsoil, viscous clay, and porous limestone into fine white sand that contained a plentiful aquifer that would provide cool, pure water for many years.

Before he began the well-digging project, Franklin had asked Lonnie to help him. His request was met with Lonnie's stock response: "You can't make me do anything! You ain't my daddy, and I ain't your slave." And another brawl had almost erupted.

With respect to the well-digging project, Lonnie and Franklin had reached something of a compromise. Franklin had agreed to purchase needed supplies from a man in the well supply business, who lived two miles south of Cayce. Lonnie had agreed to take Franklin's team of mules and wagon to pick up what he would need to complete the project.

A few days before Franklin and his neighbors finished digging, Lonnie informed him that he needed to haul some of his belongings to his grandfather's house in Cayce. Franklin agreed for Lonnie to use his wagon and team of mules on the condition that Lonnie would pick up the well supplies Franklin had purchased. It was an opportune time for Lonnie to get moved out and to bring back well pipe, a strainer, the well head, and pump equipment. *For once, Lonnie is being helpful,* Franklin thought. He told Lonnie to take Joshua with him in case he needed help to unload his things and then load the well supplies onto the wagon.

In the days before Lonnie moved out, he and Franklin settled on an unspoken arrangement whereby each would ignore the other as much as possible. That settlement seemed to lessen tension in the household and give both parties reason to hope for better times in the future.

Joshua did not object when Franklin asked him to go with Lonnie. But he dreaded the trip. It would cover a distance of six miles each way, with stops at Lonnie's grandfather's house in Cayce and at the well supply place two miles beyond. The accord between Lonnie and Franklin had not ended Lonnie's harassment of Joshua. Even on the rare occasions when

Lonnie acted with civility toward him, there was something diabolical in his smile and something sinister in his demeanor.

Joshua walked out the back door and across the yard toward the barn. Lonnie had already hitched the team, a horse and a mule, to the wagon. The little horse named Bert and Ole Joe, the mule, had actually belonged to Lonnie's mother, Maggie, before her marriage to Franklin. The two animals represented part of her contribution to the newly formed household, but neither one was prized stock. In fact, Joshua had heard his dad describe Ole Joe as "a little drawed-up old mule."

"You ready to go, you little pissant?" greeted Lonnie.

"I'm as ready as I'll ever be."

"Well, climb yore little butt up in this here wagon. You an' me is gonna have a time," said Lonnie with a smirk. "Be sure to give a little wave to yore pappy 'fore we leave. He prob'ly don't like for you to go without you wave bye-bye."

Joshua sat in the seat with Lonnie but scooted over as far away from him as possible. He pulled his cap down so that it was snug on his head, and he stared straight ahead and rode in silence.

From their house to Cayce was approximately four miles, but the team was slow, and Lonnie didn't seem to be in any hurry. They passed the Starr house and then the Henrys' place, where Joshua noticed at least four turtles sunning themselves on a fallen tree trunk on the edge of their pond. The air was still, but the movement of the wagon created a breeze on Joshua's face, and that was welcomed relief from the August heat.

At the junction of their lane with the Fulton-Hickman road, Lonnie geed the team to the right to turn west. The wagon bumped and swayed through the ruts of the dirt road. After traveling about two and a half miles over the rolling hills, Lonnie pointed his finger forward and broke the silence.

"Down yonder is where I'm gonna feed you to the snakes and the muskrats," he said, glancing menacingly at Joshua.

The wagon was moving down a hill toward a low-lying area known as the Willingham Bottom. It consisted of a series of sloughs and marshland, heavily wooded with cypress trees and other wetland vegetation. It was a dark, watery area full of mosquitoes and crawling with cottonmouth moccasins that had always given Joshua an eerie feeling. He shuddered to think of being thrown into any part of the Willingham Bottom, but he ignored Lonnie's threat.

"I betcha they's even lots'a alligators in that swamp," said Lonnie with a laugh. "I might hang you over the edge of this here bridge, an' see if one of 'em will come gitcha." He reached out in Joshua's direction as if to push him out of the wagon. Joshua flinched but said nothing.

"Oh, don't worry, little feller, I wuz just jokin' with ya. You an' me are gonna be big buddies." Lonnie laughed, and both he and Joshua were silent as they traveled two more miles to Cayce.

Cayce was a little town with two stores, one school, one church, a post office, a barbershop, a doctor's office, a stock pen, and a train depot. The town's name had become immortalized in a song about its most famous citizen, John Luther "Cayce" Jones, a passenger train engineer who had grown up there.

In 1900, Cayce was at the throttle of the New Orleans Special, an Illinois Central Railroad passenger train better known as the Cannonball Express. He rammed it into the back of a freight train just outside the little town of Vaughn, Mississippi, and he was killed in the collision.

By 1920, there was confusion about the connection between the common name of the town and the engineer. Some people knew that the man was named for the town, and others thought the town was named for the famous engineer they sang about. But eventually, everyone who came to this little town heard about its local hero.

Lonnie dropped Joshua off at Brinson's General Store to kill time while he went to his grandfather's house on the edge of town. Without explanation, he told Joshua he preferred to pick up the well supplies alone. Joshua was elated to have some time apart from Lonnie. Although he was not a frequent visitor to Cayce, Joshua knew Lloyd Brinson to be a man he could trust, and he would enjoy looking around in his store.

"How ya doin', young fella? Are you here with Mr. Franklin?" Mr. Brinson looked down at Joshua through his black-rimmed glasses. He was a short man in his fifties who shaved what little bit of hair he hadn't lost to baldness. His full, bushy beard compensated for his clean-shaven head.

"No, sir, I'm here waitin' on my stepbrother to get back from his grandpa's house," replied Joshua.

"Well, I'm mighty proud to have you in the store. Did you get some candy?" he asked.

"No, sir, I don't care for candy." Joshua didn't want to admit that he had no money.

Brinson reached over Joshua's head to a jar on the counter, removed the lid, and pulled out two pieces of peppermint candy.

"Here, put these in your pocket for later when you might have a hankerin' for some." He grabbed Joshua's hand, placing the jawbreakers in his palm.

"Thank you, sir. But …"

"I can't help but notice that you have some warts on your finger," Brinson interrupted in a kindly manner. "Do you want me to get rid'a those warts for you?" he asked seriously.

Joshua pulled his hand away quickly and examined the two warts that had grown on the outside of his index finger. He blushed, but realized that the storeowner had made a genuine offer to help. "Well, I guess so. But what do you hafta do to get rid of warts?"

"Well," said Mr. Brinson with a laugh, "I don't aim to cut your finger off, if that's what's worryin' ya! Just come back here with me and let me get my special towel."

Brinson turned quickly and walked toward the back of the store. He stood to the side of a doorway and reached with both hands to sweep aside two full-length pieces of cloth that hung there, allowing Joshua to enter his sitting room.

"Just make yourself to home, young fella," he said, "whilst I grab that towel."

Joshua wondered if he had been wise in following Mr. Brinson to the back of his store, and he surely had no idea of how the man was planning to remove his warts. Immediately, Brinson returned carrying a small, faded green towel.

"Let me see them warts again," he said, almost in a whisper.

Slowly, Joshua raised his hand, looking over the top of Brinson's glasses as he bent over to get a close look at the warts. Joshua thought about closing his eyes until the strange medical procedure was done, but he squinted and watched as Brinson gently rubbed his faded towel over the warts.

"Now, you just forget about those warts, young man, an' pretty soon, you won't have 'em no more," he instructed.

When the wart doctor stood up and motioned toward the doorway, Joshua knew that the deed was done. *What was on that towel?* he wondered. *It felt dry, and there was nothing visible to make it unique. Can this guy really remove warts, or was he just foolin' with me 'cause I'm a boy?*

"Thanks," he said sheepishly as he stared down at his warts and then left the room. He walked quietly through Brinson's General Store to the front porch, glanced back over his shoulder, and sat down in one of three empty rockers. He was relieved to see that Mr. Brinson had not followed him out of the back room. After a brief wait on the porch, he returned to the store to look around.

Most of the store was devoted to groceries. A cracker barrel stood at the end of the display case where gumdrops, lemon drops, candied raspberries, peppermints, and other goodies were sold out of glass jars. Baby Ruth and Butterfinger candy bars were three cents each.

Flour, brown and white sugar, coffee, and tea were bulk items kept in containers on shelves behind the display case. On a customer's request, a store clerk transferred the desired amount of these goods to brown paper sacks that were weighed, priced, and secured at the top with a white string.

A large slab of cheese called a hoop was kept in a wooden container with a lid to keep it fresh. Like slices of a pie, wedges cut to customers' specifications were weighed, packaged, and sold by the pound. Joshua was particularly fond of cheddar cheese, a fortunate taste because that was the only variety sold at Brinson's. On rare occasions, his father would buy a pound or two and dole it out like candy, to be eaten on crackers or by itself.

In season, apples, pears, oranges, lemons, and other fresh fruits delivered by train were available in bins. A small stalk of bananas hung from the ceiling where they continued to ripen until they were all sold.

Canned goods and a full line of toiletries were displayed on shelves attached to the wall behind the counter. Joshua enjoyed the blend of scents emanating from Palmolive soaps, talcum powders, and other fragrances that stocked the shelves. Evening in Paris and Lily of the Valley were popular brands, but he was most fond of the distinctive smell of Jergens Lotion because that was what his mother had used.

Butter, eggs, and lard were brought into Brinson's by farmers who exchanged them for other merchandise in the store. Due to lack of space in the front, these items were stored a back room with kerosene and vinegar.

One long shelf behind the counter displayed tobacco, corn-cob and briar pipes, cigarette papers, matches, and other tobacco use products. Chewing tobacco came in plugs, while several varieties of loose tobacco for roll-your-own cigarettes and pipes, along with snuff, came in tin cans, cotton sacks, or small boxes.

Joshua turned up his nose at the thought of tobacco use. On a few occasions, he had sneaked cigarette paper from Franklin's bureau drawer, filled it with Prince Albert tobacco poured out of its skinny, oblong, red can with a flip-up top, and rolled his own smoke, partly to see what it was like, but mostly because he thought it was manly. Each time, his cigarette had had some kind of deformity. Sometimes it was too short and fat, and other times it turned out skinny and crooked. But regardless of its shape, each one of his cigarettes had made him sick.

Snuff was out of the question. The only times he had seen his Aunt Bertha, a great-aunt on his father's side, she had had brown ooze visible from the corner of her mouth to her chin. Even worse, she was a big kisser and hugger. His rare experiences with Aunt Bertha had convinced Joshua to stay away from snuff forever.

Brinson's had a limited supply of piece goods, thread, needles, thimbles, and other sewing supplies. Joshua counted four bolts of fabric leaning up against the wall in the front corner of the store. Before her death, his mother had used material purchased there to make dresses for Jessie and herself.

As Joshua made his way toward the front of the store to watch for Lonnie, he stopped at the display case for watches and knives. That was his favorite spot in the store.

If I ever have money of my own, he thought, *I'll surely buy me a good knife and a gold pocket watch.*

Brinson's sold Case and Barlow brands, all two- and three-blade pocket knives. Hunting knives and other larger ones were kept in the back. Of those shown in the case, Joshua's favorite was the Vintage Case 3.5-inch XX triple blade pocket knife 6332. It looked the best to him, and he dreamed of coming back some day to buy it.

The selection of pocket watches included four that were heavy, thick, sturdy, and less expensive. Preferred by farmers and workmen, they were plain, with very little or no engraving, but they gave years of good service. Two of them were open-faced Waltham watches made of coin silver, and the other two were closed-face Elgins made of silver plate with brass to resemble gold.

At the bottom of the case was a gold, open-face watch that was more striking than the others. Below the watch was a small card on which was printed, "Hamilton Watch Company. Guaranteed to pass railroad inspection. $75."

Who could afford such an expensive watch? I'll never be able to afford one like that, he thought.

Someone was shouting his name. Joshua looked around the store for a moment before he realized the yell was coming from outside. For a few fleeting moments, he had forgotten about his return trip with Lonnie, but without further hesitation, he raced through the door and jumped from Brinson's porch into the wagon.

"Why weren't you lookin' for me, you little turd?" demanded Lonnie. "First I hafta load all this stuff for your pappy by myself, an' then you ain't even ready."

"You said you didn't want me to go."

"Just sit there an' shut up. I ain't in any mood to listen to you yappin'!"

Joshua was happy to comply, and neither he nor Lonnie said anything until they were back in the Willingham Bottom. The wagon clattered over the rough planks of a wooden bridge, one of two long spans over wide sloughs connecting the swamp on either side of the road. When they cleared the first bridge and were back on the dirt road, Lonnie suddenly grabbed the cap off Joshua's head and slung it out of the wagon. It caught a gust of wind and sailed onto the shoulder of the road.

"Hey, that's my cap," protested Joshua. "Stop!"

"Okay, little feller. I wuz just a-kiddin'." He reined the team to a stop. "Go on an' git yer cap. I'll wait fer ya."

Joshua jumped out of the wagon, ran back a few yards, and found his cap lying on the edge of a ditch. He slapped it against his pants leg to remove dirt and some muddy water, and then he began to walk back to reboard the wagon. Just as he neared the back wheel, Lonnie slapped the reins down hard on the team and yelled for them to go. They broke into a run, leaving Joshua in the dust of the wagon's wheels. As he sprinted after them, he could hear Lonnie's revolting laughter and shouts of derision.

"Come on, Joshie! Is that as fast as you can run?" he chided.

He allowed the horse and the mule to slow down just enough for Joshua to gain ground, but just as he neared the back of the wagon, Lonnie slapped the reins down on their rumps again and raced out ahead. Joshua continued to run as fast as he could. He tried to catch up to the wagon, but Lonnie continued to slow down and then speed up when he got close. After a series of attempts to catch the wagon, Joshua stopped in total exhaustion and aggravation as the wagon proceeded ahead. He began to walk, resolved to let Lonnie go on without him. *I'll still make it home before dark,* he thought.

Lonnie stopped the team and yelled back to Joshua, "Come on. I ain't gonna go off an' leave you out here in the bottom—least not this time!"

Joshua continued to walk toward the wagon. He did not trust any of Lonnie's promises, and he was determined to walk home alone.

"Whatsa matter, little buddy? You tired? Can't run no more?"

As Joshua caught up with the back of the wagon, Lonnie slapped the reins on the team to get them moving, but only at a walk to keep pace with Joshua.

"I know what's wrong with you, Joshie. Yer a bastard son-of-a-bitch!"

Joshua continued to walk and stared straight ahead.

"It ain't your fault you're a sissy—it's your mama's fault. I think your mama turned you into a Chicken shit! If she hadn't died, you could'a kept on bein' a …"

Before Lonnie could finish, Joshua jumped into the back of the wagon and grabbed him around the neck in a choke hold.

"Don't ever talk about my mother!" he screamed. Driven by rage, he released the hold on Lonnie's neck and began to flail with both fists. He landed blows to Lonnie's head, neck, and shoulders before Lonnie could tie up the reins and turn to defend himself.

Lonnie whirled around, struck Joshua in the ribs with his elbow, and jumped into the back of the wagon to stand over his young stepbrother, who had been knocked down by the force of the blow.

"You just made a big mistake!" Lonnie glared down at Joshua and then kicked him hard in the thigh. "I ought'a beat the shit out'a ya and dump ya in the swamp!"

Joshua remained on his back in silence, fearful of what Lonnie would do next.

Lonnie dropped down on top of Joshua. He straddled Joshua's body, grasped his wrists, and used his legs to pin Joshua to the floor of the wagon.

"If I beat you up like I want to, yore daddy'll kill me. So I'm gonna teach you a lesson an' hope fer yer sake you don't fergit it!"

With his superior size and strength, Lonnie reversed his position on top of Joshua so that his legs were now on top of Joshua's arms and he was facing Joshua's feet. He grabbed each of Joshua's legs just above his knees to keep him pinned down. In this new position, Lonnie's butt was suspended only an inch or two above Joshua's face.

"Here's what I think of you, you little Son-of-a-bitch!" Lonnie strained hard and farted directly into Joshua's face. Then he did it again. "I hope you liked that, 'cause there's more where that came from!"

When Lonnie got up, Joshua continued to lie still. His eyes were closed, and he had not made a sound. He was determined not to cry.

He heard Lonnie say, "If I wuz you, I'd not say nothin' to yore pappy about our little fun, or next time you might git to see what nights is like in the Willingham Bottom!"

As Lonnie climbed back into the seat to drive the team back home, Joshua sat up, leaned back against the front of the wagon bed, and faced the rear for the rest of the ride home.

5
CHAPTER

WINTER DIED A SLOW death as it gave way to the gradual rebirth of spring. White blankets of snow were replaced by drab quilts of late-winter browns and tans. Ditches that had been filled to the brim with drifts were now rivulets of water. Roads made impassable by deep banks of snow were now somewhat usable again, but only for those daring enough to move about through axle-deep slop.

Outside chores that remained on the Jennings family's daily agenda now required twice the time to complete. Freed from confinement in barns and sheds, their livestock had created an ankle-deep mixture of malodorous mud and manure in feedlots adjacent to the barn.

The stinking mire was Joshua's dreaded enemy. On one occasion, he had tried to move through it too quickly and without measuring his steps. The muck's suction-cup tentacles had grabbed his boots and socks and held on, seeming to laugh as he took his next steps barefooted before landing in it on all fours.

One late afternoon, as Joshua and his father sloshed toward the barn to milk and feed livestock, they heard the sound of a horse-drawn wagon. A lone passenger steered the wagon into the Jennings property and waved as he approached. It was Lonnie Crandall, returning from two days with his grandfather.

"Hey, Franklin! Hey, Joshie!" Lonnie stood as he reined his horse to a stop beside them.

"Did y'all miss me? I bet you couldn't wait fer me to get back home."

Franklin nodded, trying to avoid being drawn into a conflict.

Lonnie dropped the reins onto the floor of the wagon and jumped out as the horse lurched forward. Joshua stepped back quickly to avoid being hit by the wagon wheel.

"What would ya do 'thout me here to take care'a ya?" Lonnie said to Joshua, grabbing his cap off his head and pretending to throw it away.

"I made it fine without you."

"Nah, I bet you was lonesome as can be 'thout ole Lonnie, wasn't ya?"

"Leave him alone," demanded Franklin.

"Aw, I was just a-kiddin' with him. I don't mean no harm."

Lonnie put the cap back on Joshua's head, pulled the bill down over his eyes, and headed toward the house.

"You got anything to eat in this place?"

"Yeah," said Franklin, "but you better do somethin' with that horse an' wagon."

"I'll get to it later," shouted Lonnie as he disappeared into the back door.

Franklin shook his head in frustration as he and Joshua walked to the barn in silence. Joshua wanted to tell his father about his trip with Lonnie to get well pipe. He wanted his father to know how he dreaded every moment he spent in Lonnie's presence. But his aversion to the conflict between Franklin and Lonnie made him hold his tongue. He feared what his father would do if he knew the whole truth about Lonnie's abusive behavior. Finally, choosing his words carefully, he spoke out.

"There's somethin' about Lonnie that worries me."

"What d'ya mean?"

"I dunno. Sometimes he just acts kind'a—crazy."

Franklin sighed. "Yeah, I know."

"I guess we just don't get along too good," admitted Joshua.

"Well, I 'spect he didn't want to come here to live in the first place." Franklin placed his hand on Joshua's shoulder. "Maybe he won't stay around here too much longer. Maybe he'll go stay with his grandpa permanent."

"I hope so."

The next three weeks were relatively peaceful. Lonnie seemed preoccupied. For the most part, he stayed to himself and ignored the rest of the family.

"I'm goin' to Fulton this mornin' to see about a pump for our well," Franklin announced as he got up from the breakfast table. "I hear tell he's got a newfangled pump that runs on gasoline—an' the best thing is that his price is good."

"Can we afford a new pump right now?" asked Maggie with a frown. "The other day, you said we was runnin' short."

"I 'spect I won't be buyin' one today. But I aim to talk about gettin' one later on if the crops are good. Matter'a fact, I need you boys to do some things around here while I'm gone."

"You mean we won't hafta pump the water by hand anymore, Papa?" asked Jessie.

"Yeah—well, if I can get us a pump, we won't. Now, what I was sayin', I want you boys to go out to the barn an' clean up all that straw an' manure where the cows were bedded down during the snow. There's pitchforks an' a shovel or two already out there. Just load it on that old wagon, an' then we'll spread it on the field before plowin' time."

"Just who you talkin' to?" asked Lonnie as he finished his milk.

"I mean you, an' Joshua, mostly. No reason you can't do a little work around here. It won't take all day if you work steady." Franklin stopped in the doorway as he was about to leave.

"Matt, you can go along with 'em. You're gettin' big enough to help a little."

Lonnie rose from his chair and wiped his mouth with his shirt sleeve.

"I ain't shovelin' no cow shit!" he said, pursing his lips and shaking his head. "An' you ain't gonna make me, either."

Immediately, Franklin lunged toward him in anger, but Lonnie darted away. He yanked open the back door and ran out, pushing the screen door with such force it swung open and banged loudly against the outside of the house. As Franklin stumbled over a chair, Lonnie ran into the cabin and shut the door behind him, securing it with its sliding bolt lock.

Franklin had promised Maggie and himself that he would not be drawn into another altercation with Lonnie. As he reached the back steps, he saw that Lonnie had locked himself in the cabin. For a fleeting moment, he thought about getting his rifle, but just as quickly, he took a deep breath, turned, and went back inside.

"I don't aim to deal with this right now. I'm goin' to town," he announced sternly. He put on his coat and hat, walked out of the house, started up the old Model T, and left.

Maggie nervously began clearing dirty dishes off the table, and the girls joined in to help. No one said a word. Joshua motioned with his head for Matt to follow him to the door. On tiptoes, he reached to pull his coat and Matt's off the wooden pegs where they hung during winter months. They dug their brown cotton gloves and stocking caps out of their coat pockets and put them on as they left the house.

"Why'd ya do yer head like that?" asked Matt, mocking the way Joshua had motioned for him.

"I wanted to get us out'a there," explained Joshua. "It makes me feel sick at my stomach when Papa and Lonnie fight like that. I felt like I had to get out."

"You reckon Papa can throw him down?"

"I don't know—an' I don't care, neither."

"What d'ya wanna do now?"

"I 'spect we ought'a go an' clean out that barn, like Papa said."

"Why? Lonnie's not goin'—an' if Lonnie doesn't hafta do it, why do we?"

"I'm glad Lonnie's not goin'! I don't like Lonnie, an' I don't like bein' around Lonnie."

"I don't see why we hafta clean the barn."

"You don't. You prob'ly can't handle a pitchfork, anyway. I just feel like workin' to take my mind off Lonnie. You can do what you want."

"All right. I'll go."

Joshua continued across the backyard toward the barn with Matt close behind. They crawled under the gate separating the yard from the feedlot surrounding the barn. Sometimes they would unlatch the gate, swing it open, pass through, and then close and latch it again. But usually, they either crawled under or climbed over.

As Joshua entered the feedlot, a young filly stood in his way. As he had done many times before, he picked up a soggy, mud-covered corncob and threw it at her to chase her away. It hit her solidly on her rump. In a swift and unexpected reaction, she kicked with both hind legs. One of her hooves caught Joshua squarely on his forehead, just above his right eye. As he lay dazed on his back, blood gushed out. His flesh was laid open down to his skull.

Matt ran to him, wide-eyed and speechless with fear at the sight of his brother's head and face covered with blood. Joshua began to blink, covered his face with his hands, and screamed as blood ran down the sides of his face and onto the front of his coat. Matt ran ahead, unlatched the gate, and continued toward the house, yelling for help.

Maggie heard their screams, and she knew it was an emergency. She met Matt on the back porch and grabbed him by the shoulders. Breathless, he muttered and stuttered, but his words were incomprehensible.

"What's wrong, Matt? Are you hurt? Matt, slow down and tell me—what happened?"

"It's Ja—Ja—Joshua …" he began, but he couldn't speak.

Maggie saw Joshua as he struggled to sit up. Blood dripped from his face.

"Oh, Joshua!" she shrieked as she ran to meet him. "Joshua, what happened? Let's get you inside."

Joshua continued to scream and couldn't talk. Maggie put her arm around him and held him close to her as she rushed him to the house. Lonnie emerged from the cabin, standing just outside the door.

"What'sa matter with Joshua? Why's he cryin' like a girl?"

"You go back inside," his mother said sternly. "This is all your fault!"

She rushed Joshua inside. Naomi, Reba, and Jessie, who had congregated at the back door, gasped and cried at the sight of Joshua's bloody face.

"What happened to Joshua?" cried Jessie.

"I don't know yet. Get some cool water and some towels."

The girls shuffled out of the way and hurried to comply. Maggie took Joshua to the bed in the room adjacent to the kitchen. Gerthy hobbled into the room.

"Help me get Joshua onto the bed," Maggie whispered.

"What happened?"

"I don't know yet. He's covered with blood. I—I think his head's cut."

"Take it easy, Joshua. You're gonna be all right," Gerthy assured him. He and Maggie lifted the boy onto the bed.

Joshua continued to hold his forehead in his hands. Gerthy grasped Joshua's hands and gently pulled them away, exposing the deep cut above his right eye. Maggie dipped a towel in the basin of cool water that Jessie held for her, and she began to wash away the blood from Joshua's face. Seeing the gash that continued to ooze blood, Naomi and Reba gasped aloud and ran from the room, nauseated by the sight.

"We're gonna need the doctor," said Gerthy quietly. "Call Dr. Beeler."

Maggie handed her towel to Gerthy. She rushed to the telephone on the wall in their sitting room, took the receiver off its hook, and turned the crank for one long ring.

"Central."

"Get me Dr. Beeler, and please hurry! This is Maggie Jennings."

"What'd he say?" asked Gerthy as Maggie reentered the bedroom.

"Said he'd jump in his buggy and come right on over."

Doc Beeler kept his horse hitched to his buggy for emergencies just like this one. He looked in his bag to be sure he had a needle and suture material, said goodbye to his wife, who doubled as his nurse, and rushed out the door to his buggy. From Crutchfield to the Jennings house was a distance of three miles. Allowing extra time for the climb up Dixon Hill, the doctor knew he would make the trip in twenty to twenty-five minutes.

Dr. R. E. Lee Beeler was a man of slight stature in his midfifties. Most folks called him Doc Beeler, but his close friends called him Lee. He was a native of Fulton County who, after graduating from Murray State Teachers College, had decided to forego his teaching career for the medical profession. He went to Memphis, where he completed his medical training at the University of Tennessee Medical School. Then he returned to practice in his home county, where he was totally devoted to his family, his friends, and his patients. Only his patriotic devotion to his country and its military forces had lured him away. He had served a two-year tour of duty as a medical volunteer during the World War.

His graying hair was neatly parted and combed, but he had a bald spot on the back of his head about the size of a jar lid. Some people described him as "bug-eyed" because his eyes were constantly wide open, as if he was afraid he would miss something. His lips were thin and straight, but he constantly worked them back and forth from a pucker to a smile—and back to a pucker again.

Not only did he constantly move his lips, but also his whole body was perpetually in motion. He swayed, shuffled from one foot to the other, fidgeted, scratched, and waved his hands as he talked. When he was a boy, his nicknames had included Skeeter, June Bug, Dragonfly, and Snake Doctor (a name he particularly deplored as an adult).

Doc Beeler's patients acknowledged that he was not the most knowledgeable, up-to-date physician in the state—or even in the county, for that matter. But he was a caring, devoted doctor who knew their personal histories and their special needs like no one else possibly could, and they trusted themselves to his care. When money was scarce, his patients paid him with chickens, hams, beef roasts, vegetables from their gardens, and fruits from their orchards. To the folks in that part of Fulton County, there could be no better physician and friend than was Robert E. Lee Beeler. He was always available when and where he was needed, and sooner than expected, he knocked on the back door of the Jennings house.

"Thanks for coming so soon," greeted Maggie as she opened the door. "He's in that first room there, just through that door."

Doc Beeler went through the door where Maggie was pointing. He shook hands with Gerthy and greeted him quietly before walking over to the bed.

"Hello there, my friend," he said to Joshua, extending his hand.

"Hi."

"Miss Maggie tells me you got a cut on your head. Let me have a look at it so we can get you fixed up."

The doctor folded back the towel covering Joshua's wound. Joshua flinched and moaned.

"I know it's a little sore, buddy, but I've gotta clean it up an' see what we've got here." He reached in his bag for some cotton.

"How'd this happen?"

"A horse kicked me."

"A horse? A horse kicked you with its back foot?"

"Yes, sir. I—I was tryin' to get to the barn, an'—an' this horse was standin' in the way. So I hit her with a cob to chase her out'a the way. An' that's when she kicked me. It knocked me down."

"I'm sure it did! Did you pass out? You know, did you know what was goin' on the whole time, or did you kind'a black out?"

"Yeah—I mean, yes, sir. I did kind'a pass out. At first, I didn't know what happened. An' then I was just lyin' on the ground, an' I couldn't see 'cause of all the blood."

As Doc Beeler continued to clean the wound, he spoke quietly to Maggie and Gerthy.

"He probably doesn't think so, but he's a very lucky young man. Let me show you." He motioned for them to get closer.

"He has a nasty cut on his head, and I'll have to sew it up. But it could'a been a lot worse. See right here?"

He pointed at the crescent-shaped cut extending through Joshua's right eyebrow.

"The horse's hoof hit Joshua right across the bone that protects the eye socket. If it had hit lower, he might have lost that eye. If it had hit higher, he could'a had a skull fracture or a bad concussion."

"Is he gonna be okay?" asked Jessie. She had remained in the room to observe in silence.

"Well, hey there, Jessie," said Dr. Beeler. "I didn't see you standin' there. Yeah, you brother's gonna be fine as soon as I get him stitched up here. Why don't you stand there by him while I talk to Maggie and Gerthy in the kitchen? Maggie, can I get a glass of water? I'm thirsty."

Maggie and Gerthy followed the doctor to the kitchen, and Maggie filled a glass with water.

"I needed to tell y'all somethin' that I didn't particularly want Joshua to hear. Don't worry—he's gonna be fine. Just watch him for the next day or two and let me know if he gets the headache, or if he gets sick at his stomach."

"Will he have a scar?" asked Maggie.

"Oh, yes. He'll have a scar there to help him remember this day for the rest of his life. There's no way I can stitch it up without leaving a scar— matter of fact, that's what I wanted to tell you. I can sew it up here, but I don't have any anesthetic with me to deaden it like I would if we were at the hospital. It's gonna be pretty painful for him while I'm puttin' in the stitches, and I 'spect you're gonna have to hold him down an' keep him still while I'm doin' it."

Without any more discussion, they returned to the bedroom. Gerthy motioned for Naomi to come back into the room to help. Doc Beeler walked back to Joshua's bedside and placed his hand on Joshua's chest.

"Joshua, I need to put some stitches in your head to close up that wound. It's gonna sting a little when I do it, but I'll be as easy on you as I can."

He got his needle from his bag and threaded it with suture material. As he approached the bed with needle in hand, Joshua started to squirm and kick. The doctor nodded to his new assistants, who knew what to do. Maggie and Jessie took responsibility for Joshua's feet and legs. First, each of them tried to hold one of his legs, but he kicked free of their grasp. Then Jessie climbed up onto the bed and sat on his legs just above his knees. Maggie went to the foot of the bed and grabbed hold of his ankles.

Naomi latched onto one arm, and Reba clasped the other. They were sympathetic to Joshua's plight, and they certainly did not want to see him in pain. But they had a job to do. Besides, their competitive spirit made them determined to show Joshua that they could hold him down.

Gerthy held Joshua's head firmly in his strong hands. It was his head, after all, that needed to be stable, and his uncle's presence close to him was somewhat comforting to Joshua.

Doc Beeler worked carefully but steadily to close the wound. Joshua screamed as the needle was drawn repeatedly through his flesh, and he writhed in pain, but he could not free his arms or legs. The girls watched at first, interested to see this strange procedure that substituted human flesh for quilts, dresses, and other apparel that they had helped to sew. They soon turned to look away, however, as they felt queasy and faint.

As the doctor completed his final stitches, Joshua lay still and quiet. He closed his eyes and gritted his teeth, determined not to cry again. Finally, the doctor announced that he had completed his last stitch. He applied tincture of iodine and a bandage and put his supplies back in his bag.

"You are a brave young man," he said to Joshua as he prepared to leave. "Your head will be sore for a few days, and I'll need to come back in a week or so to take out the stitches. I'm sure you're gonna have a black eye, but other than that, you should be fine."

Gerthy and Maggie walked Doc Beeler to the door, leaving the girls to stay with Joshua. After they thanked the doctor, made arrangements to pay for his services, and said goodbye, they discussed how to care for Joshua during his recovery. Since his condition needed to be monitored, Gerthy volunteered to set up a temporary bed in his room so that Joshua could stay with him.

In the middle of the afternoon, Joshua woke up from a nap and saw his uncle seated in a rocking chair reading a book.

"What are you readin', Uncle Gerthy?"

"Oh, I'm reading *The Adventures of Tom Sawyer* for the umpteenth time. It's a book that makes me smile inside, so every once in awhile, I read it again. Actually, it's a book written for boys and girls, so I'll loan it to you, an' you can read it for yourself."

"Do you think I'd like it?"

"Not a doubt in my mind. Matter'a fact, I was just getting to the part where Tom's aunt gives him *painkiller* 'cause he's all down in the dumps."

"Maybe you ought'a give me some painkiller. My head's really …"

"Gerthy! Gerthy, are you in there? Is Joshua in there with you?" Franklin shouted.

"Come on in, Franklin."

"I just got home, and Maggie told me a horse kicked Joshua. Are you all right, son?"

"I'm okay, I guess. But my head hurts a little."

"How'd you get kicked by a horse? Which one of the horses kicked you?"

"It was Betsy. Me an' Matt, we were goin' to the barn to clean it—like you said. Betsy was standin' …"

"You an' Matt were goin' to clean the barn by yourselves? Without Lonnie?"

"Yeah—I mean, yes, sir."

"Well, I never meant for you boys to clean the barn without Lonnie. You could help, but you can't do it by yourselves."

"Well, when Lonnie ran off to the cabin, an' you went to town …"

"This is all Lonnie's fault. He won't do anything around here, an' now because of him, you get hurt! I think it's time we got this settled once and for all."

Franklin stormed out of the room, red-faced with anger. He strode down the hall to his bedroom and reached up on top of his chest of drawers, where he kept a loaded 22-caliber rifle. As he turned to go back through the kitchen to the back door, Gerthy stood in his way. He looked straight into Franklin's eyes and reached out to take the gun.

"Franklin, I can see you're upset. You go settle things with that stepson'a yours. But leave the gun with me."

Franklin started to resist and moved to the side to pass by his brother, but Gerthy held his arm firmly.

"Franklin," he said again, "give the gun to me!"

Franklin looked at Gerthy and took a deep breath. He extended the gun, and Gerthy took it from him.

"I'm goin' to have a talk with Lonnie," declared Franklin as he squeezed past his brother and headed through the kitchen toward the back door.

Franklin walked to the cabin and knocked on the door.

"Who's there?" shouted Lonnie.

"It's me, your father."

"You ain't my father! You ain't never been my father, an' you ain't never gonna be my father. Now go away an' leave me be."

"Okay. It's Franklin. Open the door! It's time you an' me had a talk."

"I ain't interested in talkin' to you. Now go on away."

"Lonnie, open the door! I was a mind to come out here with my gun. I left it in the house. I don't have my gun with me now, but I can go back an' get it. An' I can get through that door one way or another. Now, you want me to come in there with my gun or without my gun?"

Franklin waited. In a few moments, he heard Lonnie unbolting the door. The door swung open as Lonnie walked back to sit on the edge of his bed.

"I'm gonna make this short," said Franklin. "I want you out of here by tomorrow evenin'."

"What? You want to kick me out? You can't kick me out! I live here."

"Not anymore, you don't."

"Where you plan on me goin' to live?"

"I don't plan on anything except havin' you out of here. You'll have to find someplace to live."

"You brought me here to live when you married my mama. Now you're stuck with me. I ain't leavin'."

"You're right about one thing. I brought you here. An' I treated you like one'a my own. It's just I expected you to help with the work an' do your share like everybody else does 'round here."

"Maybe I'll start helpin'."

"Too late for that now. Start packin' up your things an' get out'a here. By tomorrow evenin', if you're still here, I'll be back with my gun."

"What does my mama say about this?"

"It don't matter what your mama says about it. Just get your things together an' leave. An' I never want to see you around here ever again."

Without waiting for any more conversation, Franklin turned and walked out the door, closing it behind him.

"You'll see me again, for sure!" Lonnie screamed. "It ain't over—I guarantee you, it ain't over," he muttered to himself.

The next day, Lonnie put his belongings in his grandfather's wagon and left.

6
CHAPTER

MAGGIE TURNED DOWN THE wick to extinguish the kerosene lamp that sat on a small table beside the bed. She slid under the covers carefully to avoid waking Franklin, who had been in bed for almost half an hour. Normally, he preceded her to bed, and as a rule, he was already asleep when she retired for the night. She was surprised when Franklin rolled over onto his side and propped himself up with his elbow digging into the featherbed.

"I don't want that boy'a yours to ever come around here again," he declared. "He better be gone for good."

Maggie sat up and fumbled for a match to relight the lamp.

Franklin squinted. "What are ya doin'? I don't aim to have a long discussion about it. I just want everybody to know I'm through with that boy, that's all."

Maggie sat up and pulled the covers up under her chin. "He's gone, Franklin. He left this mornin'. I don't know what else you want me to do."

"Just make sure he doesn't come back, that's all." Franklin sighed heavily and shook his head. "I took him in an' treated him just like one'a my own, an' all he's done is cause trouble. I just don't want him around here no more."

Maggie wiped her mouth and chin nervously. "Well, he's gone for now, an' maybe he won't come back, but ..."

"There's not gonna be any buts about it," interrupted Franklin. "For his own good, he better stay away from here."

"It's not easy for Lonnie, Franklin," pleaded Maggie. "He's only a seventeen-year-old kid. He doesn't have a place of his own."

"He had a place to live here, an' plenty of food to eat, too," barked Franklin. "But he wouldn't work, an' all he did was fight an' cuss an' cause trouble."

"He's gone to his grandpa's to live with him for awhile. But his grandpa is more than eighty years old, an' he has trouble takin' care of his self—an' he only has one bed. Lonnie's gonna hafta sleep on the floor, I guess. It's just ... I just don't know how long he can stay there, that's all."

"Well, he better figure out a way to stay there. I swear, I think there's somethin' bad wrong with him. I never saw a boy that seemed so mad all the time. I never saw him look happy the whole time he's been here."

Maggie wiped her face again with her drawn, arthritic hand. "He's had a hard life, Franklin. I never told you what all of us went through livin' with Harley before he died. Never really wanted to talk about it."

"Well, it must'a been bad if that's the cause of Lonnie actin' so crazy. How did Harley die, anyway?"

Maggie adjusted the wick on the lamp to chase away some of the darkness.

"Maybe it's time I told you some things," she said. "Maybe it would make you feel different about Lonnie—an' even me."

Franklin laid his head back on his pillow and closed his eyes. "Well, it's gettin' mighty late, but I reckon I'll listen."

Maggie coughed, cleared her throat, and told about her life with her alcoholic husband Harley, hoping it would help Franklin understand Lonnie's anger and his erratic behavior.

Indeed, Harley Crandall had been a cruel, overbearing man, given to excessive drinking and violent behavior throughout the duration of their marriage. One evening, after he had had more to drink than usual, Harley had come home to find that Maggie was asleep, but there was no food on the table, and Lonnie was crying. Maggie had covered his dinner with a cloth and placed it in the cupboard. In his drunken delirium, Harley picked up a cup, glared into its emptiness, and hurled it furiously against the wall. The baby screamed louder. Yanked from her sleep by the sudden commotion, Maggie leapt from her bed to get her baby. Just as she lifted Lonnie from his little crib, Harley snatched the little one away from her and dropped him roughly back into his bed. He shoved Maggie backward against their bed, and when she rose back up in a seated position, he struck her hard in the face with the back of his hand.

"You ain't no good, woman!" he shouted with his eyes ablaze. "They ain't nothin' ta eat! No food on the table an' the baby's a-yellin', an' all you can do is sleep! What kind'a woman are you, anyway?" Harley held his hand high in the air, prepared to hit Maggie again.

"Please, Harley, don't," cried Maggie, covering her face with her arms. "I'm sorry, Harley."

"Yeah, well, bein' sorry now ain't gonna help me none. You better ..."

"There's f-f-food in the c-c-cupboard," sobbed Maggie. "I'll get it if you want."

"I'll git it myself. Looks like I'm gonna hafta do everything around here. Take care of that young'un! He's over there a-screamin', an' it's drivin' me crazy. Now git!" Harley jerked Maggie up off the bed, shoving her toward the crib where Lonnie lay screaming. He stomped into the kitchen to eat.

This scenario was repeated over and over in the Crandall home. Sometimes, after such an episode, Harley was apologetic, but most of the time, there was no discussion of the events of the prior evening. Throughout their sad marriage, Maggie suffered his abusive eruptions continuously, but for a time, Lonnie escaped with just an occasional slap on his head or swat on his behind.

The first time Lonnie experienced his father's fury was on a day when Harley seemed calm and unusually sober. They had gone outside to play catch with an old baseball that was missing some of the stitching in one of its seams. Lonnie used a cheap mitt his father had given him, and Harley played barehanded. Wanting his son to learn to play well, Harley threw a mixture of flies and grounders that Lonnie would try to catch. Then, after he caught the ball or retrieved a miss, Lonnie tossed the ball back to his father.

Harley decided to increase the difficulty of his throws to challenge his son to improve his game. He threw the ball harder, and in various directions to make Lonnie move from side to side, or up and back to make the catch. A grounder that Harley had thrown with increased velocity hit an uneven spot in the yard, bounced up, and hit Lonnie square on his nose. Blood flowed freely, and Lonnie screamed. He held his nose in his hands, and as blood ran down his arms and dripped off his elbow, tears streamed down his cheeks and dripped off his chin. Harley ran up to him immediately.

"Hey, stop that cryin'!" he yelled. "You stop that cryin' right now, you little sissy."

Lonnie looked at his irate father and cried even more.

"Didn't you hear me? Stop that cryin'!" He grabbed Lonnie by his shoulders and shook him. "You better stop that cryin' right this minute, or I'll—I'll … You little sissy! Stop it!"

Now Lonnie was hurt, scared by the sight of his own blood, and terrorized by his father's shouts and the furor in his eyes. He screamed uncontrollably.

"You better listen to me, you little sissy! Stop that cryin'. No son of mine is gonna cry like a girl just 'cause he gits hit by a ball. I said stop it. Stop it right now!" Harley continued to shake Lonnie, and Lonnie continued to bawl.

"I might as well'a had three girls. Maybe that's what I got. You're a girl! You're nothin' but a little sissy!"

When Lonnie let out another scream, Harley released his grip on the boy's shoulder and struck him in the jaw with the back of his hand, knocking him to the ground. Harley walked away.

"I'll just go git your mother. I'll git your mother an' tell her to come out here an' take care of her little girl."

From that day on, Lonnie was never the same in the eyes of his father, and Harley was not the same father Lonnie had known. Harley acted as if he had lost his son, and Lonnie feared his father's outbursts. The beatings Harley administered to his son grew in frequency and intensity as Lonnie grew older and stronger. Similarly, Lonnie's hatred for his father intensified through the years, not only because of the abuse he experienced personally, but even more because he watched as his father beat Maggie.

The Crandalls' nightmarish existence with Harley ended on a summer evening soon after Lonnie's sixteenth birthday. Lonnie slept at home, and he ate some of his meals there, but he worked during the day, and most of the time at night he was out with his friends. He worked with a crew of young men and other teenagers who hired out to help farmers put up hay.

Lonnie began as the driver. As he drove the team of horses or mules slowly through the field, other members of the crew used pitchforks to load the loose hay onto the flat bed of the wagon. When it was stacked up as high as they could hoist it, they hauled it to the barn, where it was pitched into the hayloft. As Lonnie grew larger and stronger, he graduated from being the driver to manning one of the pitchforks.

In the evenings, Lonnie and his friends congregated to develop their social skills. They rolled and smoked cigarettes, chewed twists of tobacco, and drank whatever alcohol they could get. They stayed out late every night, even though they knew they were expected to be in the fields as soon as the dew was off the next morning. They caught up on sleep on stormy days, when no work was available for them, and on Sundays, when many of the farmers would not allow work to be done on their farms.

Harley had reached the nadir of his sorry existence. He was drunk every night. Much of the time, he stayed away for periods of three or four days, never able to remember where or with whom he had been.

Late in the summer in the early hours of the morning, Harley came home from a night of heavy drinking. This was not the end of a three-day binge. Those sprees ended when he had passed out somewhere and slept for a day or so. This was one of those nights when he had been angry when he started to drink, and the liquor had intensified his anger. He had no idea why he was angry, but his ire was loaded and primed and ready to be shot off at any person or anything that crossed his path.

He crashed his six-foot-two-inch, two-hundred-twenty-five-pound frame into the back door, ripping away part of the doorframe and tearing the latch off its screws. The door was not locked. Harley just didn't want to turn the doorknob.

"Can somebody git me somethin' to drink?" he screamed, falling over one of the wooden chairs beside the kitchen table. "Hey! Didn't you hear me?" he continued. "I need a drink!"

Maggie came to the door, wiping her eyes to rid them of sleep and the tears that she could already feel welling up.

"Oh, Harley, please sit down," she pleaded. "I'll see if I can find somethin' for you."

"Find somethin'? Find somethin'? You better git somethin'! I don't …"

"Okay, Harley. Just sit down. I'm comin'," said Maggie, trying to calm him down.

"I don't aim to sit down, an' I don't aim to wait here all night. Hey! What're you two a-lookin' at? Git yer little … You better git them girls away from me, woman. I ain't in no mood to put up with them girls."

"Please, girls," Maggie whispered. "Just go back to bed."

"Where's my drink?" Harley slammed his fist down on the table and fell into the chair.

"I have some tea here. Or, if you want, I can make you some fresh coffee," Maggie said, knowing that was not what Harley wanted to hear.

"Tea?" Harley yelled. "You think I want tea?" Harley struggled to stand. "Woman, I want a drink, an' I want it now!" he demanded. As he moved toward Maggie and knocked over another of the kitchen chairs, Lonnie opened the screen door and burst into the room, gasping to catch his breath.

"What's goin' on in here? I could hear yellin' for half a mile," he panted.

"We're gonna be okay, Lonnie," said Maggie quietly.

"Oh, I should'a known! It's you," said Lonnie, looking disdainfully at his drunken father. A lighted cigarette dangled from Lonnie's lips. He had never smoked in the presence of his parents before, but he hadn't expected them to be awake, and hearing all the commotion, he had run to the house without throwing it away.

"What's that hangin' out'a your mouth?" shouted Harley. "Who told you you could start smokin'?"

"Nobody. Didn't need nobody to tell me!"

"Well, I'm tellin' you right now you ain't gonna keep on smokin'. Ain't no boy'a mine gonna smoke 'til I say he can. Put that thing down out'a yer mouth, or I'm gonna come over there an' …"

"An' what? What are you gonna do? You're drunk! An' you're a sorry old man. You ain't ever gonna do nothin' to me—ever again!"

"I'm gonna teach you that you can't talk to me like ..."

"An' don't you ever—ever—*ever* lay a hand on my mama again!" Lonnie said, pointing his finger in Harley's face.

Lonnie had finally gone over the brink with his father. He felt bold. For the first time in his life, he was not afraid of his father's wrath. But Harley was full of rage, and Lonnie's challenge to his authority was more than he could tolerate.

"So, you wanna smoke, huh?" shouted Harley, moving toward Lonnie. "Well, then, maybe I'll just help you smoke." Harley grabbed a small paper sack from the cupboard and turned it upside down, emptying four peppermint sticks onto the kitchen table. He twisted it lengthwise. Then he grabbed a kitchen match, struck it on the top of the cookstove, and lit the end of the sack. With the flaming sack in his hand and his eyes ablaze from the mixture of booze and rage, he stumbled toward Lonnie.

"Yeah. You wanna smoke, don't ya? Well, you're gonna smoke, all right." Harley held the burning bag in his hand and thrust it forward toward Lonnie like an uncoordinated fencer.

"Git away from me!" shouted Lonnie. "Git away from me or somebody's gonna git hurt."

Maggie had moved away, over by the door to the bedroom.

"Please, Harley," she cried out. "Please put that down."

"Where's that cigarette?" taunted Harley, continuing to back Lonnie toward the wall. "Come on, you little sissy, I'm gonna light it fer ya."

To Lonnie, *sissy* was the magic word. Suddenly, he was right back out in the yard with blood dripping from his nose, looking into the eyes of his father as his father ridiculed him mercilessly. Suddenly, all the rage and hatred that had boiled inside of him since that boyhood time erupted like a skyrocket.

"You'll never call me a sissy again," he screamed, and as his father jabbed at him again with the burning sack, Lonnie stepped to the side. Grabbing Harley's wrist with both hands, Lonnie pulled him forward and then pushed him headlong into the wall. Harley's head hit the wall with a dull *thud*. He stumbled but didn't fall. As he attempted to regain his balance, his fiery sack became entangled with curtains hanging at the kitchen window. Instantly, the curtains were ablaze, and Harley stumbled backward and fell to the floor.

Maggie had made curtains for every window in the house. The ones she now watched being consumed by flames were her favorite pair—heavily ruffled, and made of cotton cloth from flour sacks. Instinctively, Maggie ran to the window to put out the fire. Grabbing the curtains on the opposite side of the window from the blaze, she yanked them down, curtain rod and all. Using a dishtowel, she tried to beat out the flames.

Lonnie knelt down to check on his father, who was slumped down in the floor in a pitiful heap. He heard Maggie scream. As he jumped to his feet, he saw that a ruffle at the hem of her nightgown had caught fire. Maggie continued to scream and ran to escape the fire. By the time Lonnie caught up to her, she had run to the bedroom, where Reba and Naomi hid as they listened to the bedlam. As flames spread up the left side of her gown, Lonnie threw her onto the bed, and Naomi quickly covered her with a quilt.

"Stay here with Mama," said Lonnie. "I gotta go back out there an' take care'a the old drunk."

Lonnie went back to the kitchen and looked under the edge of the table where his father had fallen. He was not there. Lonnie looked all around the room. He thought that at any moment Harley might spring on him again with more of his fury. His father was nowhere in sight. As Lonnie pushed open the screen door to see if his father was standing on the porch, he heard a *pop,* or more like a crack—the sound of a single gunshot. It was a familiar sound to Lonnie. It was the sound of his father's 22-caliber single-shot rifle. At that instant, Lonnie knew that his father had shot himself.

After Maggie had finished talking, she stared straight ahead into the flickering darkness. She waited for a response from Franklin. He was silent. She touched his arm. He did not respond. She lifted the lamp to illuminate his face. He was asleep. Tearfully, Maggie extinguished the lamp and lay still. She wondered how much of her story Franklin had heard.

7
CHAPTER

MATT AND JOSHUA SLOSHED through ankle-deep water carrying small sacks of corn from the stock barn to a smaller hog barn. Spring rains had been heavy and frequent, often flooding the barnyard and fields already saturated by unusual amounts of precipitation since the late winter. They rushed to feed the hogs as more loud claps of thunder and dark, foreboding clouds overhead heralded a new storm.

They poured corn into the troughs as one old sow and seven shoats from her previous litter came to eat.

"Get out'a here! You're steppin' on my foot." Matt whacked a young pig with his empty sack. The pig jumped, squealed, and moved to a new spot at the crowded trough.

"We better get out'a here ourselves before that storm hits," said Joshua. "I'm gettin' sick an' tired of all this rain."

"Do we hafta help milk the cows an' feed the mules?" Matt asked.

"Yeah. I reckon. Papa's back up there milkin', but he said for us to come give 'im some help when we got done feedin' the hogs."

As the boys left the hog shed, darker clouds moved in. Billowed by strong gusts, trees swayed and bowed toward the east while lightning popped and cracked all around. The boys looked at each other, first in awe and then in fear. Joshua motioned toward the barn with his head, and they raced through the water and mud. About halfway there, a tremendous bolt of lightning sizzled through the air and made a loud crackling sound very close to the big barn. The horrified boys stopped dead in their tracks as huge fireballs rolled and skipped across the wet ground between them and the barn. They screamed in unison and felt their hair stand up, partly out of fear and partly from the electrically charged air.

"Come on!" screamed Joshua, his voice barely audible above the din of high wind and repeating claps of thunder. He turned and ran a short distance to the empty granary that stood only ten feet to the left of the path from the hog shed to the barn.

The door to the small granary was not locked, but dampness from recent rains had caused it to swell, and the boys had to shove against it together with their shoulders to burst it open. Once inside, they pushed against the door just as hard to get it shut. They were out of breath and shaking, still terrified by the lightning bolt and the balls of fire it had spawned.

"Did you see that?" asked Matt breathlessly. "What was that?"

"I dunno. I never saw anything like that before."

"Can it get us in here?"

"Naw—least, I don't believe it can."

Then, to tease him, Joshua said loudly and with mock fear, "I sure hope that wasn't a sign the world's comin' to an end!"

"Huh? What did you say?"

"I said I'm afraid that fire rollin' across the ground was a sign the world's comin' to an end."

"Naw. You don't really believe the world's gonna end, do ya? You're scarin' me!"

The storm intensified. The gale turned cracks in the tongue-and-groove walls and floors of the granary into a chorus of whistles and moans, sounds that made Joshua and Matt quiver just as the sight of the fireballs had done.

"You hear that wind, don't ya?" Joshua spoke bravely to hide his own qualms about their fate. "That's one of the signs, an'—an' fire is the other. It says so in the Bible."

"Does not! The Bible doesn't say nothin' about wind an' fire," Matt insisted. "You're just tryin' to scare me."

"Does too! Says that we won't have another flood, but next time the world's gonna be destroyed by wind an' fire. You an' I both saw the fire, and we can sure hear the wind."

Just at that moment, a strong gust of wind, or perhaps a small twister, hit the old granary, lifted it slightly off its blocks, and then settled it back down again. Rain fell in torrents, and rapid-fire claps of thunder sounded like the finale at a fireworks show on the Fourth of July. Now both boys were frightened. They stood there in the old, creaky building, staring at each other wide-eyed in stony silence.

Another gust hit the granary broadside, and the boys thought it was going over. It was lifted up higher this time but rocked back onto its foundation. The granary had been built there by Grandfather Jennings to hold wheat. Its walls and flooring were constructed of tongue-and-groove lumber to avoid losing any of the small kernels of grain stored in it. Despite cracks that had formed with age, its solid construction made it an ideal place for the boys to ride out the storm, except that it sat freely on cement blocks. Their only real danger was that it could be blown completely off its foundation.

The two brothers crouched together in a corner of the granary as gusts of wind repeatedly rocked it up and down on its blocks. Finally, as the sound of wind and rain subsided slightly, they could hear their father's frantic voice.

"Hey! Joshhuuaa! Maa-att! Where are you?" he yelled. *"Can you hear me? Joshhuuaa! Maa-att! Where are you?"*

The boys struggled unsuccessfully to open the door.

"We're in here," shouted Matt as he banged on the wall with his hand.

"Papa! We're over here—in the old wheat shed," yelled Joshua.

Finally, Franklin heard his sons' shouts and came to rescue them.

"Stand back away from the door!" After waiting a moment for the boys to comply, Franklin kicked it open.

"You boys scared me. I didn't know where you were." Franklin slammed the door and hurried the boys back toward the barn in the heavy downpour of rain.

"Is the world coming to an end, Papa?" inquired Matt.

"What?"

"Is the world gonna end?"

"Not that I know of, son. Why d'ya ask?

"Well ... Joshua said ..."

Joshua poked him hard in the ribs, and Matt knew to drop the question.

Wet weather continued for the next week and a half. Heavy thunderstorms replaced more typical springtime showers. The ground became totally saturated. Creeks, ponds, and rivers overflowed their banks. Preparations for springtime planting would have to wait.

"Come with me, Bud," Franklin said to Joshua during a slight break in the weather. "I need you to go get that section of harrow that we left over in the back field. If it ever quits rainin', we'll need it up here to harrow the garden."

It was midafternoon, and Joshua had completed his usual Saturday chores. He walked with his father across the yard toward the barn.

"Where is it?"

"It's sittin' in the edge of the back field next to the trees right by the gate. You'll see it."

The back field was across a large ditch—almost a ravine—that in some places was fifteen to twenty feet wide and twelve feet deep. It had been etched into the terrain over a period of many years by running water from natural springs and runoff. After heavy rains in the spring, the flow was swift and deep, but usually with the coming of summer, the stream would dry up to expose sandbars dotted with small pools of stagnant water. The ditch was heavily vegetated, with trees and small bushes clinging to its banks with their talon-like roots. Rotten tree trunks lay across it randomly, forming natural spans traversed by small animals and daring children.

The ditch was a popular place for the Jennings children to explore. It was their playground. Its sandbars of fine, white sand were perfect for make-believe road construction and farming, its pools were good places to wade, splash, and catch tadpoles, and there were plenty of trees to climb. With its canopy of sycamores, hickories, and water oaks, this meandering passageway was a natural haven for curious children. It sparked their imagination and transported them to new worlds of make-believe each time they played there. Its natural wonder beckoned: "Follow me around the next bend." Its serenity whispered, "Sit on my sand with your feet in the water." And its eeriness warned, "Beware of what might be hiding here." It spoke to them in many voices, so they gave it a name—the *Big Ditch*.

"How am I s'posed to get the harrow?" Joshua asked.

Franklin put his hand on his boy's shoulder. "I'm gonna put the harness on Ole Dick an' let you take him over there to pull it back. It's just one section of harrow. You won't need more'n one horse just to drag it back up here to the shed."

"Can I get across the Big Ditch? With all this rain, there may be water in it."

"If it's full'a water, just come on back, an' we'll get the harrow some other time. I'd go back there with you, but I need to carry Maggie down to Cayce to buy her some things she needs."

Joshua trotted ahead of his dad into the barn. He reached up, yanked a bridle off one of the wooden pegs that held gear for the horses and mules, and went out into the adjoining field to find Ole Dick. The horse was standing about fifty yards away, scratching his neck against a walnut tree in the fencerow. He was a medium-sized gelding with a brown coat, a black mane and tail, and a splotch of white on this nose. He was the farm's most reliable horse. He was easy to manage, powerfully built, and a tireless worker.

Joshua pulled the horse's head around and placed the bit between his lips. Ole Dick took the bit in his mouth without hesitation, and lowered his head to allow Joshua to slip the bridle behind his ears. Sensing that there was work to be done, he willingly followed Joshua back to the barn, where Franklin was waiting to put on his harness. The trusty horse stood still but turned his head to watch as Franklin selected the collar with the initials *O D* scratched into its crusty leather covering. That identification was necessary because the collar was sized specifically to fit Ole Dick. The other horses and mules had their own collars.

As they had done many times before, Franklin and Joshua worked together putting gear on the horse. First, Franklin unhooked the top of Ole Dick's collar and slipped it up onto his neck, buckling it into place firmly against the horse's withers. Joshua picked up a pair of hames, curved pieces that fit into slots on each side of the horse's collar, to which trace chains would be attached. He handed one to his father, who dropped it into place and attached it with a hame string. Joshua walked around the front of the horse, climbed up on an old crate, and reached up as high as he could to attach the other hame to the left-hand side of the horse's collar. Then, on opposite sides of the horse, each one attached one end of a trace chain to the hame, pulled the other end to the back of the horse, and attached it to a singletree, a swinging bar to which the harrow would be attached by a clevis. Finally, as his father had taught him to do, Joshua walked around the horse to make certain that all the gear was attached securely. It was.

Joshua took the reins, gave them a gentle slap against Ole Dick's sides, and headed out of the barn toward the path that had been worn down by livestock as they paraded in single file going to, and coming from, the back part of the farm. Franklin returned to the house.

"Joshua, remember what I said," shouted Franklin as he stopped and turned to look back at his son. "If that ditch has too much water in it, or if it starts to storm again, just come on back to the house." Then, as dark clouds rolled in once again and a clap of thunder echoed a warning, Franklin looked up at the darkening sky and frowned.

"Maybe you'd better come on back now an' forget about that old harrow. Look's like it's gonna come another storm!"

"I'll be okay, Papa. I'm already wet, anyway. It won't take me an' Ole Dick long to get that harrow back to the barn."

Franklin glanced back at the clouds, and he thought about insisting that his son come back. But he turned back toward the house, shook his head and muttered to himself, "I s'pose it won't hurt him to get a little wetter than he already is."

Joshua was not worried about the storm. At least there weren't balls of fire rolling across the ground. He was excited to be out in the wind and rain with thunder as sound effects both in front of and behind him. He didn't mind that drops of rain were being blown against his neck. He could feel water actually running down his back as his loose-fitting shirt ballooned out in the strong wind.

Since his twelfth birthday back in February, Joshua had begun to feel differently about himself. More confident. Happier at school and more comfortable with his friends at church. He worried less about his old and rather shabby clothes. His stomachaches were gone, and he had slept better since Lonnie left.

"Whoa, Dick!" Joshua yelled as they came to the edge of the Big Ditch. He tied the reins to a small bush and walked down the steep bank to inspect the water's depth and to decide whether the horse could pull the harrow back across.

"Yeah," he said to himself. "Me an' Ole Dick can get through that!"

Quickly, he retraced his steps, untied the horse, and urged him down the slope into the ditch. He held tight on the reins as the horse lowered his rear and braced against his forelegs for added stability going down the hill.

Ole Dick was not skittish to move into the flowing water as Joshua slapped the reins on the sides of his rump. Joshua stepped out into the knee-high current. He coaxed his dependable horse through the stream and up the other side without incident.

Joshua had been only wary of the storm, not afraid. But worsening conditions and chilly rain caused him to shiver. Crackles of lightning and rumbles of thunder intensified and persisted. Wind-driven rain pelted Joshua's face with stinging force, and dark gray skies turned black. Joshua squinted to keep drops of rain from hitting directly against his eyeballs. He shivered again as cooler winds chilled his soaked body, and he became more anxious in the squall.

The harrow he and Ole Dick were there to retrieve sat just where his father had said. He reined the Ole Dick around it and then pulled back hard on the reins to urge him to back up into position for Joshua to hitch the harrow to the singletree. The horse obliged and stood in relative calm as Joshua made his way to the front of the harrow to connect it. Then he hurried to the back again to grab the reins for the trip back across the Big Ditch.

Suddenly, amidst the storm's growing fury, a bolt of lightning hit the top of a tall hickory tree not more than 150 feet from where the boy and the horse stood. The tree was split into two parts with a resounding explosion that knocked Joshua to the ground. Ole Dick reared up in terror. Twisting in a ninety-degree pirouette, he dashed away, jerking the harrow up onto its side and yanking the reins out of Joshua's hands. He ran helter-skelter, first toward the downed tree and then away from it, past the opening coming into the field from the ditch. Wild with fear, he made an arc through the edge of the field and finally ran into an old, rusted-out fence that still stood there on the property boundary. His harness and the harrow tangled in the fence, slowing him down, but Ole Dick didn't quit running until he had ripped up two old, half-rotted posts and a long section of fence wire.

In disbelief and fear, Joshua raced through the mud to where Ole Dick was entangled. The horse's eyes were glassy, as he, too, was terrified. He flinched and began to move backward as Joshua approached. Joshua reached up to offer a reassuring pat on the horse's nose, but his hand shook and Ole Dick jerked his head to the side.

Joshua had lost track of time. As he worked to free the horse, he glanced up at the sky. It was getting dark. He wondered whether the darkness was due to the storm clouds or whether night was falling. He worked faster. Just as he extricated one part of the horse's harness, Ole Dick would move forward or backward or sideways to extricate himself. Each time, he got snarled all over again.

Physically exhausted and emotionally drained, Joshua finally freed the horse from the fence. With a tight hold on the reins, he took a deep breath and cried out meekly, "Come on, Dick, let's go!"

The horse jumped. Once again free to move, he broke into a trot, but Joshua hung on to restrain him. They headed for the Big Ditch. At its edge, Joshua stopped to assess his chances of getting back across. He was afraid as he peered down into the gulch. The water level had risen, and its current appeared swifter than before. Spontaneously, he yelled for help. Over and over, he called out as loudly as he could, but he realized his yells would not be heard. He was too far away from the house.

"What are we gonna do?" he uttered, perhaps to the horse.

Often his father had told him to have a plan for doing his work.

"Always think about the best way to do something before you do it," his father would say. "Use your mind to plan your work, and you will save your muscles a lot of pain," his father would say. "When you learn the best way to do something, do it that same way every time," his father had said.

Ole Dick is big enough to wade through the current, he reasoned. Most of the water would simply rush around his strong legs and under his belly. Perhaps he could ride the horse across the ditch. Joshua dismissed the idea. To his knowledge, Ole Dick had never been ridden. He was spooked already by the storm, and there was no point in doing something else that would cause him to go wild. Moreover, Joshua had never tried to ride a plowhorse, and he was unsure whether he could control Ole Dick unless he held onto the reins in the customary manner.

Instead of riding the horse through the water, Joshua decided to stand on the harrow to ride it across. It was a metal implement, an open grid with rows of teeth, or spikes, designed to break clods of dirt. It would be heavy enough to be dragged through the water across the sandy bottom of the ditch without capsizing. Joshua studied the harrow to see if he could stand on it without having his feet swept away by the swift current. There, on top of the harrow, was a metal frame mounted to hold levers used to adjust the angle of the tines against the ground. He stepped onto one of the crosspieces and tucked the toes of his heavy work boots under the framework. By pressing down with his heels and up against the underside of the frame with his toes, he could maintain his balance riding through the water.

Lightning and thunder had now moved off to the east, but like an aftershock, a deep rumble made Ole Dick jump and dance forwards and backwards nervously. Joshua feared that at any moment the horse might plunge down into the roaring chasm, just as he had plowed headlong into the wire fence.

"Take it easy, boy. We're gonna go in a minute."

He knew his planning time was used up. Water continued to rise. Soon, the fleeting remnants of daylight would be gone completely. Joshua knew he had to go now, or not at all.

He gently urged his horse to inch forward until he was standing directly on the edge of the ditch. Intent on his work, he was unaware of a loud roar that rumbled in the south, to his left and upstream, as he faced the Big Ditch. Joshua stepped onto the harrow. This was it. Now it was the real thing. He looked up into the darkened skies. Rain struck him in the face. Quietly, he said, "Dear God, help me an' Ole Dick get across the Big Ditch. Amen."

He took another deep breath and slapped the reins against the horse's sides. Ole Dick moved forward slowly with measured, careful steps. His rear legs momentarily slipped underneath him, but he quickly regained his balance and continued his descent. Joshua pressed his toes hard up against the harrow's frame in another test to be sure that he could hang on in the current. Instinctively aware of hazardous conditions, the big horse moved very slowly. His forelegs were now almost to the water's edge, but he seemed undaunted by its rushing flow under his nose. Joshua stared straight ahead. His grip on the reins made his knuckles white, and his calf muscles were taut as he pressed his toes upward. He tapped the reins against Ole Dick to encourage him to continue his forward movement into, and then through, the flowing water.

Faint, distant rumbling sounds that Joshua had ignored earlier quickly intensified to a deafening roar. Looking to his left, Joshua shivered and lost his breath. The noise coming from just around a bend in the ditch about fifty yards away was as loud as the clatter of freight trains he had heard as they passed at full speed through Cayce. But compared to the rumble of the trains, this was a much more menacing roar punctuated by the cracking of trees being snapped in two. Joshua shook, but his feet would not move.

In another instant, a wall of water plunged down upon him, and he had no time to react. He, and Ole Dick, and the harrow were engulfed in the torrent and swept along the Big Ditch like pieces of driftwood in ocean surf. The horse was knocked off his feet. He tumbled and bounced across the sandy floor with the harrow still attached to his harness, acting like an anchor.

Joshua lost his grip on the horse's reins, but in the rushing tide, his right foot lodged under the frame of the harrow as the harrow flipped over. As he tumbled under the surface of the water, he felt something snap in his ankle, and a sharp pain darted up his leg. For what seemed like an eternity, he was dragged along the bottom of the ditch, completely submerged and still entangled with the harrow. Finally, as it settled in the sand, he managed to work himself free and struggle to the surface.

He gasped for air as the rush of water continued to thrust him along. Joshua was not an experienced swimmer. In fact, he feared being in water more than knee-deep. He kicked and flailed his arms. He reached out for something—anything—to hold. Once again, he was sucked under. As he fought desperately to resurface, he choked and coughed up some of the muddy water that had been sucked into his throat. His work boots felt like cinder blocks attached to his legs. His arms ached with fatigue. He was scared.

As the rushing current pushed him around another slight bend, he was washed toward the side of the ditch. He grabbed onto a tree limb. It was large and buoyant enough to bear his weight, but it, too, floated free in the rapid surge. Joshua squinted to see through encompassing darkness. He looked back upstream for Ole Dick. His favorite horse was not in sight.

In another bend in the ditch, the tree limb he was riding snagged the top of another fallen tree and spun around a full 180 degrees. Dislodged from his perch for a horrifying instant, Joshua groped frantically in the blackness and found another part of the limb to hold onto. But just as he felt around for a stationary branch to grab, the surge grabbed his floating tree again and pulled it loose.

The Big Ditch had become a small river. Although he was blinded by the darkness, Joshua felt pieces of debris brush against him as he continued to hang on to the limb.

Soon, he sensed he was following a straighter course. And the absence of trees directly overhead indicated that he was now beyond the confines of the Big Ditch. But the raging current was no more shallow. His feet had not touched bottom since he had extricated himself from the harrow.

Panic-stricken, he clung tightly to his tree-limb raft. He had no idea where the flood was taking him, nor did he know whether he would survive.

8

CHAPTER

MAGGIE HAD BEEN ASKING Franklin to take her shopping for more than a week. She had no more flour and sugar, two of the few staples that they had to buy, and she needed fabric for spring dresses for herself and the girls. So with a final glance at the sky to assess the weather, Franklin cranked the old car for a quick shopping trip to Brinson's General Store in Cayce. Matthew went along for the ride, but the girls, Jessie, Reba, and Naomi, stayed behind to complete their Saturday house-cleaning chores.

Usually, Franklin did not drive through wind and rain. His car was difficult to handle in a crosswind, and it leaked. He fought the steering wheel as the car's narrow tires squished through deep mud and bumped against the sides of deep ruts in the road.

"I sure hope that boy is okay gettin' that harrow back up to the shed," he said as the new storm moved in. "I kind'a wish I'd made him turn around an' come back to the house."

"Where is Joshua?" asked Maggie.

"He went back to the field across the Big Ditch to get a section of harrow we'd left back there a while back. I told him to go get it when it looked like the weather was clearin' up. I didn't know it was gonna storm again."

"He'll prob'ly be okay," said Maggie. "I wouldn't worry about it."

"You should'a let me go with him," said Matt.

"Nope. It's bad enough that he's back there. I don't need to be worr'in' about both of y'all bein' out in this rain."

Franklin parked his old Model T in front of Brinson's. Saturday was the day most people did their shopping, but few others had come out in the inclement weather. The Jenningses tiptoed through mud puddles onto steps that led to the store's covered porch. They used a short-handled broom Lloyd Brinson had provided to brush excess mud and slop off their shoes. Maggie and Franklin went inside. Matt sat down in one of the old rocking chairs that stayed on Brinson's porch day and night.

Maggie gave her grocery list to Franklin so that she could select dress fabric while he filled the order for staples and food items. First, he laid a twenty-five-pound sack of Gold Medal flour on the counter, and then he quickly stepped over to the sugar barrel to measure out ten pounds of refined sugar into a paper bag. He selected the remaining items in the order they appeared on Maggie's list: three pounds of coffee beans, a five-pound sack of white cornmeal, two tins of canned salmon, three cans of sardines, one pound of crackers, a two-pound wedge of cheese, and ten sticks of horehound candy.

Maggie was pleased to find a broader selection of fabrics than was available the last time she had visited Brinson's store. She bought four yards of a pastel blue calico material for her dress and selected various gingham print fabrics for the girls' dresses. As an accomplished seamstress, she didn't need new patterns. Four yards of fabric for each dress would leave useful remnants.

Lloyd Brinson emerged from a storage room in the rear of the store. He rushed out, wiped his hands on his white apron, nodded to Maggie, and shook hands with Franklin.

"Afternoon, Franklin. Afternoon, Miz Jennings. I'm sorry—I didn't hear y'all come in the store. Did ya find everything you need?"

"Yep. I reckon we have everything we came for," said Franklin. "I just hope we can get it all back home. We almost got stuck a couple'a times gettin' here."

"Is that right?" responded Lloyd. "I'll tell you what's the truth. This stretch of bad weather has almost killed my trade. That's why I didn't know you folks was in the store. Hardly been anybody in here all day."

"Tell Thelma I sure do like the new dress material y'all have in now," Maggie said as Lloyd continued to add up the bill.

"Why, thank ya, Miz. Jennings. I 'preciate you sayin' so. An' I sure will tell Thelma, too. She's the one that picked out the new stuff. Them's mighty purty ones you got here. These all fer you?" he teased.

"Oh, no. Only the blue one. The gingham is for new dresses for the girls."

"Did the mail come in on the train last night?" asked Franklin.

"Yep, it shore did. Came in just after midnight. But won't be no more mail 'til Monday night."

In addition to operating his general store, Lloyd Brinson was responsible for getting outgoing mail from the Cayce post office to the train, and he carried incoming mail from the train to the post office.

Although the train didn't stop in Cayce and other small towns, there was a system to expedite mail service without stops. Outbound mail collected at the post office was placed into a specially designed pouch for transport by rail. The pouch was made of waterproofed leather with a rigid loop, or handle, protruding from its side. A hook designed to hold the mail pouch was affixed to a pole, and the pole was firmly planted adjacent to the train tracks. The pole's height and location allowed a designated member of the crew on the passing train to extend a hook to snag the pouch and pull it on board. Incoming mail was dropped to the ground.

Lloyd's job was simple. Each time a mail-carrying train was scheduled to pass through, he took the pouch filled with outgoing mail to the tower, suspended it there, and waited for the train to come for pickup. As the train passed at full speed, a crewman hooked the outgoing mail sack, dropped the incoming mailbag to the ground, and exchanged waves and verbal greetings with Brinson.

Lloyd dutifully carried incoming mail back to the post office and locked it up. He was well-known as the person to ask about mail delivery and train schedules. In twenty-two years, he had never missed a scheduled connection with the mail train.

Franklin paid his bill, and he and Maggie loaded their supplies into the back of their car. He was anxious to head back home without further delay.

Maggie gave a stick of candy to Matt as a reward for his good behavior, and they drove off. Franklin was quiet during the trip home. Maggie's attempts to begin a conversation with him were in vain. He was too preoccupied to talk.

Franklin stopped his car close to the back porch, killed the engine, and headed toward the house as the old Ford sputtered and coughed to a stop.

Jessie and Reba came to meet him at the back door. "Where's Joshua?"

"I dunno," Jessie replied. "We haven't seen him. He didn't go with you to the store? We couldn't find him, so we thought he had gone with you."

Franklin shuddered. He walked quickly to Gerthy's room and found his door open. Gerthy was sitting in his rocking chair reading a book. His old briar pipe, still smoldering with unsmoked tobacco, lay in an ashtray on the small table beside his chair.

"Hey, Franklin. What's the matter?"

"I need your help, Gerthy! I fear somethin' bad could'a happened to Joshua."

"What d'ya mean? What could have happened to Joshua?"

"Come on. I can tell ya as we go. Get your coat and bring your lantern."

Franklin went to the cabin to get a kerosene lantern he kept hanging on a nail just inside the door. It was almost full of fuel. He checked to be sure he had matches in one of the pockets in the bib of his overalls. Just as he was about to yell for his brother to hurry, Gerthy limped out the back door.

As they began to walk away, Maggie leaned out the back door and yelled,

"Do you want me to come?"

"No," said Franklin. "You stay here with the kids. But maybe it would be a good idea to give a call to Vernon Starr. I hope we won't need him. But we might."

Gerthy had moved on to get a head start to compensate for his slow, gimpy gait. When Franklin caught up, the two men proceeded together as quickly as Gerthy's crippled foot would allow. They walked in silence, as neither man was inclined to express his growing concern.

Their lanterns flickered and their shadows jumped as they walked. At the edge of the Big Ditch, they raised their lanterns above their heads to get a better view.

"Oh, dear God in heaven," Gerthy murmured.

Franklin stared in disbelief.

They had seen swift currents in the gully on many occasions, especially in the springtime. But never before was the water fully to the top of the ditch. But on this night, they saw clear evidence that the water had overflowed. Debris was visible on both banks. Weeds and other tender vegetation lay flat on the ground. The men stood in silence as they surveyed the damage, trying to imagine the force of the water that had caused it.

Injecting a ray of hope, Gerthy suggested that Joshua might not have crossed the ditch. "Maybe he's still somewhere on the other side."

Franklin seized the possibility.

"Jaaa-shuuu-aaaa!" he yelled. *"Jaaa-shuuu-aaaa! Jaaa-shuuu-aaaa! Can youuu heeeer meeeee?"*

"Please, dear God. Let him be okay," whispered Gerthy.

Franklin's words echoed, momentarily filling the emptiness of the night but not the void in their bellies. After another period of silence and unexpressed fears, Franklin suggested that they should move downstream along the bank to check for any sign of Joshua or Ole Dick. They moved in tandem. Unable to climb up and down the bank, Gerthy stayed on level ground just at the edge of the ditch. He held both lanterns as Franklin climbed down to the water's edge only two or three feet beneath the rim. They moved quickly but searched thoroughly, trying to uncover any sign of Joshua.

For about fifty yards, they combed the gully's edge without any sign of the boy or the horse. Then, once more, Franklin lowered himself down toward the surface of the water with a firm grip on the exposed root of a large tree.

"Look there, Franklin," Gerthy exclaimed. "Over to your right a little. I think there's something stickin' up out'a the water."

"You mean, over here?"

"Yeah, right in there. Here, let me move the light so you can see a little better."

Placing one of the lanterns on the ground, Gerthy brushed aside some branches to illuminate the spot where he had seen a protrusion from the water. Franklin spotted the curious-looking object, but he couldn't identify it. Moving closer but still holding the root, he leaned out as far as his short arms would allow and touched the object.

"God help us," he moaned. "It's the horse!"

"You sure?"

"Yeah. I'm sure. See? This is his nose. You can barely see his nostril stickin' up out'a the water. He's dead. See? He's dead," said Franklin as he moved the horse's nose up slightly and then let it fall gently back into the water.

"*Jaaa-shuuu-aaaa!*" he yelled. "*Jaaa-shuuu-aaaa! Jaaa-shuuu-aaaa. Can youuu heeeear meeeee?*"

Again, only the echo of his words reverberated through the swishing sounds of water pushing its way around fallen branches and dripping from trees above.

Franklin climbed back up the bank. He and Gerthy sat down on the wet ground facing each other with their lanterns between them. Their shadows danced on the ground and on small trees and bushes behind them. They were silent for a few moments as they contemplated what to do next.

"You know what this means, don't ya, Gerthy?"

"Yeah, I reckon so."

"It means Joshua did try to cross the ditch with Ole Dick."

"Uh-huh. But that doesn't necessarily mean we won't find him somewhere on further down," Gerthy said.

"Looks to me like Ole Dick got washed away in the flood. How else would he have gotten all the way down here? He must have drownded."

"Yeah, I 'spect you're right. But what we've got to figure out is what happened to Joshua."

"D'ya s'pose Joshua could'a seen the water comin' an' stayed on the other side?"

"Could be. Hard to tell exactly what happened. Franklin, can Joshua swim?" Gerthy realized that the boy had never been around water much except for farm ponds.

"He doesn't swim very much," Franklin answered. "He never seemed to like the water, an' … Gerthy, what are we gonna do? We gotta find Joshua. I can't lose my boy this way."

"Someone's coming," Gerthy said quietly.

Striding as swiftly as they could without breaking into a trot, Vernon Starr and Elmer Dixon approached, each carrying a lantern. Maggie had called Vernon, their closest neighbor, and he had recruited Elmer, who lived about three quarters of a mile down the road from the Jennings family, on the opposite side of their farm.

After a quick exchange of greetings and handshakes, Franklin thanked them for coming and tried to explain why Joshua and Ole Dick were out in the storm in the first place. He told them about finding his drowned horse and related his fears that Joshua had been swept away in the current with Ole Dick. Gerthy reminded Franklin and their neighbors of the glimmer of hope that the boy would be found on the other side of the Big Ditch.

Holding his lantern high, Franklin shuddered and groaned, "Just look," inviting the newcomers to examine the destruction.

"I can tell ya why so much water came flowin' through this ditch," suggested Vernon. "My wife went down the road to check on Miz Wilkins after the storm. Y'all know her—she's that widow woman who lives on the old Stanton place. Anyway, she told Rosie that Mr. Tom Parker's dam broke. That big lake he had is now empty. With all this rain we've had, his levee must'a gave way, and all that pond water just gushed out. That pond sits on the back side of his place, an' it would have flowed right into the ditch."

"It must'a been like an awful flash flood," said Elmer. "But that doesn't explain why there's so much water still flowin' through here. Somethin' else must'a happened to allow for that."

"Whatever happened, it was awful, all right." Franklin was weary of talk. "What we gotta do is figure out how to find my boy."

Heavy cloud cover remained, but the rain had stopped and winds had died down. The night air felt cool.

The men agreed to work in pairs. Gerthy teamed up with Elmer, a younger, stronger man, leaving Franklin and Vernon to search together. With water so high, there was no place to cross the ditch to search on the other side, especially in the darkness. They walked downstream to the spot where Ole Dick lay submerged in the water, and before they split up, they looked again for any sign of Joshua. From there, they decided to search hundred-yard segments in pairs, leap-frogging each other to save time. Gerthy and Elmer began searching at the spot where they stood. Franklin and Vernon walked a hundred steps down the ditch to begin their search. Vernon tied his red bandana handkerchief to the limb of a tree to mark the place where the search by the other team should end.

Section by section, they looked along the bank for any sign of Joshua. Occasionally, one of the men would call his name, hoping for a response. They found nothing to indicate his presence or his passing. The only sounds they heard were persistent, rhythmic noises made by katydids, locusts, and other nocturnal insects and rippling sounds of floodwater rushing over, around, and through debris in the Big Ditch.

With only an occasional pause for rest, they continued to search and call out for Joshua until three o'clock in the morning. Like the fuel oil in their lanterns, they were almost exhausted. They decided to go back home to rest until daylight, when they would recruit additional help and resume their search.

9
CHAPTER

JOSHUA FOUGHT SLEEP AS the storm surge carried him out of the Big Ditch into a natural drainage basin. It was a deep vale that meandered through open fields, flowing slowly toward Chapman's Creek.

He shivered and his teeth chattered involuntarily as his body fought the night chill. He had swung one leg up over the biggest part of the tree limb and pulled himself up so that the full length of his torso rested on it as he floated along. His arms and shoulders ached, and his hands were numb. Occasionally, the big limb he was riding would pitch and roll, and he began to doubt whether he could hang on.

Like other farm boys, Joshua was trained to gauge the time by the position of the sun during the day and the moon at night. But on this night, there was no timepiece, as the evening planets hid behind the veil of heavy clouds.

Perhaps it was his will to survive that kept Joshua alert. But disconnected thoughts and questions flitted through his mind like butterflies with no place to land. *Where am I? Is this a bad dream? What is in this water with me? I wish I were in my bed in the cabin. What happened to Ole Dick? My leg hurts. Does Uncle Gerthy's leg always hurt? How does it feel to drown? When will daylight come?* Plenty of questions, but no answers. So much that

Joshua did not know. But he was certain that he should not have tried to cross the Big Ditch in the storm, and he knew he was scared.

Sometime before the light of dawn brought his surroundings to life, Joshua sensed that he was moving more quickly again in a resurgent current. The storm water had dumped him into a stream known as Chapman's Creek. It was more than a creek or a stream. Its depth, breadth, and swiftness should have qualified it to be a river. It was fed by numerous springs and supplemented by runoff during rainy seasons, flowing year-round from the eastern part of the Fulton County to the west, toward the Mississippi River. It flowed into the swampy area known as the Willingham Bottom.

Willingham Bottom was a marshy area that flooded each spring. During other parts of the year, water from Chapman's Creek and other smaller tributaries flowed unimpeded through the swamp and into the Mississippi River. But in the spring, there was no room in the big river for any new water. It would fill up and sometimes overflow its banks, and the Willingham Bottom became a vast holding tank, ready to accept water from all sides. Due to unusually heavy winter and spring rains upstream along the river basin, the flood had come earlier this year, and the Willingham Bottom was abnormally engorged.

Under the dim light of early dawn, Chapman's Creek spat Joshua out into the swamp. He bobbed gently in open shallow water dotted with cypress trees, cypress knees, and a few tupelo and water oaks. The eastern sky had now turned yellow with hints of red among wispy clouds just above tree tops in the distance. The long-awaited coming of daylight rekindled Joshua's spirit. The dim outline of trees and shoreline flanking him on both sides lifted his hope for survival.

Grasping the limb with his right arm and his uninjured leg, he began to paddle and kick, trying to escape the tug of the current, to reach the shore. But a sharp pain reminded him that his leg was not usable to propel his craft. He grimaced and cried out, aware again of his throbbing ankle and radiating pangs up through his calf.

After drifting farther into the marsh, Joshua spotted a small mound of earth—a little island covered with scrub myrtles and marsh grass—located about twenty yards ahead and ten yards to his right. It was oval-shaped, and it covered an area of about five hundred square feet. He shifted his body around on his limb and pulled and pushed himself from tree to tree until he was finally able to reach it. He rolled off of the tree limb and crawled through shallow water and mud onto the little island. In the center of the island, he rolled over on his back and collapsed. Unaware of flying and crawling insects whose habitat he had invaded, he fell into a deep sleep. And he dreamed.

In his vision, Joshua was transported back to the old home place where he was born. He had lived there until after his mother died and the family moved into the house that had belonged to his grandfather Jennings. In his dream, he walked along a narrow lane that stretched from behind their little house past their chicken house and their barn, down a small hill, and to a wooded area in which there was a small ditch. Another wooded area lay on the left of the lane, with a small field on the right. The woods at the end of the lane belonged to a neighbor, but Joshua had spent many hours playing there.

In his dream, Joshua walked into the woods at the end of the lane. The ground was covered with a thick layer of freshly fallen leaves, displaying their fall colors all around. They crunched under his feet as he moved through the dense stand of trees and underbrush. He continued to walk until he came to a small clearing on the side of a hill. In the clearing there were rows of earth that had been raised up in ridges that ran perpendicular to the slope of the hill. The ridges reminded him of the ones he had helped his father make in their garden for planting sweet potatoes or peanuts. Like the ground throughout the woods, these ridges were covered with leaves.

Joshua ran down the hill, jumping across each ridge of earth. As he did, people of unknown identity and clad in strange clothing rose up out of the ground through the layer of leaves and ran away into the deep woods.

His dream ended abruptly. A muscle spasm made him kick violently, and his foot struck hard against the base of a small shrub. Once again, sharp pains radiated up his leg, and his ankle throbbed. He was hungry. His lips, tongue, and throat were parched. *Extreme thirst should not be a problem for one surrounded by water,* he thought. He crawled to the edge of the mound, dipped his fingers into the water, and placed it on his lips. With a few more drops, he bathed his eyes. He considered taking a drink of the muddy, smelly stuff. But he was not yet thirsty enough to put it past his lips.

As before, questions of survival and issues of insignificance invaded his mind. *Should I yell for help? Can't hurt.* "Help! Help me! Hey, can anybody hear me?" *Not a chance. Where am I? What will I say to my father when he finds me? What happened to Ole Dick? What would Uncle Gerthy say? Is he worried? What time is it? What are Matt and Jessie doing right now? How will I get out of this swamp?*

Before he could answer one question, another had already replaced it. He wished the questions would go away. He wished for food and clean water. He wished for his family. Finally, not knowing what else to wish for, Joshua covered his face with his hands and wept.

When his tears dried up, Joshua tried to be positive. "God will take care of you," he had been taught. "Your mother up in heaven still watches over you," he had been promised. But doubts overruled these assurances. *How did God let this happen to me?* he wondered. *What can my mother do for me now?* he asked.

Joshua rolled onto his side with his knees tucked against his chest like a young colt trying to stay warm in the snow. His thoughts about his mother lingered. He remembered how she looked and smelled, how she talked and walked, and how she laughed and sang. He remembered her touch, how she combed his hair, the food she cooked, and the clothes she gave him to wear. And he even recalled when she first taught him and his siblings to play pretty bird.

Abruptly, his thoughts turned to his memory of the days surrounding his mother's illness and her eventual death. It had been a dark and mysterious period in his life, but he remembered specific parts of it vividly.

"You and Matt feed the hogs and mules while I milk," his mother had instructed early one evening as she walked quickly toward the barn. She coughed deeply and wiped her mouth with her apron.

"Where's Jessie?" Joshua asked. "Why isn't she doin' anything?"

"She is. She's in the house fixing supper. I need everybody to pitch in and help me, especially until your father gets back home."

Hannah poured a measured amount of sweet feed into a wooden trough. Dutifully, the cow came to eat and be milked. With an old crate for a stool, Hannah sat down, washed the cow's teats and udder, and began to squirt streams of warm milk into her clean bucket.

"Where is Papa?" Joshua asked.

"He's taking care of some business down in Mississippi."

"Why?"

"Well, I can't explain it all to you right now, son. He and Mr. Faulkner went to look at a farm in Mississippi."

"Is that far from here?"

"Yes, it is. It's all the way down through Tennessee."

"When's he comin' back?"

"Oh, I don't know for sure—probably in a few more days. Now, don't ask me any more questions. It's getting cold out here. You and Matt get the feeding done, and then we'll go eat supper."

Hannah Jennings was doing the work of at least two people. She fulfilled her usual responsibilities to provide meals and clean clothes for her children. She got them off to school in the mornings and tucked into bed at night. She drew water from the cistern. She brought in wood for the stove. She washed dishes and cleaned her house. In Franklin's absence, she was responsible for outside work as well—feeding, milking, and tending to livestock. Her children helped, but the responsibility was hers alone.

A few months earlier, Franklin had expressed his desire to move to Mississippi. His yearning to leave Kentucky was fueled by discussions he had repeatedly with Sam Faulkner, an acquaintance who farmed a piece of land about four miles away, just west of Fulton. He was impressed by Sam's description of his experience growing up on a farm in north Mississippi, close to Corinth. Franklin had never been to Mississippi. But in listening to Sam's stories, he had conjured up an Eden-like setting with rich, loamy soil; lush pastures; tall, deep-green stalks of corn; clear, sparkling streams; and plenteous yearly harvests.

Gradually, Franklin's thoughts of moving to this veritable paradise evolved from fantasy to genuine longing. It was no longer a mere fascination; it had become a fixation. He waited for the opportunity to move his family to this wonderful place that, in his heart, he knew would provide a superior existence.

On a Sunday morning late in September after morning worship services, Sam Faulkner motioned for Franklin to join him under a large sycamore tree toward the rear of the graveyard.

"I've got good news, Franklin," he began as the men shook hands. "I got a letter from my sister down in Mis'sippi. She says there's a big farm that's gonna be sold purty soon, an' she's tryin' to get me an' my family to come back down there."

"That's good news, Sam," said Franklin, nodding. "I think you ought'a buy it. From what you say, it's great land, an' I know you've been wantin' to get back down there awful bad."

"Well, that's not the whole story." Sam placed his hand on Franklin's shoulder. "The farm that's for sale is too big for me to buy. I wouldn't ever be able to come up with that kind'a money. An' my sister says they prob'ly won't sell half of it an' keep the other half. I was just wonderin' if you'd be interested in buyin' it with me."

"Well, I don't know, Sam. How much are they askin'?"

"I dunno, exactly. But I believe land is about the same there as it is here. If you sell this place, you could prob'ly get that one for about the same money."

Franklin closed his eyes and scratched his head. He turned away from Sam and took a few short steps through the fallen leaves. Then he turned quickly back toward Sam.

"We'd need a house to live in."

"Well, I thought of that. If we move back there, me an' my wife will move into the old house I grew up in. My mama's not doin' too well, an' that's one reason my sister wants me back down there. All I need is the extra land to farm. You could take the house that's on the place."

"I dunno, Sam. It sounds good—but I just don't know."

Franklin turned and started to walk toward his buggy.

"Hey, I know what," yelled Sam. "Let's us go down there an' look at it. Won't do no harm just to take a look at it. An' then we can both decide if it'll work out. What d'ya think? Won't do no harm to look!"

Franklin stopped walking and turned back toward Sam.

"Well, maybe you're right. Maybe I ought'a at least go down there to take a look at it."

"Okay, then. That's what we'll do. But we need to go as soon as we can. A farm like that won't be for sale long. If we want it, we better go quick."

Exactly one week after they had discussed it, Franklin and Sam headed south across the state of Tennessee, fully determined to purchase a farm somewhere close to Corinth, Mississippi.

Everything about their father's departure and absence was mysterious to the Jennings children. He announced to them simply that he was going to Mississippi and that he would be gone for a few days. He said for them to be sure to help their mother while he was gone. Hannah was reluctant to discuss details of his plans with the children because she did not want them to be unduly alarmed or excited at the prospect of moving. She told them that their father had to go to take care of some business and that he would be back soon.

Joshua and Jessie knew that their mother was sick. Her cough had grown progressively deeper and more persistent, and she seemed unusually tired. She wasn't laughing and singing as she normally would, and one morning before school, she had raised her voice to scold Matt for an offense that usually would have gone unnoticed. The night before their father returned, they were especially concerned when they saw her wrapped tightly in a blanket but shivering as she sat in her chair.

"Are you okay, Mama?" asked Jessie.

"I'll be all right, honey."

"Can I get you anything?" asked Joshua.

"Maybe a wet washcloth," she said softly. "There's one on the table in the kitchen."

Joshua got the cloth from the table and dipped it in a basin of water sitting on the cupboard. He wrung it out and took it to his mother. She wiped her eyes and then her forehead and handed the cloth back to her son with a faint smile.

"Will Papa be home soon?" asked Jessie.

"I hope so," whispered her mother. "I really hope so."

Franklin and Sam returned to Kentucky the following day, excited to share good news with their respective families. They had negotiated a deal to swap their farms in Kentucky for the one in north Mississippi. It seemed to be a trade that would benefit all parties involved. Owners of the property there wanted to come to Fulton County, and Sam and Franklin were impressed with the quality of the land they would get in Mississippi. The deal would be finalized pending an inspection of their farms by the folks from Mississippi.

When Franklin returned home about midafternoon, he was distraught to find Hannah in such ill health. It was apparent that she had fever, and she was too weak to get out of bed. He called Doc Beeler, who came within the hour to check her condition. He said she had influenza, and that she was dehydrated. He prescribed complete bed rest and plenty of fluids.

About three days later, Joshua became ill with symptoms similar to Hannah's, and Doc Beeler's examination confirmed that he was suffering from the same malady. One minute he burned with fever, and then he shook with chills. It seemed that every muscle in his body ached. His joints were stiff, and his eyes burned. He arose from his bed only to move far enough to relieve himself, and with his fever and dehydration, that was not often. He passed in and out of sleep, knowing that occasionally someone would come to wipe his brow or to offer him some water or broth. At times, he was too sick to bother to identify who was there to help.

Joshua's condition worsened. His fever remained high throughout the day, and he had begun to cough uncontrollably. Doc Beeler was called back to reexamine him, and he arrived soon after suppertime. Although he could not open his eyes, Joshua was aware of the doctor's presence, and he could recall each step in the examination procedure.

The doctor's stethoscope felt cold, but refreshingly so, as he placed it under Joshua's nightshirt and moved it strategically around on his chest and then on his back. Offering no resistance, Joshua voluntarily opened his mouth when he felt the doctor slide the tip of a wooden tongue depressor between his lips. He felt the doctor's strong fingers as he probed from under his ears to his throat and back again. The doctor's hands seemed to transmit a sensation of healing to Joshua, and he was sorry when Doc Beeler pulled his covers back up and tucked them under his chin.

Joshua lay still and listened intently, determined to hear the doctor's prognosis.

"The boy is very sick, Franklin. I can hear some noise, particularly in his left lung. I'm afraid he has pneumonia. It's not as bad as Hannah's yet, but we have to watch him real close."

"What do you want us to do, Doctor Beeler?" a female voice asked. Not recognizing the voice, Joshua tried to open his eyes to see whose it was, but he decided it didn't matter.

"Just keep doin' what you're doin'," replied the doctor. "I don't know much else to tell you. Unfortunately, it's like I told you with Hannah. It seems like there's a three-day period that's critical. With pneumonia, if a person gets through the third day okay, then they usually make it fine. Just say your prayers."

"Oh, we will, Doctor Beeler. We will!" That same soft female voice indicated that some God-fearing friend or relative had come to help him pull through his illness.

Doc Beeler had diagnosed Hannah's double pneumonia two days earlier. Thus, according to his three-day cycle theory, she was in that critical third day. Her sister, Bess Tisdale, had come all the way from Missouri to be by her side. Joshua was aware that his mother was very ill, but not until he overheard the doctor say that his pneumonia was not as bad as his mother's did he know the real gravity of her condition.

The small Jennings house resembled a hospital ward. Hannah was in the living room/bedroom, one of the two rooms in the front of the house. Joshua lay in a double bed in the parlor, the other front room, just across a hallway from his mother. Neighbors came in shifts to sit around the clock with both Hannah and Joshua. Vernon Starr's wife, Rosie, was there daily. Emily Dixon, Earlyne and Ivylene Smith, Sarah Faulkner, and Doc Beeler's wife, Patricia, all came to the Jennings house regularly. Those who could not come to sit brought food—plenty of food.

Joshua's high fever was still with him the morning after Doc Beeler's visit. Rosie Starr sat by his bed, bathing his face with a cool, wet towel. He had slept through most of the night, but now he was restless.

When he closed his eyes, he was transported into a strange and frightening universe of distorted reality. He saw beings of unrecognizable form and movement. He saw bright lights, he heard brassy sounds, and he witnessed eerie activities involving twisted shapes.

He opened his eyes and stared at the wall. The interior walls of this crudely constructed house consisted of a heavy cardboard material fixed to poplar boards with large tacks. The cardboard was light blue. When he first stared at the walls of his room, Joshua was soothed. He thought he was gazing at the blue sky. Then his focus narrowed from the breadth of the entire wall to the head of a single tack. He tried to refocus on the calm blue of the cardboard wall, but his blurry sight was drawn back to the tacks. Each tack seemed to expand, growing slowly at first and then rapidly until it filled his entire field of vision. He blinked and turned his head to the side to rid himself of the disturbing vision, but invariably his eyes found another tack.

"What is it, Joshua? Are you having a dream?" asked Rosie.

"Uh-huh, I guess so," Joshua muttered.

"Here, let me wipe your face off with this towel. Does that feel better?"

"Yes'm. That feels good."

"Would you drink some water? You need to drink all the water you can 'til that fever comes down."

She placed one hand under Joshua's neck for support and raised his head slightly so that he could sip water from the cup she held up to his lips. He drank slowly, licked his chapped lips, and lowered his head back to his pillow. Her words, the towel touching his face, and the water on his lips helped Joshua clear his mind of his disturbing hallucinations. He saw Rosie's round face, her kindly eyes, and her curly hair. He saw the old pump organ that his grandmother Jennings had once played in its place against the opposite wall from his bed. He looked at a circular brown stain on the wall close to the ceiling in the corner of the room. He was comforted as Rosie held his hand in hers and stroked his forearm. He closed his eyes and rested.

The door separating the parlor from the hallway was slightly ajar. Joshua could hear sounds indicating heightened activity both in the hallway and in the room where his mother lay. He could hear voices, sometimes muted and sometimes loud. He listened to the sounds of footsteps, sometimes taken slowly and at other times quickened. He detected his father's voice, then Doc Beeler's, and then his father's again.

Doc Beeler had returned to see his mother again. Even in his befuddled state, Joshua tried to make sense of what he heard. *Is my mother worse? Who is that I hear? Oh, yeah. That's Aunt Bess. She's crying. I like Aunt Bess. She's a lot like my mother. Uncle Gerthy? Why is Uncle Gerthy in with my mother? What is he saying to Papa? Why have all these people come at the same time?*

With his eyes closed and feigning sleep, Joshua withdrew his hand from Rosie's. He turned onto his side facing away from her. She sat back in her chair and remained silent. The sound of footsteps down the center hallway indicated that some of the people were leaving. Conversations ceased, and suddenly the house was quieter than it had ever been before. Finally, out of the silence that had enveloped Joshua like a heavy fog, he heard the sound of muffled sobs and then his Aunt Bess's screams.

"Oh, dear God, no!" she wailed. "Not Hannah. Please, not our dear Hannah."

There were more sobs. And then, for the first time in his memory, Joshua heard his father cry. Rosie stood quietly, walked to the door, closed it quietly, and returned to her chair. Joshua was relieved that she thought he was asleep. He did not want her to see his tears as they streamed down his face and soaked into his pillow. He knew he would never see his mother again. He knew he might follow her soon. And at that moment, he did not care.

Hannah Jennings was buried two days later as Joshua fought to survive. On this day, the critical third day of his cycle, he was much too sick to know about his mother's funeral, much less to attend. Rosie Starr insisted on staying with him so that Franklin and other family members could attend Hannah's funeral. Doc Beeler was there, too. Franklin asked him to sit with his son just long enough for him to attend his wife's simple burial.

"If something happened to that boy and I wasn't even there to call you for help, I don't know what I'd do," he had told the doctor.

All during the day and into the night, Joshua's fever remained high, and he seemed to be failing. Franklin and Bess stayed with him after they returned from Hannah's interment. They feared that they would be back soon to retrace those steps with Joshua.

Around midnight, his fever broke, and his condition improved slowly but steadily thereafter. When he made it into the fourth day, his family had renewed hope that he would survive.

Joshua remained in bed for another week and à half. Slowly, he regained color in his face and strength in his muscles, but his bout with pneumonia left him very thin and weak.

Before she left to return to her home in Missouri, Aunt Bess sat down beside Joshua's bed.

"I'm glad you are feeling better," she said.

"Thank you."

"It looks like you are going to be just fine real soon. I sure would like for you to come see me in Missouri sometime." She patted the back of his hand.

"Maybe I can." Joshua was not really sure how far it was to Missouri or how he would get there.

"Before I go, there's something I have to tell you," said his aunt. "I don't know if …"

"I already know," interjected Joshua. "You don't have to tell me."

With tears welling up in her eyes and spilling out onto Joshua's bed, Aunt Bess leaned over and kissed him on the forehead. Then, cupping his hand between hers, she said, "You are a dear boy, Joshua, and don't you ever forget it."

She released his hand and walked toward the door, but she stopped just before leaving the room.

"Now, remember what you promised. You come to see me in Missouri."

"Yes, ma'am. I will."

Aunt Bess left the parlor and closed the door behind her. Joshua was alone.

On his little island on the edge of Willingham Bottom, Joshua sat up and wiped his eyes. His fingers passed over a piece of mud that had hardened on his face. He scratched it off with his fingernail, letting it fall on the ground. He stretched his arms above his head. Looking around at the marsh now fully illuminated by the morning sun, he shook his head to yank himself back into consciousness. For a moment, he didn't know whether he had been dreaming or whether this place and this circumstance was his dream.

He tried to remain calm and positive. He was still alive. He had survived the water, and he had survived the frightening darkness of a night in the swamp. *Surely they will come looking for me,* he thought. *Surely, before the end of the day, they will find me. Dear God, please help them find me,* he prayed. *And help me to be strong until they do. Amen.*

10
CHAPTER

TWO HOURS OF SLEEP were plenty. So Vernon Starr and Elmer Dixon returned to the Jennings house at daybreak to help Franklin and Gerthy map out a plan of action. They had called their closest friends and neighbors to join the search, and as the news spread, many others would come voluntarily.

Maggie dumped wet coffee grounds into a bucket sitting on the floor next to her cookstove, replaced the lid on her percolator, and poured freshly brewed coffee for the men and then for herself. She pulled up a chair to join them around her kitchen table. Vernon removed a plain white sheet of paper and a pencil from his shirt pocket.

"Franklin, if you want me to, I'll make some notes so we can plan an organized search for Joshua."

"That would be real good," said Franklin, nodding. "I was kind'a hopin' you'd do that."

Vernon opened his pocketknife and began sharpening his pencil. He slid the bucket Maggie had used for coffee grounds over next to his feet to catch the shavings.

"First, I think we need to talk about what we're gonna need," Vernon began. "Any ideas?"

"We need a way to get across the ditch to look on the other side," suggested Gerthy. "Who has a boat?"

"I think Tom Parker still has a rowboat," said Vernon. "He's already agreed to come, anyway. We'll ask him to bring his boat."

"After we use the boat to get people to the other side, it might be a good idea for somebody to float in it down the ditch," said Elmer. "That way, we'll have people lookin' for Joshua on each bank and in the middle, too. D'ya know what I mean?"

"Good idea," said Vernon.

Maggie refilled coffee cups while Vernon made notes. Franklin got up from his chair, paced back and forth across the small kitchen, and then stopped to gaze out the window. He shook his head and sighed loudly.

"Don't worry, Franklin. We're gonna find Joshua," said Gerthy.

"Where does the ditch end?" asked Elmer as Franklin returned to sit at the table again. "I mean, what does it empty into?"

"That's hard to say," said Franklin, shaking his head. "It's never had this much water in it. I 'spect it just runs out into the farmland between here and the Willingham Bottom—you know, down south of old man Sheldon's farm, and close to the Pascal place."

"Well," said Vernon, "that's another good reason for somebody to take that boat as far as they can go in it. Maybe it'll just float to where Joshua got carried by the flood. Will Tom Parker's rowboat hold two men?"

"Yep. It's a pretty good-size boat," said Elmer. "I remember seein' Tom an' his uncle out in it on his pond, fishin'. Tom's a big man, an' his uncle must weigh over two hunderd pounds."

"Who's a good one to put in the boat with Tom?" asked Vernon.

"What about Joe Smith, Dossie's oldest boy?" suggested Franklin. "He's big and stout. He ought'a be able to row a boat from here to Hickman."

"That's what we'll do, then," said Vernon, writing it down on his paper.

There was a pause in the conversation as the men glanced at each other. They finished off the last of their coffee and tried to think of what else needed to be done.

"Anybody need any more coffee?" asked Maggie, holding up the percolator. "There's a little bit left in here, an' I can even make more."

"No, thank you, ma'am," said Elmer as the other men shook their heads.

"Vernon, I feel like it would be a good idea to have us work in teams," interjected Gerthy. "You know, to have at least two people searchin' together. That way, if we find him an' need to send for help, the other one can stay with him."

"That's a good idea, Gerthy. I'll make sure everybody knows to do that."

"There's a bunch of people comin' into the yard," said Maggie as she put dirty coffee cups into a washbasin. The men rose from the table in unison and followed Franklin to greet those who had come to help.

By daybreak, the thunderstorms had moved to the southeast. The air was crisp and cool, and the West Kentucky sky was crystal clear. New leaves on oak, maple, and gum trees growing in the yard fluttered as gentle breezes blew out of the northwest.

Livestock took turns drinking at a watering trough in the feedlot just on the other side of the fence from the yard. Franklin's cows mooed persistently, perhaps to remind him they had not been fed. Chickens wandered throughout the yard and mingled with the guests, too busy scratching out their usual breakfast of bugs and grubs to be afraid.

"Thank y'all for comin'," Franklin said as he met the volunteers at the edge of his back porch. "Vernon here is gonna take the lead in organizin' everybody so we can spread out an' cover every inch of ground 'til we find my son. I'm much obliged for your help!"

"I'll make this brief so we can get out an' start our search." said Vernon. "Tom, do you still have a rowboat?"

"Yep. Still have it. Just fixed it up an' repainted it last week. Want me to go get it?"

"Yes, if you don't mind. We need it right away to get some folks across to look on the other side of the ditch."

"I'll go get it right now."

"Yeah, you take off. But before you go, here's the plan. Franklin and I will go to the other side of the ditch to look over there. After you get us across, we want you an' Joe Smith to paddle down the ditch and go as far as you can to see where all this water goes. That'll tell us where else we need to look if we don't find him in the Big Ditch. Joe, you want'a go with Tom to get his boat?"

"Yep. Suits me."

"Okay. Franklin and I will wait for you here."

Tom Parker and Joe Smith trotted off to get in Tom's wagon to get his boat. Vernon looked down at his scribbled notes and continued his instructions.

"Elmer Dixon and Gerthy are going to look along this side of the ditch. We looked there last night, but we want to be sure we didn't miss any sign of Joshua, and they'll be able to go further down than we did in the night. Ivylene, do you want to go along with Elmer and Gerthy?"

"Sure. I just wanta help any way I can."

"Good! Okay. Well, I guess we're all set. Y'all can go on ahead an' get started. Franklin and I will wait for Tom to get back with the boat, an' then we'll get goin' on the other side. I guess that's …"

Vernon's words were interrupted by the sound of an approaching wagon being pulled by a team of horses at a fast clip. Everyone turned to see. The horses slowed to turn from the road toward the house, but their pace quickened again in response to slaps of the reins against their sides.

"Why, I believe that's Lonnie!" Gerthy whispered to Franklin. "Do you want me to talk to him?"

"Nope! I'll talk to him myself." Franklin jumped off the porch and walked past his neighbors. "Thank y'all again for comin'."

"Hey," shouted Lonnie as he jumped down from his wagon. "I heard about Joshua bein' lost."

"I thought I told you never to come back here again!"

"But …"

"I meant what I said," insisted Franklin. "Now go on back."

"Hey, I just came to tell my mama goodbye. You don't hafta keep yellin' at me!"

"All right, then. But make it quick! Why do you need to tell your mama 'bye'?"

"Matter'a fact, I've got me a job. I'm gonna go to work on the river. I'll be …"

"What do you know about workin' on the river?" interrupted Franklin.

"Nothin'. They said they'd train me. Like I tried to tell ya, I'm supposed to go to Hickman first thing in the mornin'. A man is gonna take me an' another feller to Memphis to work on a dredge."

"Have you told your mama about this?"

"Nope. I ain't talked to Mama since I left."

"Well, she'll be glad to hear you're tryin' to do somethin' with yourself."

"I'll go tell 'er now."

"Well, I guess a feller can change his ways. Maybe it's a sign you're finally growin' up."

"Uh-huh. I guess so."

Vernon had stepped aside to let Franklin and Lonnie talk privately. As Lonnie walked to the house, he approached Franklin.

"We could use another helper," he said. He reminded Franklin that Doc Beeler had agreed to help, but a prior commitment to one of his patients made him unavailable until midmorning. They could recruit Lonnie to drive his wagon to the doctor's house so that as soon as he had completed his early morning responsibilities, the two of them could ride together to search the edge of Willingham Bottom.

"What are you doin' for the rest of the day?" Franklin asked Lonnie as he walked back toward his wagon.

"Nothin'!" Lonnie snapped back. "But first thing in the mornin' I gotta go to Hickman. "Don't worry, I'm not gonna git in yer way. I'm leavin' right now."

"I wasn't tryin' to make you go," Franklin said with a conciliatory tone. "The reason I asked is that we can use your help to find Joshua. Vernon here can tell ya what we need you to do."

"Aw, I see," growled Lonnie. "First you don't ever want ta see me again, but now you and Vernon are gonna tell me what to do. All you ever want to do is order me around."

"I'm not orderin', I'm just askin'," conceded Franklin. "I'm worried about Joshua, an' I need all the help I can get."

"Say please!"

"Okay, please."

"Awright. I'll do it. But I don't aim to forget how you treated me when I was here, an' after I do this, don't ask me to do nothin' else, ever again."

Franklin nodded and walked away to let Vernon tell Lonnie what to do. He was to go to Doc Beeler's house, wait for him to keep his early-morning appointment, and then proceed with him to Binford Road, a seldom-traveled logging road that extended back along the edge of the swamp in Willingham Bottom. There, they were to look to see if floodwaters had reached the marsh, and of course, to look for any sign of Joshua. Lonnie assured Vernon that he understood his assignment, got in his wagon, and left.

The swamp known as Willingham Bottom was a long shot. Neither Franklin nor Vernon thought it likely that Joshua would be found there. But since they would soon have search teams on each side of the ditch and a boat to explore the floodwaters as far down as possible, there wasn't any other place to look. It was worth a try.

Not long after Lonnie left, Tom reined his team of mules and wagon into the lane and stopped for Franklin and Vernon to get in. His rowboat with its fresh coat of bright-green paint glistened in the early morning sunshine. It was loaded upside down, with its bow sticking out the rear of the wagon. Joe was beside Tom in the wagon's only seat. Vernon and Franklin climbed into the wagon bed. They sat on top of the rowboat, one on each side.

As Tom slapped the reins against his mules' behinds, the men heard shouts from the back porch of the house, and the screen door slammed shut.

"Wait, Papa. Wait for us," yelled Jessie. She and Matt ran to catch up with the moving wagon.

"Hold up a minute, Tom," exclaimed Franklin. "Let me see what these kids want."

Jessie and Matt pranced nervously beside the wagon as it came to a stop.

"Can we go with you, Papa?" begged Jessie. "Please, can we go to help find Joshua?"

"I'm a good looker!" declared Matthew. "I bet'cha I can find 'im."

Franklin looked down at his children. He could see that they were both anxious and excited, and he knew they had genuine concern for their brother's well-being. He almost relented but quickly thought better of it.

"I know how bad you want to go with us," he began, "and I allow that you could help us look for your brother. But Mama's going to need your help here at the house. Jessie, I need you to help her any way you can. Matt, I need you to be the man'a the house while I'm gone. So y'all run on back now an' let us get started."

"Aw, please, Papa …"

"Nope."

"Mama said it was all right with her."

"Don't argue. You can't go. Now get on back."

Tears welled up in Jessie's eyes. "Is Joshua gonna be okay?"

"Is Joshua drownded, Papa?" asked Matt.

Franklin leaned out over the side of the wagon. He placed one hand on Jessie's head, and with the other, he gently grasped Matt's shoulder up close to his neck.

"Let me tell you kids somethin'. Look at me—look up here at me. I know you are worr'in' about Joshua. But we're gonna find him. We couldn't see him in the dark last night, but we'll find him now that it's daylight. Now go on back in the house an' do all you can to help your mama. An' quit worryin'."

The children returned to the house before Tom Parker's wagon disappeared down the lane toward the Big Ditch. Quickly, the men unloaded the rowboat and set it afloat in the muddy water. As Joe held the boat firmly against the bank, Franklin got in, sitting down in the stern. Tom got in next, taking the middle seat by the oarlocks. Then Joe stepped into the bow and shoved off. Tom deftly turned his boat and rowed quickly to the other bank. Joe grabbed the limb of a fallen tree to hold the boat steady against the bank while Franklin stepped out. Just as quickly, Tom steered his craft back to get Vernon and deposited him on the other side with Franklin.

"Good luck," Tom shouted as he and Joe shoved off to begin their float down the ditch.

Franklin and Vernon searched the bank as they had done on the other side only a few hours earlier. The search went more quickly in the daylight. As they had done the night before, they yelled Joshua's name intermittently in case he might be somewhere within earshot.

As they expected, Ole Dick was still where he had been found the night before, his head and part of his neck now exposed. Vernon looked at Franklin and shook his head, but neither man spoke. For a moment, Franklin wondered how he could pull the dead horse from the ditch and dispose of its carcass, but he dismissed that as a trivial matter for another time.

Foot by foot, section by section, Franklin and Vernon probed along the bank of the ditch. Occasionally, they were startled by yells for Joshua coming from the other side of the ditch, and they surmised that their own yells were just as startling.

The men searched on and on. As Franklin climbed out of the ditch to move to a new spot, he sighed audibly.

"You want a short break, Franklin?" asked his partner. "We've been goin' at this pretty hard. We could take a rest if you want to."

"Naw, I'm fine. Let's keep lookin'."

"Try not to worry. We have a lot more area to cover, and I'm sure we'll find Joshua okay."

"I can't help but worry. I'm happy we haven't found him dead, but I can't help but worry that we haven't found him alive, either."

"I know what you mean. To tell you the truth, I hoped we'd find him right away. I kind'a figured maybe he'd crawled out into the field somewhere and gone to sleep."

"Yeah," agreed Franklin. "Right before I woke up, I dreamed he was waitin' for us there at the crossing. Dreamed we put him in a wagon an' took him home."

"Well, don't give up. I still believe we'll find him. He's a smart boy, and he'll do whatever it takes to take stay alive 'til we can find him."

"Yeah. I hope an' pray you're right. I sure don't want nothin' to happen to that boy."

After they had searched another thirty yards or more, Vernon, who was up ahead, shouted for Franklin to come. Franklin pulled himself up the side of the bank and ran a few steps to where Vernon was standing, pointing out to an object caught on the limb of a tree floating in the water.

"Is that Joshua's cap?" he asked. "I think that's a cap—see it right there, caught on that branch? I can't tell for sure, but it looks like a dark brown cap."

"Yeah. Joshua had a brown cap, all right. An' I'm pretty sure he was wearin' it yesterday when he went back to get that harrow. My Lord, Vernon, why did I let him go after that harrow in a rainstorm?" Franklin began to shake uncontrollably.

"Quit worryin' about that. What's done is done. Here, help me find a stick that's long enough to reach out there an' get that cap."

Franklin took his knife out of his pocket and opened the longest of its three blades. He cut off a branch that was approximately one inch in diameter and ten feet long. He stripped it of its little twigs and leaves. He handed it to Vernon, who had positioned himself so that he could hold to the base of a small tree and extend himself over the water. With Franklin's freshly cut branch, he lifted the cap and swung it around onto the ground beside where Franklin stood.

"No doubt about it," uttered Franklin in a low voice. "This is Joshua's cap, all right."

Clutching the cap in both hands against his chest, Franklin began to scream.

"*Jaaa-shuuu-aaaa!*" he yelled. "*Jaaa-shuuu-aaaa! Jaaa-shuuu-aaaa! Jaaa-shuuu-aaaa! Jaaa-shuuu-aaaa! Can youuu heeeer meeeee?* Oh please, dear God, let him hear me."

Vernon stepped over to face Franklin and grabbed his shoulders firmly.

"Take it easy, Franklin," he said. "Here, sit down for a minute so we can talk about this."

The two men sat down together on the damp ground.

"Finding Joshua's cap doesn't mean anything we didn't already know. He was in the floodwaters, and he lost his cap. But that's to be expected. It doesn't mean he's not alive. It just means he lost his cap. That's all it means."

"Yeah. I know, Vernon. I just don't want to think about anything happenin' to my boy."

"Then don't. Let's just think about how happy we'll be when we find him. Come on. Let's get back to work."

Tom Parker and Joe Smith soon learned that their boat was much too heavy and cumbersome to negotiate twists and turns in the flooded ditch. It got hung up on submerged logs and fallen treetops, and the men had to grab limbs and pull, push with their oars against anything stable, or rock the boat back and forth to free it.

"Just what are we lookin' for?" asked Joe abruptly.

"Huh? We're lookin' for Joshua, I guess," responded Tom. "Or maybe anything that would show that he was here."

"If he's alive, wouldn't he just climb out'a the water an' walk home?"

"Well, I 'spect he would—unless he was hurt, or somethin'. Maybe we'll find him hangin' onto a tree limb."

"I kind'a think he must'a drownded."

"Why do you think that?"

"Well, for one thing, everybody has been yellin' out his name every three or four minutes, it seems like. An' if he was still alive, he would'a answered. He would'a either walked home or yelled for help."

"Well, maybe he's on down further, an' he can't hear us an' we can't hear him. We hafta keep on lookin'."

"Are we s'posed to be lookin' for his body?" asked Joe, totally unconvinced that Joshua could be alive.

"I believe they want us to look for anything—him, his body, his clothes—just anything."

"How're we s'posed to find his body in all this stuff? If he drownded, will he be on the bottom, or will he be floatin'?"

"How do I know?" shouted Tom. "What's wrong with you? Why are you wonderin' about whether he'd be floatin' or not? You're just like your daddy!"

"You leave my daddy out'a this. I was just wonderin', that's all. Nothin' wrong with wonderin'."

Tom realized Joe's questions were valid. But he was not ready to deal with the thought of finding Joshua's body submerged or floating in the muddy waters. It was his levee that had broken, and his lake water that had helped to create the flash flood that had swept Joshua away—or worse. Even though he tried, Tom couldn't dismiss those thoughts from his mind.

"Let's just keep on lookin' the best we can," he said. "Maybe we'll find him still alive. If we don't, then we'll prob'ly hafta come back an' look for his body after the water goes down."

The two men resumed their search without further conversation. Ponderously, they worked their way along. Judging by the sun's position, they figured the time to be midmorning. After searching for another half hour or so, they heard voices on the eastern bank of the ditch about fifty yards ahead.

"That must be Gerthy an' them," said Joe as he pushed against a fallen tree trunk to steer the boat away from the bank.

"Yeah. It's gotta be them—wouldn't be anybody else out here."

"Hey!" yelled Joe. "Y'all found anything yet?"

"Hey! Who's …? Is that you, Tom?"

"Yep. It's us, all right—me an' Joe. Y'all wait up! We want ta talk to you."

Joe reversed his paddle stroke in the water on his left side, forcing the nose of the boat to swing around and bump up against the bank just below where Gerthy, Elmer, and Ivylene stood. A short rope attached to a ring in the bow was lying at his feet. He grabbed it and tossed it to Elmer, who tied it to the base of a sapling.

"Have y'all found anything?" Elmer asked.

"Nope. Have you?" responded Tom.

"Nothing—well, we did see the horse, of course. But there is no sign of Joshua," said Elmer.

"We're taking that as a good sign," Gerthy interjected. "At least we haven't found any reason to believe that he's not still alive."

"I'm real glad you brought your boat, Tom," said Elmer. "Did you get Franklin an' Vernon over to the other side?"

"Yeah, we left them over there way back early this mornin'. Far as I know, they're still huntin' for Joshua on that side of the ditch."

"Can y'all keep goin' some more?" asked Elmer.

"I reckon we can. That's what we come to do—you know, keep lookin' 'til we find him," said Joe.

"Yeah," agreed Tom. "It's good weather, an' there's no reason we can't keep goin' as far as we can."

"Yeah, well that's the reason I asked," said Elmer. "Ivylene walked ahead to see how much further this ditch goes. An' she says … Well, I shouldn't be tellin' it. Ivylene, go ahead—you tell 'em what you saw."

"Well, okay. Well, ya see … uh … Mister Gerthy said that he thought it'd be a good idea for us to see how much further this ditch goes. An' we was wonderin' what we'd find—uh, you know, where it ends. And uh, well, I said I'd be happy to be the one to go—you know—since it'd just be walkin' an' all, 'cause I'm a real good walker. I kind'a like walkin'. Always have. Joe, you recollect when you an' Jolene would gripe an' complain about havin' to walk to school. I never did mind it. I liked walkin' to school an' back more'n I liked school. An' I'd usually be the first one home. I could walk real fast. Matter'a fact, my daddy always said I could walk faster'n any girl he ever saw, an' I reckon that's the truth. I never did mind walkin', an' ..."

"For God's sake, Ivylene! Just tell us what you saw!" insisted Joe. "Quit your ramblin' on about how good a walker you are!"

"It's okay, Ivylene. Go ahead and tell us," said Elmer.

"Well, okay. Well, uh, I must'a walked a little more'n a mile down yonder, an' that's where the ditch ain't so deep anymore. It kind'a—uh—you know, levels out. The water runs out in a big field. I never seen so much water'n all my life. Well, you know—maybe when we went down at Hickman an' saw the river all flooded up against the side'a that big hill. That was lots'a water. There was water all the way out to where the river was, an' more on the other side. I 'spect that was the most water I ever saw. I don't rightly know for sure 'cause that was a long time ago, an' I may have forgot ..."

"Ivylene!" her brother yelled. "You're ramblin' again!"

"You just shut up, Joe!" she yelled back. "Well, anyway, water's everywhere down there."

"How deep is it, Ivylene?" asked Tom. "I'm wonderin' if we can get through it in this boat."

"Well, I never waded out in it to see," she said. "But it looks pretty deep to me—but not like it is here in this ditch. It's just spread out all over everywhere. I never in my life saw so much water."

"Ivylene, we really appreciate you walkin' down there an' back to scout it out," said Elmer.

"Yeah, thanks, Ivylene," said Gerthy, patting her on the shoulder.

"Oh, you're welcome," she said, smiling broadly.

"Tom, why don't you an' Joe head on down the ditch right now. Check out the floodwater to see if it's deep enough for you to get through. An' see if you can tell if maybe Joshua could'a washed all the way down there."

"Yeah, we can do that. What d'ya say, Joe? You ready to go again?"

"Yep. I guess so."

Elmer untied the rope and shoved the boat away from the bank with his foot.

"Y'all be careful," Gerthy yelled as they paddled away. "I guess if none of us finds anything, we'll all meet back at the house sometime later this afternoon."

"Good luck to you, too," shouted Tom. "We'll see y'all later."

11
CHAPTER

JOSHUA LOOKED ALL AROUND for anything edible. Perhaps berries or a plant he recognized. Nothing! Nothing but ferns, marsh grass, and some scruffy-looking shrubs. He would have to wait to eat.

His ankle had swollen to at least twice its normal size, and it throbbed constantly. He found slight relief by submerging it in the cool swamp water. He licked his lips with the scant saliva he could manufacture. The image of a few sips of cool well water from the silver-colored dipper that hung by the well back at the house only intensified his thirst. He looked down at the water where he soaked his foot and ankle. It was brownish, but not totally opaque—especially away from where his foot had agitated the muddy bottom. Mud wasn't the only impurity in the water. Tadpoles were abundant, too. They darted helter-skelter, propelled by their little temporary tails. *Surely there'll be plenty of frogs in the bottom this year,* he thought.

Joshua dipped with his hands to examine the water. It was clearer looking in his hands than it appeared in the swamp. He hesitated, and the water leaked out between his fingers. Taking a deep breath, he dipped up another double handful, raised it to his lips, and sniffed it. It reeked with the odor of mud mixed with rotting vegetation, but its fishy stench made it particularly repugnant to Joshua. He released the remaining drops onto the ground and decided to wait to drink.

Hunger, thirst, and his painful ankle intensified his fear and loneliness. Anger and self-pity dominated his mood.

"Where is everybody?" he yelled. "Hey! Hey! Does anybody even know I'm out here? Does anybody care? Does anybody care that my ankle hurts? Hey! Hey! Can anybody hear me? My ankle hurts! Does anybody care?"

He shouted to the sky, the trees, the air and water, as if nature could be his captor and his confessor simultaneously. Joshua broke a limb off of a scrub tree. He beat it against the remaining limbs on the tree and then used it like a scythe to mow down ferns and marsh grass. When there was nothing else to hit, he hurled the limb as far as he could into the swamp.

"Hey! I'm hungry! I need help! Is anybody out there?"

Joshua covered his eyes and dropped to his knees in the soft earth.

"Please, somebody come an' get me out'a here. Somebody come an' take me home!" he cried.

"Dear God, please help me," he prayed. "Please help me."

In the ensuing silence, Joshua remembered a hymn that Uncle Gerthy sang often as he did chores around the house or sat in his room. In the silence of his mind, Joshua sang the familiar tune.

> Be not dismayed whate'er betide.
> God will take care of you-ou.
> Beneath His wings of love abide.
> God will take care of you.
>
> God will take care of you
> Through every day,
> O'er all the way,
> God will take care of you.
> He will take care of you.

Because he could not remember the words to the second stanza, Joshua repeated the first stanza and the refrain over and over again. As he sang the words or hummed the tune, he was calmed. His attention was diverted from the pain in his ankle and pangs of hunger and thirst in his belly to recollections of past events in his young life.

He recalled in vivid detail the first time his father took him to hunt rabbits. He remembered his surprise and utter excitement when Franklin unexpectedly asked him to get his coat and hat to go along. It was wintertime, and Joshua remembered that a thin layer of moist snow covered the ground. And it must have been prior to his mother's death because he recalled that she had smiled at him as she buttoned the top button of his coat, adjusted his cap, and advised him to be careful.

Hunting was a way of life in the country. Rabbits, squirrels, doves, quail, and even possums and raccoons were hunted regularly to supplement the food supply. Every young boy eagerly anticipated his first hunting trip. It was one of the important rites that signaled his gradual advance into manhood. Joshua was no different in that regard. On many occasions, he had asked his father to take him along on one of his frequent trips. Franklin's stock response was, "One of these days when you are older, I'll take you." Accustomed to that answer, Joshua had ceased asking, content to wait until his father considered him to be old enough. Then, without warning, that day came. Because it was such a momentous occasion in his life, he soaked it all in. Every detail of that first hunting trip with his father was indelibly imprinted on Joshua's memory.

Franklin was a skillful rabbit hunter, and he was a good teacher. He knew where rabbits were most likely to hide, and his keen vision allowed him to spot the white fur of their bellies against the brown earth or the brown fur of their heads against a white snowbank. Hunting rabbits with a rifle, as he and Joshua did that day, required finding and shooting them in their hiding places before they were flushed out to run away.

Joshua leaned back against the base of the little scrub tree he had previously tried to defoliate. Closing his eyes, he relived the hunting trip.

"Can I carry the rifle?" he asked his father.

"Yeah, I'll let you carry it. But let me show you first." Franklin held the butt of the rifle in his right hand and rested it on his shoulder military style, with the barrel pointing up at the sky behind him.

"Some folks like to carry a gun like this," he said. "But I carry mine different. Here, let me show you."

"I already know how to hold a gun, Papa."

After he checked to see that the safety was on, Franklin handed the rifle to Joshua. He took it from his father and pointed it down toward the ground away from him. It was not as heavy as he had imagined it would be, and he held it confidently. He could hardly wait to shoot it for the first time.

Joshua walked beside his father toward the fence situated on Vernon Starr's property line. Wet snow squeaked beneath their boots. The air was still, but it was damp and cold, and it bit the exposed skin of their faces. As they neared the fence, Franklin stopped and motioned with his hand for Joshua to stop as well.

"Shhh," signaled Franklin with his finger on his lips. "Be quiet. We're gonna look for rabbits hidin' in this fencerow. They like to hide in the grass. See, look right over there." Franklin pointed at clumps of grass in winter browns that had drooped over to form natural shelters from the weather and the rabbits' natural predators.

"Give me the rifle." Franklin held out his hand as he began to move quietly along a parallel path about twenty-five feet from the fence. "Keep your eyes peeled. I bet ya there's a rabbit sittin' in there, an' you might see him before I do."

Joshua trailed along. He moved stealthily and peered into the clumps of grass and bushes. He hoped to spot a rabbit before his father did. As he checked every possible hiding place, he wondered, *If I was a rabbit, where would I hide?* On first glance, every different color and every different shape and form he saw looked like a rabbit. Twice he stopped abruptly, pointed, and blurted, "There's one!" and "I see a rabbit!" Upon closer examination, one of his "rabbits" was a large leaf nestled amongst the grass, and the other was just more grass.

After they had moved about fifty feet, Franklin held up his hand. He switched the rifle to his left hand and pulled Joshua close to him on his right.

"Look right in there. There's one sittin' just to the left of that post." He pointed so that Joshua could sight along his arm and finger to the exact spot where the rabbit was hiding. "D'ya see him? See the white spot down next to the ground? An' you can see his ears stickin' up. He's lookin' directly at us."

"Yeah, I see him! Can I shoot him?" Joshua shivered at the thought.

"I'll shoot this one," answered Franklin. "You watch how I do it, an' then I'll let you try the next one."

Franklin raised the rifle slowly, released the safety switch with his trigger finger, and aimed. Joshua watched as he squeezed the trigger firmly with no other movement to alter his aim. He heard a sharp *crack* and then a dull *smack* as the 22-calibre cartridge hit the rabbit in the neck. It flopped out of the tall grass, kicked its legs a couple of times, and lay still.

"You got it! You got it!" Joshua ran toward the dead rabbit.

"Shh—wait!" called his father. "Don't ever run out in front of someone who's holding a gun! And don't yell like that. There might be another one hidin' in there close."

Joshua quickly returned to his father's side. "I'm sorry, Papa. I just wanted to see the rabbit."

"It's okay. You can go get him now if you want to. I brought a sack to put him in."

Joshua ran to get it, but he stared down to examine it before he picked it up.

Franklin called out, "Pick him up by his hind legs. That's the best way to carry a dead rabbit."

Joshua held the rabbit high to keep its ears and head from dragging on the ground.

"I didn't know a rabbit would be so long."

He dropped it into the sack his father was holding. Franklin tied it up, looped the knotted end under his belt, and allowed the sack to dangle behind him.

He reloaded his single-shot rifle and motioned for Joshua to follow him along the fence, as they had done before. Now Joshua was even more intent on spotting a rabbit because his father had promised him that the next shot would be his.

Franklin walked more quickly toward the corner of the field, and Joshua trotted to keep up.

"Come on," said Franklin. "Let's climb over this fence an' I'll show you my favorite huntin' place."

He climbed over the fence and then parted two strands of wire to make a space for Joshua to crawl through. A few feet from the fence, they entered a wooded area, where Franklin led his son through the barren trees and down a gradual slope to a gully that had cut a long, sweeping *s* through the woods. A light smattering of snow partially covered the thick layer of leaves that had fallen from maple, birch, sweet gum, hickory, sycamore, oak, and elm trees. The snow glistened like rhinestones. Randomly scattered cedar trees added touches of greenery.

"Here's where we'll find some rabbits," said Franklin, pausing at the edge of the gully. "Let me tell you where to look, an' you might find one yourself."

"If I find one, can I shoot it?"

"I'm gonna let you shoot the next one, whoever finds it. I want to see you kill your first rabbit. Now, all along the banks of this little ditch, you're gonna see where the dirt has been washed out from under part of the roots. See? Look at that little oak tree over on the other side. See how some of the roots stick out? Rabbits like to get up in under there to hide an' to stay out'a the wind an' rain."

"I think that's where I'd go if I was a rabbit," Joshua said.

"You would, huh? Good. Here, you take the gun. Be careful with it, an' if you find one, remember to switch the safety off before you try to shoot him."

Franklin stepped back to let Joshua lead the way. He watched as the boy moved slowly and stared intently under every tree that had exposed roots. *You're gonna be a good hunter,* Franklin had said.

Joshua continued for several yards without seeing any game. He was about to move around a large sycamore tree when Franklin tapped his shoulder and pointed toward a clump of bushes on the edge of the gully.

"Look close in those bushes."

"Where?"

"Right there! See those bushes growing right there beside that rotten tree trunk?"

"Oh, yeah. I see 'em. Oh! There's a rabbit! I see it! I see it!"

Joshua raised the rifle to his shoulder and switched off the safety lock. He felt his heart beat. He gulped, aimed, moved slightly, aimed again, and then squeezed the trigger firmly. He jumped as the gun discharged, but the bullet found its mark. A big male rabbit flopped out of the brush and tumbled into the ditch.

"Good shot! You just killed your first rabbit!"

Joshua stood in wide-eyed amazement. He was speechless, first looking at his father and then back to the rabbit he had just killed.

"Is he dead?"

"Yep. He's dead, all right! I think you got him right through the head. Couldn't'a been a better shot."

"Can I go get 'im an put 'im in the sack with yours?"

"Sure. He's your rabbit."

Joshua handed over the rifle and ran to claim his prize. Proudly, he picked it up and held it as high as he could to show it off to his father.

"Mine's bigger than yours!" he shouted.

"Yeah? Well, I don't know about that," Franklin muttered to himself.

"Can we go home so I can show it to Matt?"

"Yeah. Come on. Put it in the sack, an' we'll go dress 'em. Maybe your mama will fry 'em up, or make us some rabbit stew for supper."

Joshua remembered how excited he had been to show off the rabbit he had killed. His mother gave him a big hug and a kiss. From Jessie and Matt, he received more envy than praise. They ran to ask their father when he would take them to hunt rabbits.

Recollection of his first rabbit-hunting trip with his father helped Joshua pass the time while he waited and hoped to be rescued. It helped him to ignore pains in his ankle, his hunger, and his loneliness and fear. But with no help in sight, he felt more worried than ever about how he would escape from Willingham Bottom.

"Help! Somebody please help me!" he yelled. "Help!"

Joshua struggled to his feet, trying not to put any weight on his sore ankle. He began to think more seriously about how to get off the little island and out of the swamp on his own.

There was no dry, solid ground visible. To his right, he could see another clump of vegetation much like that on his own little island. It was about twenty yards away, and it appeared even smaller than where he was. Beyond that, all he could see was more water. A thick stand of cypress trees and knees was to his left, but he could not see what lay beyond them.

If only I could swim, he thought. *If only I could swim.* But he was afraid of the water, and his recollection of stories about snakes and other inhabitants of the swamp made him shudder. He reconsidered. He had not seen any snakes so far, and now his biggest fear was to remain alone in the swamp for another night. *I must get out'a here,* he thought. He looked at his ankle. Still swollen, it had begun turned black, blue, and even yellow from the top of his foot to his calf. He wondered if he could tolerate the pain of wading through the muddy bottom of the swamp if the water was not too deep. Joshua stripped another limb from the scrub tree. He reached out as far as he could and dipped it to test the water's depth. At the outer limits of his reach, the water was about two feet deep. He looked again at the thicket of cypress trees and cypress knees just to his north, about twenty-five feet away. The water around those trees looked to be relatively shallow. He decided to venture off the island, using the limb to test the depth of the water ahead of him, and to test the strength of his ankle with each careful step.

Barefooted, he limped to the water's edge, used his stick to test for depth once more, and gingerly stepped in. Mud swallowed his foot up to his anklebone—not any deeper than he had expected. His next step would test his sore ankle. Although the soft mud cushioned it, sharp pains radiated up his leg as his weight shifted. Quickly, he took another step. Water was now waist deep, and his measuring rod indicated even deeper water ahead.

Step by step, he moved away from the island until he had nearly reached the midpoint between it and the cypress trees. Pausing to rest with his weight on his good leg, he reached as far out as he could to test the water's depth before moving on. When the full length of his measuring stick could not find the bottom, Joshua's forward momentum caused him to fall face-first into the water. He released the stick and flailed his arms to regain his balance and to come up for air, choking and coughing up the vile swamp water. His feet were mired in the mud well above his ankles. Careful not to lose his balance again, he retraced his steps. He crawled back onto the mound that had become his home. Dazed, soaked, cold, and frightened, Joshua crawled away from the water, sat down, and stared up at the sky.

12
CHAPTER

LONNIE LET HIS TEAM walk at an easy pace, splashing through the sloppy mud and leaning hard against their collars to pull the wagon through deep ruts in reddish-brown muck. He was in no hurry to get to Doc Beeler's house because the doctor had an appointment to keep before he would be free to go.

Lonnie daydreamed about his plan to work on the river. He had been told that he would be a deckhand on a dredge barge working for the Army Corps of Engineers. He knew that the work was in Memphis, but he had forgotten that the man who hired him said he would be on the *Iota* dredging out the Memphis Harbor. The "army" part was confusing. He was pretty sure he had not joined the army, but his mind was fuzzy about a military connection. He wondered what it would be like to do something other than farm work.

High ground along the road to Crutchfield was covered with lush, green spring grasses nourished by recent heavy rainfall. Trees were bursting with new leaves. Puffs of wind and gentle breezes carried scents of honeysuckle, jasmine, and clover as if vaporized from some gigantic atomizer.

As his team approached the crest of Dixon Hill, Lonnie grabbed the long wooden lever to brake against the wagon's momentum. His horses slipped and slid, stiffening their forelegs for added balance. Although it was slippery, the mud in the road was so deep that it inhibited the wagon wheels from sliding too far in either direction toward the side ditches. Lonnie and his team reached the bottom of Dixon Hill with less trouble than he had anticipated.

At Doc Beeler's, Lonnie stopped his horses to wait in the shade of a large pecan tree beside his house. In about fifteen minutes, he saw Doc Beeler emerging from his back door. The doctor blew a kiss to his wife, turned, bounded down the steps of his stoop, and trotted to Lonnie's wagon, holding his wide-brimmed hat in one hand and his black medical bag in the other. He wore khaki work pants and a long-sleeved khaki shirt.

The doctor climbed into the wagon and extended his hand. "You must be Lonnie."

"Yep, that's right. My name's Lonnie Crandall."

"Well, I'm pleased to meet you. My name is Robert E. Lee Beeler, but most folks just call me Doc Beeler."

Lonnie pulled hard on the left rein and coaxed his horses to circle out to the road for their trip toward Cayce. Seemingly full of pep, the team sprang forward with a jolt, causing Lonnie and the doctor to rock backward against the hard wooden back of the wagon seat.

"I understand we're supposed to go down to the bottom to look for Joshua." Doc Beeler drummed his fingers against his leg.

"Yep. That's what Mr. Vernon told me this mornin'."

"It's hard for me to believe that he'd be all the way down to the Willingham Bottom."

"Uh-huh. Me too. I believe they think he's still up there somewhere along the Big Ditch, but they wanted to check out the bottom just in case."

"Well, that's what we'll do. Let's see now, you're Franklin's stepson, is that right?"

"Yep. He married my mama about ... a little more'n two years ago."

"I don't remember seeing you there at the house when I went there to sew up Joshua's head."

"Nope. I was at my granddaddy's house down at Cayce."

"Do you still live with your granddaddy?"

"Uh-huh. But I'm fixin' to go to work on the river," Lonnie said proudly. "I'm s'posed to be down at Hickman in the mornin' to report."

"Is that right? Well, good for you!" Doc Beeler gave Lonnie a congratulatory slap on the back. "Who are you going to work for in Hickman?"

Lonnie shook his head. "I'm not gonna be workin' in Hickman. I'm workin' on the river—on a barge—I think it has somethin' to do with an army of engineers."

"Oh, you must mean the Army Corps of Engineers," said the doctor with a chuckle. "They are responsible for dredging in the Mississippi River."

"Yeah, that's it. Is that part'a the army?" asked Lonnie.

"Well, not the military part of the army, if that's what you're askin'."

Lonnie was glad to get assurance that he had not enrolled in the military. But the vaguest use of the word *army* in the presence of Doc Beeler was like poking a nest of yellowjackets.

"You might be wondering why my name is Robert E. Lee Beeler," the doctor began. "Well, both my father, Dameron Beeler, and my uncle, Thomas Beeler, served in the Confederate forces in the Civil War. Although neither one of them served directly under General Lee, my father had the utmost admiration for him, and he gave me his name. You know all about Robert E. Lee, don't you?"

"Uh-huh."

"Good! Well, let me tell you first about my uncle Thomas. He was a little older than my father. I never had the good fortune to meet him because he was killed at Shiloh in a battle at Pittsburg Landing, in April of 1862. First, he served with troops commanded by General Albert Sidney Johnston, but when General Johnston was mortally wounded, General P. G. T. Beauregard took over. My uncle Thomas was part of the army that took many Union casualties in a battle they called the Hornet's Nest. But then, General Beauregard didn't realize that Major General Don Carlos Buell of the Union army had brought his forces to help General Grant.

"He ordered a counterattack, not knowing that his forces of about thirty thousand men were outnumbered by more that forty thousand Union troops. It was there at Shiloh, on April 7, 1862, that my uncle died, along with more than ten thousand other Confederate soldiers. Am I boring you with all this, son?"

"Uh-uh."

"Well, that's good. I'm glad you're interested. Now, let's see. I want to tell you about my father. My father joined up after the war had started. He was not with the same outfit as his brother, my uncle Thomas. As a matter of fact, it was in March of 1864 when he joined up. He was put in with a small group of soldiers commanded by Lieutenant General Nathan Bedford Forrest. General Forrest had come up from Columbus, Mississippi, through West Tennessee and into West Kentucky to recruit and re-outfit Confederate soldiers. Immediately after he joined, they went up to Paducah, a town they quickly occupied. You ever been up to Paducah?"

"Nope. I reckon not—but I heard of it."

"Yeah, well, Paducah is not very far from here. Anyway, what I was sayin', when I was a boy, my father told me about how they rounded up some fine horses and mules that belonged to the Union army. Then, in an assault on Fort Anderson on the edge of town, he was slightly wounded, but his injury wasn't bad enough that he had to come home."

Lonnie yawned and wiped his eyes. He slapped his horses with the reins to quicken their pace.

"I'll bet you're not interested in all this about my family, are you?"

"Huh? Oh, yeah. It's pretty interestin', all right."

"Well, I'll cut it short. But I did want you to hear about my father fighting at Ebenezer Church down in Alabama, outside of Selma. That was in March of 1865, close to the end of the war. My father was still with troops under the command of Lieutenant General Nathan Bedford Forrest, and they were trying to defend Selma from the advance of three divisions of Union cavalry commanded by Major General James H. Wilson.

"As you may know, three divisions of cavalry include about thirteen or fourteen thousand men. Although they were greatly outnumbered, the Confederate troops valiantly held off the Yankees in a long-running battle at Ebenezer Church before they were finally defeated. Fortunately, my father was able to escape with General Forrest and a small number of troops, and he was one of the few lucky men who came home to his family. That's why I'm here today. I know, I went on and on, and I probably bored you silly."

"Naw. You really know some stuff."

"Yeah. Maybe some day I'll tell you about my two years in the medical corps during the war."

"Okay."

"Did you say we're supposed to go to Binford Road?"

"Yep, that's what Mr. Vernon said. It's about two or three more miles down the road."

"Well, good. We'll be there soon. I sure hope they have found Joshua somewhere along that ditch. If not, I hope we find him down here."

"Uh-huh. Me too."

Bright sunshine felt warm against their faces as the men bounced along noisily. A couple of floorboards that had come loose at the rear of the wagon clattered against its frame each time the large wheels rolled stiffly over a bump or a pothole. Both men were splattered with mud the horses kicked over, around, or through the wagon's partially rotted splatterboard.

Characteristically, Doc Beeler glanced nervously about, drummed his fingers against his legs, and tapped his toes rhythmically against the floor. He would have preferred to drive the team himself, as he was never content to sit with nothing to do with his hands—even to ride for a short distance in a wagon.

As Lonnie steered his team around a small bend, a woman dashed out from under a roadside tree and waved her arms up and down frantically. As they approached, she yelled for the men to stop.

"Stop, Lonnie. That's Mrs. Samples," said Doc Beeler. "It looks like she needs some help."

Lonnie reined his horses to slow them to a walk and then veered off the road into her yard.

"I'm so glad to see you, doctor," she gasped. "I called for you at your house, and your wife said you were already headed this way. It—it's Brent. He's having another fit or somethin', an' I don't even know if he's still alive. Please hurry!"

Dorothy and Lester Samples had six children, all under the age of twelve years old. Doc Beeler had delivered every one of them. Brent, their two-year old, was next to the youngest. He had been a sickly child almost from birth with a propensity for rare ailments. During his most recent episode of high fever and convulsions about six months back, Doc Beeler had informed the boy's parents that he didn't expect him to survive.

Neither Doc Beeler nor other doctors that the Samples had consulted in nearby Union City, Tennessee, could determine the exact cause of his continuing problems.

Doc Beeler edged forward, already prepared to jump out. "Take me up to the house."

Lonnie urged his horses to trot to the front of the Samples' small home as Dorothy ran behind them. By the time the team stopped and the doctor jumped out of the wagon with his medical bag, she had caught up to accompany him into the house. Lonnie waited in the wagon.

Doc Beeler gently pushed one of the older Samples children aside to get across the small living room to the sofa where Dorothy Samples had placed her ailing baby.

"You kids go to the other room," she ordered.

Doc Beeler saw that the child's body was rigid. He shook with convulsions, and by touch, the doctor determined that the boy had high fever. Quickly, he opened the child's mouth. His tongue looked slightly swollen, but it did not obstruct his breathing.

"Get me some cool rags. We have to get his fever down."

Dorothy ran to the kitchen. The doctor looked at the boy's ears, peered into his eyes, and examined his throat carefully. Then he pulled the baby's little shirt up to expose his torso. When his mother returned with cool rags, he bathed the little boy's chest and back. He reached into his pocket for his gold watch. It was attached to a gold chain hooked around one of the belt loops at his waist. He flipped open its cover and held the baby's wrist between his thumb and forefinger to take his pulse.

"What's wrong with my baby, Doctor Beeler?"

"Honestly, I don't know." The doctor continued to bathe the baby's torso. "His fever is even higher than it was when I was here with him the last time, and we must get it under control. I need a tub about half-full of freshly drawn well water. Can you get that for me?"

"Sure!"

"I'll be right back. I'll go out and tell Lonnie to go on without me. I need to stay here with your little boy."

"Oh, thank you, Doctor! Thank you!"

Doc Beeler rushed out to Lonnie's wagon. He explained that he had to stay to try to help the Samples' baby survive.

Lonnie frowned and stomped on the floor of the wagon. "I came down here to help you," you he shouted. "Nobody said I'd hafta do this by myself!"

"I'd sure go with you if I could," assured the doctor. "But this baby is really sick, and I can't leave. Do yor know where Binford Road is?"

Lonnie gritted his teeth and nodded. Accepting his fate, he assured Doc Beeler that he could find Binford Road and that he knew what he was supposed to do to search for Joshua. Doc Beeler reminded him to pass back by the Samples' house or to come get him if he found Joshua in a condition that required the doctor's help. Lonnie agreed that he would, and he turned his team to leave. Then, as Doc Beeler started back toward the house, he turned abruptly and yelled out at Lonnie.

"There's another little lane that leads back toward the edge of the swamp. I've been back there to hunt and fish. It's located about half a mile further down. If you don't find Joshua along Binford Road, you ought to go check it out."

"Yeah. I reckon I'll do that." Lonnie drove his team away and headed toward Willingham Bottom, but he began to brood. His mood had changed. Earlier in the day, he had felt important to be part of the search team. Now, he was not so sure. Feeling abandoned by Doc Beeler, Lonnie stewed at the thought of having to spend his last day alone before going to work on the river first waiting for the doctor at his house, then listening to his boring stories, and finally waiting for him to return again. Although he had turned sullen and despondent, he continued toward Binford Road.

Lonnie could tell from the sun that it was almost noon. He was hungry. He turned his team onto a dirt lane along a small levee. Although there was no sign to identify it as Binford Road, he saw two big water oaks that Vernon Starr had said would mark its entrance, and it did run alongside the swampy area where he had been told to look. He decided to drive his team as far back into the bottomland as he could go and to see what he could see.

The water was well above its normal level. All along the first quarter mile of Binford Road, constant trickles of water spilled over the levee. To his right was tillable land that under normal conditions remained dry. Now it was completely flooded. To his left was swamp. Normally, numerous cypress knees protruded well above the surface of the water around each cypress tree. Now, however, only a few of the cypress knees were visible, their tips sticking out of the water like giant sharpened pencils without any lead.

Farther along the lane, water spilling over the road was deeper and deeper. About a half mile into the marsh, Lonnie had to stop. Surging floodwaters had totally washed away the road. A rivulet with surprisingly swift current continued to flow through the gap in the levee road, emptying some of the vast pool of water in the fields into the already swollen swamp.

Unable to go any farther, Lonnie's only option was to turn around and return along Binford Road to the main road leading through Willingham Bottom. As he glanced back at the tracks his wagon had made along the levee, he realized he had made a serious error in judgment. The top of the levee was barely wider than his wagon and team, and there was deep mud or water on each side. *How will I ever turn around and get out'a here?* he wondered. *Why did I agree to come back into this awful place?* Lonnie slapped his hat against his leg and swore.

Backing up a team of horses hitched to a four-wheeled wagon was next to impossible. Even with a good team and an experienced driver, the task would be difficult. Lonnie's team was makeshift at best, and he an inexperienced handler.

"Josshh-uu-aaa!" Lonnie yelled, just on the slim chance that Joshua might be near enough to hear him. *"Joshua! Can you hear me?"*

Lonnie froze as he heard a response in the distance. He cocked his head slightly and turned like an antenna being rotated to receive a weak signal.

"Joshua, is that you?"

Again he heard a response—and again!

Lonnie strode in the direction of the sound. Now it was repeated in a staccato-like rhythm, and he realized the sound was merely a birdcall.

Lonnie turned to reassess his situation. A turn to the left was out of the question. The drop-off at the edge of the levee was only four feet or so from the wagon wheels. It was steep, and the water was deep. After removing his shoes and socks, Lonnie waded out into the floodwater to the right of the lane. At a distance of about six feet out, he was knee-deep in muddy water, but the ground seemed surprisingly solid under his bare feet.

Lonnie figured that his only option to turn the wagon was to back up to the left as far as he dared to go and then to turn as sharply to his right as possible to move forward through relatively shallow water.

Lonnie climbed back into the wagon and grabbed the reins.

"Come on back!" he yelled at the team, pulling back hard on the right rein to urge the horse on the right to back up while other horse was more stationary. That would swing the tongue of the wagon to Lonnie's left, pushing the rear of the wagon in the same direction. Both horses moved backward together, so Lonnie stopped them to begin the process anew. He slapped the left rein against the flank of the horse on that side and pulled hard on the right-hand rein. This time, the horse on the right moved back quickly, pushing the wagon's tongue hard to the left. Quickly, Lonnie urged both horses to back up, and when they did, the wagon lurched backward, almost over the edge of the levee into deep water of the swamp.

"Whoa, you dumb bastards!" Lonnie bellowed. He released the reins to stop their backward movement just in time. He caught his breath, gasped, and swore again—this time at the team, the wagon, and his predicament. He wiped sweat from his forehead with the upper part of his sleeve.

With a yank on the rein of the horse on his right to swing his head around, Lonnie used the left-hand rein to slap the other horse, urging him to move forward through the water. As the outside horse in an arc to the right, he had farther to travel and more load to pull. Tossing his head defiantly, the horse balked at first, but then both horses obeyed Lonnie's command to move. In an effort to avoid deep water and uncertain ground, Lonnie turned the team as sharply as possible to the right. The wagon's right front wheel scraped against the frame as it rolled slowly forward. As Lonnie yelled at his team to continue their forward progress, they splashed water and mud all over him and into the front of the wagon.

Just as he thought the wagon would reach the flat ground atop the levee, the right wheel dropped into a deep hole and lodged there. Lonnie shouted at the horses and urged them to pull even harder, but the wheel did not budge. If he coaxed the team to continue to pull, they would likely snap the wheel from its axle or break the wagon tongue. Lonnie swore loudly and splintered the top of the splashboard with the heel of his shoe.

Lonnie was ready to quit. He could abandon his horses and wagon and walk out to the main road to flag down a passerby for assistance or a ride home. Then he thought to use the team to pull the wagon out backwards. He unhitched the horses and walked them around to the rear of the wagon. With an old logging chain his grandfather had taught him to carry along for emergencies, he hooked the horses to the frame of the wagon where floorboards had popped loose. With surprising ease, the horses extracted the wagon from the mire and back onto the levee.

After he hitched his team up to the wagon once again, Lonnie drove them back out to the main road. They kicked up water and mud as they trotted at a quickened pace. It didn't matter. He was already wet and muddy, and he wanted his nightmarish trip down Binford Road to end. At the main road, Lonnie had begun to turn to the left to return to the Samples' house to get Doc Beeler. Then he remembered the doctor's suggestion that he check out another road running into the marsh. He knew the doctor would ask if he had looked there, so he turned to head farther down the road toward Cayce and farther into Willingham Bottom to check it out.

Within a few yards, the swamp was no longer visible from the road. It was separated from the roadway by higher ground, a natural berm that was at least fifty yards wide in most places. The lane stretched back into the swampy area along the natural levee. It was nothing more than a trail, just wide enough for a team of horses and a wagon. Unlike Binford Road, it was lined by a thick stand of trees instead of water. It provided access for hunters and fishermen to explore the swamp to catch fish, turtles, frogs, waterfowl, and other game. Not far down the lane, Lonnie stopped, tied the reins to a tree, and continued on foot.

Dry ground extended back for a distance of more than one hundred yards from the road. Up ahead of him for another fifty yards or more, he could see that the trail stretched along a small peninsula of high ground that narrowed quickly to a point. He quickened his pace. Swamp water flanked the strip of land, and its color and lack of vegetation made it appear to be deep. As he continued to walk along the trail, Lonnie jumped, startled by the sudden dash of two fox squirrels—one chasing the other in circles around the trunk of a tree. He watched them continue their romp. They knocked bark off the tree trunk in their haste and then demonstrated their aerial agility as they jumped from limb to limb in the upper part of the tree.

As he watched them disappear into the top of an adjacent tree, Lonnie heard another sound. It was too faint for him to identify, but he stood still and concentrated, and he heard it again. He walked quickly along the trail until he reached its end at the tip of the peninsula. Standing there, with water on three sides now, he listened intently.

"Help!" came a faint but pleading cry from somewhere out in the swamp ahead of him.

"Who's there?"

"It's me! Joshua! I need help!"

"Joshua. Finally." Lonnie called back. "I was about ready to leave."

"Who are you?"

"It's me. Lonnie." And then louder, "It's Lonnie. Lonnie Crandall!"

"Lonnie ... Lonnie? I thought you had left for good."

"I did. But I came back. An' yore pappy talked me into comin' to find you."

"I need help. I can't stop shakin'. You gotta get me out'a here."

"Naw, I don't gotta do nothin'," insisted Lonnie. "Don't start orderin' me around like yore pappy does. Where are you?"

"Over here!" Joshua attempted to stand and waved his arms in the air.

Lonnie turned toward the sound and moved the limb of a bush for a better view. "Yeah. I see ya now."

"Get me out'a here, Lonnie."

"You orderin' me again?" yelled Lonnie.

"No—I'm just askin'. I'm cold, Lonnie. I'm beggin' ya."

"Can ya swim?"

"Uh, what?"

"I said, 'Can ya swim?' Whatsa matter with you? Are ya deaf?"

"I—I can't swim."

"Awright. But I can't see no way to get ya off'a that island without a boat. You can't swim, an' I can't swim, an' ..."

"Please hurry!" pleaded Joshua. "I'm cold an' wet an' tired."

"Awright. I'm a-goin'."

Lonnie turned and walked back down the trail to his wagon. He untied the reins and headed his team back toward the Samples' house, where he had left Doc Beeler. It was now midafternoon. Even if the doctor was ready to go back with him, it would take at least half an hour for them to get to the Jennings house. He coaxed his horses into a steady trot, and within a few minutes, he was back at the Samples' home.

As he was tying the reins to a low-hanging tree limb, Lester Samples approached him from behind the house.

"Howdy, you must be Lonnie," he said politely.

"Yep, my name's Lonnie."

"I'm Lester Samples. Doc Beeler said for me to tell you that he can't go just yet. Our baby's worse." Lester turned from Lonnie to hide his tears. He pulled a handkerchief from his hip pocket and wiped his eyes, and then he turned back to Lonnie.

"Our little boy ain't doin' too good, an' the doc says he's gonna stay with him for a while longer. Said for you to go on back without him."

"Awright," said Lonnie. "I'll just head on back by m'self."

Without any more conversation, Lester walked back to the house, and Lonnie untied his horses, climbed back in his wagon, and left. As before, he felt abandoned. He knew the little Samples boy needed help, but he was tired of having to work alone. Once again, he grew despondent and angry.

Lonnie slapped the reins against his horses' rumps. They broke from a fast walk into a trot. He hit them again. Then, yelling, *"Haaaaaa,"* he hit them again, and they broke into a dead run. Lonnie stood in his rickety old wagon, bracing himself against the splashboard in the front and the wagon seat behind him. Like a madman, he yelled and slapped the reins up and down. He ran his horses all the way to the base of Dixon Hill, where they could run no more. The team strained to pull the wagon up Dixon Hill, and Lonnie allowed them to walk the rest of the way to the Jennings house.

13

CHAPTER

I N THE EARLY AFTERNOON, members of the search team regrouped at the Jennings house to report their findings and to get new marching orders. Vernon Starr was in charge. From his potato crate podium, he offered an update.

"Okay, everybody," he began. "Let me report briefly about the search. First of all, thanks for all your help. I know Franklin, Gerthy, and the rest of the Jennings family really appreciate what you've done. The bad news is that we have not found Joshua. We've now searched both sides of the Big Ditch, and except for his cap, we haven't found anything."

"We found the horse!" Joe Smith interjected.

"Yep, that's right. As Joe says, we did find the horse. And, I might as well throw this in—after Joe an' Tom came back up the ditch in the boat, Joe jumped in an' felt around to make sure Joshua wasn't caught up in the harrow. The harrow was there, all right, but there was no sign of Joshua. And that leads to the good news. The good news is that we haven't found any sign that the boy is dead. We still believe that ..."

"Tell 'em 'bout what we seen in the boat," interrupted Joe again.

"Yeah—okay, Joe. Just a minute an' I'll cover that. What I was sayin' is that we still believe that Joshua's out there somewhere, an' we'll just keep lookin' 'til we find him. Now, what Joe is referrin' to is that he an'

Tom went all the way to the end of the ditch an' then out into the flooded field in Tom's rowboat. They saw some trash that must have been washed out by the flood. We figure that everything may be flooded all the way to Chapman's Creek. That means we need to pay special attention to Chapman's Creek and the Bottom. Doc Beeler and Lonnie were supposed to go down there, but they aren't back yet. We'll wait to hear what they say, but that's where Joshua is bound to be. Now, any questions?"

"Yeah, what are we gonna do next?"

"Good question. I see Franklin's comin' back from the house. I'm gonna let him tell you."

Franklin walked out from the back porch. He had been trying to reassure Maggie and the children that Joshua would be found soon. His eyes were puffy and red, and his shoulders drooped. He spoke quietly, with a raspy voice.

"Thank y'all for all you've done. We appreciate it more than we can say. Sheriff Ridley and a couple'a his deputies will be here any minute now to give us some help from here on. When they get here, we'll turn things over to them to see what to do next."

"There comes somebody now," said Gerthy. "But that can't be the sheriff. It's somebody in a wagon—it looks like Lonnie."

Standing and holding the reins like a charioteer on his victory lap, Lonnie steered his wagon into the yard.

"I wonder what happened to Doc Beeler," Franklin said.

Franklin hopped off the crate and rushed over to Lonnie's wagon.

"What took you so long to get back? Did you go to Willingham Bottom? "Where's the doctor? Any sign of Joshua?"

"Hey, hey, hey! Wait a minute. Can't I get down out'a my wagon before ya hit me with all them questions? Who are all these people? What are they doin' here?"

"They're here to help look for Joshua. Everybody's been reportin' on what they found. We're waitin' on the sheriff to get here. Now tell us. Did you find any sign of Joshua?"

"Well, I 'spect if everybody else gave a report, I ought'a give mine. I've got a report to give. That's for sure."

Franklin moved closer to Lonnie's wagon and glared up at him. "Tell me. Did you go to Willingham Bottom or not? Did you find any sign of Joshua?"

"I'll get to that. I'll answer all them questions, Mr. Jennings. Just let me tell it to everybody."

Lonnie jumped to the ground. He strutted through the crowd like a young rooster amidst his flock and stepped up onto the crate that Vernon and Franklin had used when they addressed the group.

"Uh, uh, well ... most'a y'all know I'm Joshua's stepbrother. An' when I heard he was missin', an' Mr. Franklin asked me to help, I did. Uh ... that was this mornin'. Well, Mr. Vernon, there, he told me to go down to get Doc Beeler, an' for us two to go lookin' in the Willingham Bottom. Well, uh ... that's what I done. I drove my team over to Doc Beeler's house an' waited on him. An' ... uh ... when he fine'ly come out, me an' him rode down toward the bottom like Mr. Vernon said. But ... uh ... along the way, Miz Samples come runnin' out, an' she started screamin' for the doctor to help her with her young'un. Said he had a fever or somethin'. So Doc Beeler ... uh ... he told me I should go on ahead an' look by myself for Joshua. An' ... uh ... well, that's what. ..."

"Just get to the point!" yelled Tom Parker. "Did you see any sign of Joshua, or not?" Murmurs and nodded *amens* spread through the crowd.

"Uh ... yeah. Well, that's just what I'm tryin' to tell ya. I looked for Joshua up an' down Binford Road. Matter'a fact, water was over the road, an' I couldn't hardly get through it. I must'a gone maybe a half a mile before it got so deep, I couldn't go no further. There was no sign'a Joshua anywhere."

Audible sighs were offered in unison, and looks of dismay spread throughout the crowd. Some began to talk quietly amongst themselves, and one or two of the men ambled away from the group.

But Lonnie was not finished.

"Then, uh ... when I tried to get my team turned around, uh ... that's when I got my wagon stuck in a deep hole. You should'a seen what I had to go through to git it out. Uh ... uh ... that's when I yelled out his name. I yelled his name an' called out for him to answer me if he could hear the sound'a my voice. Uh ... well, I never heard nothin' but a couple'a birds. So then, I got my rig out'a the hole, an' I come on back home. I'm tellin' you the honest truth—I looked high an' low, an' it's for sure. Joshua ain't in the Willingham Bottom."

Lonnie stepped down off the crate and began to walk through the crowd back toward his wagon. He glanced over at Franklin as he passed, but Franklin's head was bowed, and their eyes did not meet. Vernon Starr stepped out into Lonnie's path.

"Wait a minute, Lonnie. I want to ask you a couple'a questions, if you don't mind," he said.

"Naw, I don't mind. I ain't got nothin' to hide. Ask me all the questions you want." Lonnie shifted his weight from one foot to the other and glanced around at the eyes focused directly on him.

"Where's Doc Beeler? Did you leave him at the Samples' house?"

"Yep. 'Cause when I come back by there, Mr. Samples … uh … he come out to tell me that the doctor was a-stayin' there with his young'un. An' that's when I headed on back here."

"Did you try to walk any further down Binford Road? It's plain to see from your overalls that you got all wet. Did you look for Joshua any more that just along the half-mile stretch of Binford Road?"

"Nope. I didn't. Water was too deep to go no further. It was up to my knees right there where I was stuck in the hole."

"Did you go on down any further toward Cayce to look down there?"

"Nope. I shore didn't."

"When the sheriff gets here, I want you to tell him where you looked. Hang around here 'til he comes so you can tell him the same thing you told us."

"Uh … uh … well, I'd shore like to, but like I said before, I hafta go. I hafta be down at Hickman early in the mornin' to go to work on the river. I told y'all I got me a job, didn't I?"

"I don't remember you tellin' me that," Vernon said.

"Uh … well, it's the truth. So I'm gonna be goin' on. I'm gonna go tell my mama bye, an' then I gotta go."

Lonnie went quickly to the back door and disappeared into the house. In only a few moments, he reappeared, and without another word, he climbed into his wagon, turned his tired horses toward the road, and headed off.

"I shore do hope y'all find Joshua!" he yelled back as his wagon turned onto the road and rattled off.

Just as the sound of Lonnie's horse-drawn wagon dissolved into the wind, the unmuffled noise of the sheriff's patrol car reverberated through the trees as he and his deputies approached.

More than two months prior, driving much too fast on a deeply rutted road, the sheriff had ripped the muffler and the tail pipe off his patrol car. He claimed he had been too busy to have it repaired, but as his deputies knew, he liked the sound it made, and he had no intention of having a new muffler installed.

His patrol car was a white four-door sedan with *Sheriff* painted in big red letters on each side. It was his pride and joy. Around Fulton County, people joked that his deputies spent most of their time washing his car.

The car's tires kicked up loose mud as the sheriff steered it off the road onto Franklin's property and again as he skidded it to a stop. His deputies, Harold "Hambone" Penfield and Charlie "Ducky" Brown, got out and nodded as they approached the crowd of people. They each wore navy-blue work pants and a matching work shirt onto which a name tag and a "Fulton County Sheriff's Department" decal had been stitched.

Sheriff Benny Ridley was five feet, six inches tall with a stocky build. His flat-brimmed sheriff's hat hid most of his thick red hair, but freckles dotted every square inch of exposed skin. The trousers of his khaki sheriff's uniform were pulled up well above his waistline. Behind his back, people called him Sheriff Highpockets. He seemed perpetually hurried, and harried. When he walked, he leaned forward at the waist like a man who was trying to walk against a forty-mile-an-hour headwind.

Without saying a word, he made his way directly over to where Franklin, Gerthy, and Vernon were standing. After a brief private conversation with them, he mounted the wooden crate that had now become the official speakers' platform. With his rapid-fire speech pattern that was consistent with the way he walked, he addressed the crowd.

"Okay, everybody let me have your attention. I 'spect me an' my deputies should'a been called in on this thing last night, but we weren't, an' so now that's water under the bridge, or over the dam an' all that. But me an' Deputies Penfield an' Brown are here now, an' we aim to get this boy of Franklin's—what's his name?"

"Joshua," someone yelled out.

"Yeah, Joshua. We aim to get that boy rescued before it gets dark. Now, Vernon tells me that y'all have looked up an' down every inch of both sides of the Big Ditch back yonder, all the way from the crossin' to where it empties into the fields over on the old Pascal place. So I don't see no reason to keep a-lookin' back in that area. What Deputies Penfield an' Brown are gonna do ..."

"You mean Hambone an' Ducky, don't ya, Sheriff?" ribbed one of the men. The comment prompted a couple of the men to laugh.

"Shut up, you guys! This is serious," yelled Vernon.

"Sorry!"

The sheriff continued.

"Deputies Penfield an' Brown are goin' to take some of you volunteers an' find a way to get a boat back to Chapman's Creek. We figure that when the floodwaters was at their highest, that boy could'a floated into Chapman's Creek an' ended up somewhere there along its banks. Gettin' a boat back there won't be easy, 'cause them fields is still either flooded or too muddy to cross. But if we go around toward Moscow, there's a road that cuts through the Johnson place, an' we might be able to get through there. We figure it's worth a try."

"Do you need my boat?" asked Tom Parker.

"Naw. Thanks, Tom, but we already have a little light rowboat."

"What do you want the rest of us to be doin'?" asked one of the men.

"Yeah," chimed in another, "we can't all float down Chapman's Creek in a rowboat."

"Just hold on," said the sheriff impatiently. "I wasn't through. There's plenty enough for everyone to have somethin' to do. Elmer, you an' Joe can come with me an' my boys to look along Chapman's Creek."

Sheriff Ridley paused, turning to look back at Franklin.

"I understand that stepson'a yours looked for your boy down along Binford Road. Is that right?"

"Yeah. That's what he said. Said he didn't see him. An' he said he called out his name, but he didn't hear nothin', either."

"Well, I think we better look down there again," said the sheriff. "Tom, can you get that boat'a yours down to Binford Road?"

"Yep, I shore can."

"All right, then. You an' Vernon an' whoever else wants to, go down to Binford Road an put that boat in the swamp to see if you can find him down there. Franklin, are you an' Gerthy gonna stay here?"

"I can't just sit here an' do nothin', Sheriff," said Franklin. "I aim to find Joshua. I'll go with Vernon an' them down to Willingham Bottom. Gerthy says he may stay here to see after Maggie an' the children, and be here in case anybody else comes lookin' to help."

"Good! Okay, men, let's get goin'! We're runnin' out'a daylight."

Sheriff Ridley, his two deputies, Elmer Dixon, and Joe Smith crammed into the sheriff's patrol car and roared off, heading toward the little town of Moscow, located about five miles away.

"Tom, can you bring your boat down to Binford Road?" Vernon asked.

"Yeah," said Tom. "But the only way I have to carry it is in my wagon. It'll take me awhile to get there, but like I said, all I hafta do is load it in my wagon."

"All right, then. Well, I'm gonna drive Franklin down there in my car. We'll be lookin' along the road, and we'll see you when you get there with the boat. Okay?"

Vernon motioned with a tilt of his head for Franklin to ride with him in his car. It was a 1917 Model T Ford touring car with a folding top, black body and fenders, and nickel-plated trim. Vernon had bought it only a few months back. He was quite proud of his automobile, and like his other possessions, he kept it up in good condition.

Franklin sat down and pulled the door shut as Vernon cranked the engine. It started on the third revolution, causing the entire car to vibrate until it warmed up a bit. After he released the handbrake, Vernon grabbed the long, floor-mounted gearshift lever, eased the car into first gear, and chugged off.

Initially, there was no conversation. Both Vernon and Franklin were on the edge of physical exhaustion, and they were emotionally drained. Once again, Vernon tried to think of every possible scenario that would explain Joshua's disappearance—except, of course, those outcomes that would produce his dead body. He reviewed their search plan for any oversights or holes in their logic.

A quick glance at Franklin revealed furrows of worry, dread, and fear etched on his face. He was devoid of his usual vitality. With his chin cradled in his hand, he stared motionless at his feet.

"Try not to worry, Franklin. We'll find Joshua—I just know we will."

"I can't help worryin'." Franklin opened his eyes and turned away from Vernon. "I don't know what I'll do if somethin' bad has happened to my boy."

"We'll find him. With Sheriff Ridley and his deputies and all the others out there lookin', I'm confident we're gonna find him."

Franklin appeared not to hear Vernon's optimistic words. He stared straight ahead and shook his head pensively.

"It was bad enough that God took Hannah from me. I don't know if I can stand it if He takes Joshua, too."

"Try not to think the worst."

"'Course, I should'a never let him go back there to get that harrow in the storm. I sure never thought somethin' bad like this would happen. I didn't know the storm was gonna be so bad. I never seen water rise up like that in the Big Ditch. I would'a never let him go back there if I'd'a known we was about to have a flood!"

"Quit blaming yourself, Franklin. There's no way anybody could'a known that flood was comin'. You were …"

"Why didn't I have better judgment?" Franklin slammed his fist against the dashboard. "I just didn't use good judgment."

"We'll find him. You'll see."

14

CHAPTER

SHERIFF RIDLEY ROARED OUT of the Jennings family's yard and turned onto the road without braking, causing the right rear wheel to lift up off the ground. With the vanishing hours of daylight, he had reason to hurry.

But the sheriff was always in a hurry. One of the reasons Benny Ridley had run for sheriff was his attraction to speed. On a horse, in a wagon, or in his patrol car, he loved to race. It was rumored that as a teenager he had run one of his father's horses until it collapsed and died on the spot.

As sheriff, he could run his Chevy as fast as it would go with impunity. He took advantage of the privilege, whether he was going home to dinner or chasing a suspect. Now the urgency of getting to Chapman's Creek before dark was the perfect opportunity for the sheriff to set a new personal speed record for the trip from Crutchfield to just the other side of Moscow.

Accustomed to his driving habits, the sheriff's two deputies sat back to enjoy the ride. Hambone Penfield rode shotgun, and Ducky Brown sat in the back, crammed in between Elmer Dixon and Joe Smith. The car darted from side to side in deep ruts in the road, and its undercarriage often dragged on mounds of mud between the ruts. Sheriff Ridley leaned forward in his seat and peered out just over the top of his oversized steering wheel. In a curve in the narrow road, he ran up on a flock of chickens crossing in his path. Scattering in every direction, the chickens ran, flopped, and flew to avoid being hit. One pullet jumped straight up in the air and flapped its wings in a frantic effort to fly. It gained just enough altitude to clear the hood of the car, but it smashed into the windshield and glanced off, feathers flying, into the ditch.

"Stop, Sheriff! That's a perfectly good fryer," yelled Ducky. He pulled himself forward to turn and look at the dead chicken. "Hazel could fry it up for supper."

"I ain't stoppin' for roadkill," declared the sheriff. "B'sides, we're in a hurry!"

"It doesn't seem like roadkill if you're the one that just hit it," argued Ducky. "At least we know it's fresh."

"Well I'll agree with Sheriff Ridley," said Hambone. "It's dead, an' it's lying by the road. That's roadkill in my book."

"Yeah. You always agree with the sheriff," Ducky retorted. "An' you mean to tell me you wouldn't pick up a freshly killed chicken an' take it home for dinner? The way you eat, I wouldn't be surprised you'd pick up a dead possum."

"I'll eat a possum, all right. But not one that's been hit by a car."

Ducky turned to look back once more. He sighed loudly, turned to face forward again, and slid back into his seat.

"Speakin' of eatin'," said Ducky, breaking the brief silence, "Did the deputy there ever tell you boys how he come to be called Hambone?"

"Aw, come on, Ducky," protested Hambone. "Why d'ya always bring that up?"

"I don't remember hearing that story," said Elmer.

"I didn't know his name was Hambone 'til today," Joe chimed in.

Ducky chuckled. "Tell 'em, Hambone. Tell 'em how you got your name."

"I ain't tellin' that. It ain't worth hearin'. Why don't you tell about how you come to be known as Ducky?" Hambone turned to look at the men in the back seat. "I'll give you a hint. He ain't called Ducky 'cause he can swim good! When we get out'a the car, just watch the way he walks an' you'll know why he's called Ducky!"

"Why don't you both shut up?" said the sheriff. "If I hafta listen to this one more time, I think I'll puke."

"Well, I'm sorry, sheriff, but these boys ain't heard it, an' it's too good a story not to tell. B'sides, he's already told 'bout why they call me Ducky."

Ducky scooted forward once more. He coughed and cleared his throat as if he were ready to give an important speech. Hambone shook his head in disgust, mumbling and growling unintelligibly.

"Here's the way I heard the story." Ducky had a glint in his eyes. He took great pleasure each time he told this story about Hambone.

"It was when he was a young boy—'bout eight, nine years old—an' his real name was Harold. Bad enough that folks'd name a little kid Harold," said Ducky, getting in an extra barb. "But that was his name, all right."

"Ain't nothin' wrong with the name Harold," Hambone declared.

"Anyway, as I was sayin', when Harold was little, his pappy come home one day with a big ole salt-cured country ham for the family to eat around Christmastime. They had ham an' red-eye gravy for supper, an' ham-an'-eggs for breakfast, an' ham sandwiches for dinner. An' little ole Harold, there—he could eat as much ham as any'a the rest of 'em. Matter'a fact, they found out that Harold liked country ham better'n he liked his mother's milk when he was a baby! They say they ain't never seen anybody eat country ham, before or since, like little Harold did—didn't know where a boy that size was puttin' it! They couldn't figure …"

"For God's sake, Ducky, just finish tellin' it an' shut up!" yelled Hambone.

"Yeah, well, this is where it really gets good. See, they ate up all the ham right down to the bone. All was left was just little hunks'a ham meat that hung onto the bone an' wouldn't let go. Miz Penfield—she started to throw the ham bone in a big ole pot'a beans for seasonin'. But then for some reason, she decided not to, an' so she gave it to the dog instead. Then …" Ducky tried to continue, but his words were choked out with his own laughter.

"Then …" Again he laughed, and slapped his knee. Finally, he regained enough control to go on.

"Then … then after the dog had it for maybe fifteen, twenty minutes …"

Ducky couldn't go on. He now laughed uncontrollably. Hambone glanced back at him with contempt. Amidst coughs, more laughs, and spewed saliva, Ducky continued.

"After fifteen, twenty minutes, Harold's mama an' papa looked outside, an' they saw … they saw …"

Ducky lost control again. He slapped the top of the seat in front of him, laughing so hard he temporarily lost his breath. Because of his uncontrollable glee, Elmer and Joe joined in the raucous laughter even before he got to the punch line.

"What happened? Wha'd Harold do?" asked Joe.

"Yeah, well, here's what happened," sputtered Ducky. "Harold's mama an' papa looked out in the yard, an' they saw that little ole Harold had gone out there, an'—an' he had taken the bone away from the dog! An'—an' he was gnawin' little bits'a ham off the bone that the dog couldn't even get! Took the bone away from the dog, an' showed 'im how to clean it! An'—an' that's why they've called him Hambone ever since!"

Hambone sat in silence while his backseat friends wiped tears from their eyes and continued to chortle, hoot, and holler. Soon, however, the din of laughter died down as the men became solemn again. For the remainder of their brief trip, they rode silently, pondering their task at hand.

Sheriff Ridley steered his patrol car off the road and down a narrow lane to a dilapidated barn situated behind a white frame farm house. The sheriff's first cousin owned the property, and Chapman's Creek formed its boundary on one side. The sheriff was allowed to use his cousin's rowboat to fish in the creek as he pleased, and he would come and go without notice.

The rowboat was in its usual place, leaned up against the side of the barn. Paddles were kept just inside the door.

"Will all of us fit in that boat?" asked Joe as the men walked from the car toward the barn.

"Naw," said the sheriff, "I figure it'll only hold three of us. We'll help carry it down to the creek. But then I want Hambone to take Elmer an' you in the boat with him. Me an' Ducky will drive down to Willingham Bottom to meet the others."

Elmer and Joe looked at each other and shrugged, curious about the sheriff's decision to assign them boat duty under the direction of Hambone Penfield.

With three on one side and two on the other, the men hoisted the boat upside down onto their shoulders and carried it through an open pasture down a gentle slope to the edge of Chapman's Creek. Full of muddy water to the brim, the stream was about thirty feet wide and flanked by tree-lined banks. In some spots, the depth of the water was fifteen feet or more.

"Okay, boys," said the sheriff after the boat was launched. "Me an' Ducky'll see y'all down in Willingham Bottom. Just come over to where Binford Road runs along the top of the levee, an' we'll meet ya there. If you do find the boy, bring him down there. That's where Franklin an' them other guys are gonna be lookin' for him."

The creek's current was steady and strong, but not terribly swift. Elmer and Joe managed to steer the boat into the middle of the creek to avoid tree limbs, logs, and other debris that had collected along the banks. They wouldn't begin their search for Joshua until they got farther downstream, to where the floodwater would most likely flow into the creek.

Scores of gar swam alongside the boat near the surface. Locals referred to these slender, needle-nosed fish as alligator gar. With their elongated heads and thick gray scales, they looked like baby alligators without legs. They were pests. Not only were they difficult to catch on a hook, but they were much too bony and tough to eat. Fishermen hated them especially because they frightened smaller fish away, and it was not unusual for a fisherman to lose a big catfish as a passing gar brushed up against his taut fishing line and sliced it in two with its sharp scales. Nothing angered a Chapman's Creek fisherman more than losing a prize catfish because of a no-good alligator gar.

As shadows lengthened, Elmer quickened the pace of his strokes, and Joe followed suit. There was no conversation. Joshua was neither son nor brother to any of the men. But as a member of the community, he was family. They had to find him. They had to find him alive.

Carried by steady current and smooth, strong paddle strokes, the rowboat moved swiftly through straight segments and gentle turns of Chapman's Creek. This section of the creek was heavily shaded by thick stands of mature trees on each side. The air was noticeably cooler. They passed under a single-lane bridge that rested precariously on rusty supports and rotting timbers. *Pity the unfortunate travelers who frequently use that bridge,* Elmer thought. Blackbirds noisily chased a crow from their hallowed territory, taking turns to bravely dart and peck at the much larger bird to scare it away.

In an area free of trees on one side of the creek, Elmer sat up straight to survey the surroundings carefully.

"This is about where the flood water would've emptied into the creek. We ought'a start lookin' for any sign of the boy from here on," he instructed. "Joe, you look on the left side, an' I'll take the right."

"Yeah, an' since you boys are doin' the rowin', I'll be able to look along both sides," volunteered Hambone. "You reckon we ought'a yell out his name in case he's crawled out on the bank waitin' for someone to find him?"

"Yeah," agreed Elmer. "That's a good idea. We can take turns."

Hambone paused, reluctant at first to break the silence, but then he yelled loudly.

"Hey! Hey, boy! Are you out there, boy? Can you hear me?"

"His name's Joshua!" snapped Joe. "At least call him by his name."

"Yeah, okay," said the deputy, nodding. "I'm sorry—I forgot his name there for a second."

Hambone cleared his throat and yelled out again.

"Jaa-shuu-aaa! Jaa-shuu-aaa, can you hear me?" he bellowed. Hambone's words echoed and died in eerie silence. Dutifully, each man took his turn to call out Joshua's name in desperate hope that he would answer from amongst the trees on one side of the creek or the other. There was no answer.

At the end of a rather sharp bend, the creek narrowed markedly, and its current became swift. As the boat gained speed, Joe and Elmer paddled just enough to keep it in a straight line, content to rest a bit. As Joe turned to give his fellow crewmen a "thumbs-up" to acknowledge their good fortune, Elmer noticed a trotline just up ahead of them.

Made of heavy cord, it was strung tight all the way across the creek at a height of about three feet above the surface of the water. Heavy fishing lines with sinkers and baited hooks were tied to the trotline at intervals of about three feet. They extended from the trotline down into the water at the proper depth to lure big catfish as they cruised through the muddy water looking for food.

Trotlines were popular because once the lines were baited and set, they provided around-the-clock unattended fishing. A busy farmer could set out a baited line late in the evening after field work was done and not return until the next evening to rebait empty hooks and remove any fish that had been caught. Generally, however, trotlines were set out along the bank on one side of the creek to provide access without a boat and to avoid blocking passage of other boats up and down the creek. It was highly unusual for anyone to set a line from one side of the creek to the other, and this one caught Joe and Elmer totally by surprise.

"Watch out, Joe!" Elmer yelled. Joe turned and spotted the cord directly in front of him. He quickly back-paddled, but to no avail. Caught in the swift current, the boat swung around and drifted sideways. As it floated under the trotline, each of the men ducked down to avoid being knocked out of the boat by the taut cord.

Joe and Elmer were fortunate to float between leaders that extended down from the trotline into the water, but one of the drop lines was positioned directly where Hambone was sitting. He raised his arm to protect his face from the line, but as the boat cleared the overhanging cord and continued to float downstream, the leader was pulled up out of the water, and its exposed hook penetrated his shirt and set deeply into his forearm. In an instant, Hambone was yanked from the boat. He screamed in agony and fright as Joe and Elmer watched in horror. He struggled to free himself from the hook embedded in the flesh on the underside of his forearm, and simultaneously, he thrashed to keep from being pulled under.

As Joe and Elmer paddled frenetically against the current to get back to him, he disappeared under the surface of the water. He kicked and fought like a two-hundred-pound catfish that had just been gaffed. Finally, he resurfaced, gasped for air, cried out, and was pulled under again.

Joe and Elmer paddled to get back upstream far enough for Joe to reach out and grab the trotline and hold on. While Joe held the trotline with both hands, Elmer knelt down and extended his paddle out in Hambone's direction.

When Hambone resurfaced, he grabbed the end of the paddle to allow Elmer to pull him up to the back of the boat. Hambone held on to the back transom with both hands, the fishhook still dangling from his right forearm. He coughed and sputtered.

Elmer grabbed Hambone under each arm.

"Just hang on 'til you get your breath—I've got ya." Hambone continued to cough and struggled to get his breath.

"I thought I was a goner," he said.

"I know," agreed Elmer, "It all happened so fast! I'm just glad we got back to you in time. Come on—let's see if we can get you back in the boat."

Hambone pulled as hard as he could to lift himself up onto the back of the boat. Elmer grabbed his belt in the back to lift him up and over the transom and into the boat.

"Let me see that arm, Hambone," said Elmer. "We gotta get that hook out."

Hambone's arm was a bloody mess. Set deep into his muscular forearm, the hook had torn some of his flesh as his body weight pulled against it in the strong current. In fact, Elmer could see that the hook had been straightened out, and it likely would have ripped loose from his arm in a few more seconds. Elmer cut the line off the hook with his pocketknife.

"Okay, man. Are you ready for me to get this thing out'a your arm?" he asked.

"Yep. I reckon. Go ahead an' do what you gotta do. Just make it quick!" Hambone gritted his teeth and looked away.

Not wanting the barb to tear the flesh even more, Elmer pushed the hook back in the opposite direction from the eyelet, forcing the sharp end to reemerge from the wound. Then, grasping it firmly, Elmer yanked it out quickly as Hambone screamed in pain.

"Come on, Joe," said Elmer. "We've gotta get him to where he can see a doctor."

"Yeah, I know," Joe agreed.

"Only thing I know to do is to keep on goin' down the creek to the bottom, where the sheriff will be waitin' for us. Somebody there can take him to the doctor."

"Yep. We couldn't paddle this thing back up the creek, anyway."

Hambone sat down in the bottom of the boat and leaned against the crosspiece that had been his seat before. He cradled his bloody arm against his stomach, closed his eyes, and hoped for a swift journey to Willingham Bottom. Joe and Elmer paddled harder than ever. The deputy needed medical attention as quickly as possible, but they continued to look for any sign of Joshua and call out to him along the way.

15

CHAPTER

GERTHY HAD AGREED TO stay back at the house with Maggie and the children while others searched for Joshua. Reading, his usual pastime, was futile as his thoughts strayed to the plight of his nephew. He moved to a rocker onto the front porch for some fresh air, but even the sweet scent of jasmine and a gentle breeze did little to calm his nerves. He gave up his chair to go back inside.

Maggie immersed herself in her weekly ironing. Her kitchen was overheated from the fire in the cookstove, and it smelled of burning oak mixed with the warm, crisp scent of freshly ironed cotton cloth—gingham dresses and boys' Sunday trousers. Typically, Maggie ironed in the morning, restoking the fire used earlier to bake biscuits and to fry bacon and eggs for breakfast.

"I've never seen you do your ironing in the afternoon," observed Gerthy.

"I'm almost finished. I just needed to stay busy to keep my mind off'a worryin'."

Maggie bit her lip to keep from crying. She moved her heavy, black iron back onto the burner of the cookstove. With a heavy mitt, she removed the other iron, which was now hot. Beads of perspiration dotted her forehead, and ringlets of grey hair around her face were wet with sweat.

"I know what you mean. I feel like I need somethin' to do right now, myself. I guess we're all pretty edgy."

"The children have been askin' lots of questions about what's goin' on. Maybe you could talk to them about it. I have a hard time talkin' about it without cryin', an' I don't want to get them upset."

Tears welled up in Maggie's eyes and fell from her cheeks onto the back of her hand as she moved the iron slowly back and forth. She lifted it onto a protective metal plate and lifted her apron to wipe her eyes.

"Where are the kids?" Gerthy asked. "I'll go play with them."

"They were fightin' an' wrestlin' up in the front room a minute ago. But I don't hear them now. You better go check on them for sure!"

Gerthy turned back to Maggie.

"Did Lonnie come in to tell you goodbye? He told us he's goin' to Hickman early in the mornin' to head out to begin his job on the river."

Before the words were completely out of his mouth, Maggie stopped her ironing, covered her eyes with her apron, and began to sob.

"Uh-huh," she muttered.

Gerthy put his arm around her shoulder.

"I'm sorry. I didn't mean to make you cry. I was just wonderin' …"

Maggie sniffled and wiped her eyes again.

"It's okay, Gerthy. It's good'a you to ask about Lonnie. You know I can't ever talk to Franklin about Lonnie, since the two'a them never got along."

"I'm sure Lonnie will do fine workin' on the river," Gerthy assured her. "He's big an' strong, an' I'm sure he can handle anything they dish out. It might end up bein' the best thing in the world for him—might help him grow up a little."

"I know. I know. You're prob'ly right about that, Gerthy. It's—it's just that with Joshua bein' lost an' all, an' then Lonnie goin' away to work, I guess it's got me all upset."

"Well, that's understandable, Maggie. It's never easy—especially for a mother—to see a son move away. But I bet he goes off as a boy an' then, before you know it, he'll come back to you as a man. That's what I bet."

"Uh-huh. That's what I'm hopin' for," answered Maggie with a sniffle. "But what I can't figure out is why Lonnie said what he did when he told me goodbye. I just can't figure it out, an' it's got me worried."

"What did he say?"

"Well, first he just said he had come to tell me goodbye, an' that he would let me know where he is, so that I can write to him. Then he said he hoped I would send him some cookies every once in a while, an' for me not to worry about him. Then he went to tell Reba an' Naomi goodbye."

"None'a that sounds unusual to me," interjected Gerthy. "I know you'll miss him an' all, but I sure don't think there's anything to worry about in what he said."

"Yeah, but wait, Gerthy," said Maggie, with tears beginning to fill her eyes again. "It's what he said when he came back through the room right before he left that's got me upset."

"What else did he say?"

"It was when he passed back through the kitchen after tellin' the girls goodbye. I was standin' right there by the door, an' I stopped him to give him a hug an' a kiss before he went out. An' I said somethin' like you did before—you know, like 'Well, I can't wait for you to come back here all grown up as a man.' An' that's when he pushed away from me an' grabbed me by the shoulders, and said … He said, 'Mama' …"

Unable to hold back her tears and repeat her son's words, Maggie began to sob. Gerthy put his arm back around her shoulder and tried to console her.

"It's gonna be okay, Maggie, I promise. Just try to get a hold of yourself, and tell me what Lonnie said that's got you so upset."

Maggie wiped her eyes and tried to regain her composure. "I'm sorry. He—he looked me right in the eyes an' said, 'Mama, I'm tellin' you goodbye—maybe forever. I don't know if I'll ever see you again. Maybe I can send for you to come see me sometime.' Then I asked him what he meant an' why he said I might not see him ever again. An'—an' he said, 'All I can tell ya is this. After they find Joshua, I won't be able to come back here ever again. That's all I can tell ya.' An' then he hugged me quick an' said, 'Take care'a yourself, Mama,' an' he left. Now that's what I can't figure out." Maggie starting to sniffle again. "What's findin' Joshua got to do with him not bein' able to come back here?"

"Good Lord up in heaven!" Gerthy exclaimed. He looked straight into Maggie's eyes. "Tell me again. What did Lonnie say?"

"It's like I just said—Lonnie said that he was tellin' me goodbye, maybe forever—said I might not ever see him again."

"No, not that. I mean, tell me again what Lonnie said about findin' Joshua an' all that."

"Well, he said—I remember his words exactly—he said, 'When they find Joshua, I won't be able to come back here again.' That's what he said—I heard him say those exact words."

"You sure he said 'when they find Joshua'? Are you sure?"

"Uh-huh—yes! Yes! I'm sure that's what he said. But why are you askin' me all these questions?"

"This is unbelievable. This is incredible."

"What is it, Gerthy?" asked Maggie. "Now you've got me really worried."

"Don't ya see, Maggie?" Gerthy explained. "Lonnie went lookin' for Joshua. He agreed to help. An' at first Doc Beeler was with him. But then Doc Beeler had to stop to take care of a sick baby. Lonnie ended up lookin' by himself."

"I still don't understand."

"Just listen. I'm tryin' to explain. You said that Lonnie said 'when they find Joshua,'—not 'if they find Joshua,' but 'when they find Joshua.' That means Lonnie knows Joshua is alive. An' the only way Lonnie could know Joshua is alive is if he's seen him. What I'm thinkin' is that Lonnie saw Joshua, but he didn't tell us about it. Matter'a fact, he said he didn't see Joshua. But now I'm thinkin' he probably did. Why else would he be afraid to come back here? Why else would he say that he might have to send for you to come see him?"

"Oh, no, Gerthy! I know Lonnie's not been the best boy in the world, but Lonnie wouldn't do that! Oh, surely not!"

"Maggie, I don't know for sure, but I have to find out. It might be a way to find Joshua. Do you know where Lonnie is?"

"I guess he's at his granddaddy's house. I don't know for sure."

"Can you call him on the telephone?"

"He doesn't have a telephone—says he's got no use for one."

"Well then, I've got to find Doc Beeler."

"Why?"

"He was with Lonnie when they first went to look for Joshua. I gotta find Doc Beeler. I'll explain everything later."

Gerthy limped into the sitting room, grabbed the telephone receiver off its hook, and turned the crank for one long ring to get the operator.

"Central. How can I help you?"

"Irma, is that you? This is Gerthy Jennings."

"No, Irma is out sick. This is Mary—Mary Brewer. What can I do for you today, Mr. Jennings?"

"Ring Doc Beeler for me. Would ya please?"

"Just a minute."

Gerthy listened as the operator made the connection, sending three short rings to the doctor's telephone. Silence. Then three short rings again. Silence. Once more, Gerthy heard three short rings on the doctor's party line.

"Come on—please be there," Gerthy whispered. "Please, somebody, answer the telephone."

"Do you want me to keep tryin'?" asked the operator. "I'll keep a-ringin' it as long as you want if it's an emergency."

"Thanks, but I guess he's not in. I'll call back in a few minutes."

Gerthy paced across the room, looked out the window, and then paced back to the telephone again. He caught himself involuntarily reaching for the receiver only seconds after hanging it up. He paced back to the window. He peered out, at first staring into space, focused on nothing in particular. Then he focused in on Franklin's old Ford parked in its usual spot beside the henhouse. *The car—is it possible that I could figure out how to drive the car?*

The fact that Gerthy had never driven an automobile was not due solely to his physical handicap. He had never allowed his withered leg and crippled foot to restrict what he wanted to do. When Franklin bought his Model T Ford, he had offered to let Gerthy learn to drive it. But Gerthy declined, primarily because he preferred his horse and buggy.

For him, the automobile offered no particular advantage. Most of his travel was to church and back, a trip he made at least three times a week. But he knew how much time to allow for his horse to get him there, and he was never late. Speed of travel was not a factor. In fact, although he had never shared his view with others, Gerthy considered the automobile to be an unreliable and dangerous means of transportation. He had no use for a car or the ability to drive one—until now.

Gerthy needed speedy transportation. He didn't have time to harness his horse and hitch him up for a buggy ride. He had to move quickly. Nervously, he glanced back and forth from the Model T to the telephone, and he decided to try one more call to Doc Beeler's house. As before, there was no answer. Gerthy replaced the receiver and hobbled to the back door. He paused only to tell Maggie that he intended to drive Franklin's car to find Doc Beeler and look for Joshua.

He thought it wise to test his ability to depress the clutch with his crippled leg before he tried to crank the engine. He sat down in the driver's seat, grasped his left leg with both hands, and lifted it high to swing it into the car without hitting his six-inch platform shoe on the bottom of the door frame.

He could work the clutch all right, but to move it on and off of the pedal quickly would be difficult. He decided to leave his foot on the pedal, ready to depress it when necessary, rather than move it on and off as he had seen other drivers do. With some confidence in his physical prowess to drive the car, Gerthy proceeded.

He found the ignition switch on the dashboard panel, just to the right of the steering column, and switched it on. He opened the hand throttle, located on the steering column just underneath the steering wheel, to provide sufficient gas flow for the engine to start.

Next, Gerthy reached down and felt around under the seat, where he had seen Franklin put the crank. It was under the passenger side of the musty-smelling old bench seat. He moved to the front of the car, inserted the crank, and spat into his hands.

"I sure hope I can get this ole baby started," he muttered.

On the first crank, the engine sputtered but did not start. He cranked it again, and this time it sputtered, coughed, and started to run, but then it backfired loudly and died.

"Come on, you old rattletrap! Let's get goin'," he coaxed, and he gave the crank another spin. This time, the engine started up, misfired a couple of times, and then settled into rhythmic revolutions that made the car bounce up and down on its tired old leaf spring suspension.

Gerthy hopped around the car to remove the blocks behind and in front of each of the back wheels. After setting the handbrake, Franklin would always use chunks of wood to keep the car from rolling down the hill. *I'll take my horse and buggy any day,* Gerthy thought.

Sitting erect on the edge of the seat, Gerthy reviewed the gear-shifting process. With the clutch depressed, he grasped the gearshift lever knob and moved it horizontally back and forth in its neutral position. Then he pulled it to the left toward his leg and back toward the seat for first (low) gear; forward, over to the right, and forward again for second; and straight back for third (high).

"Dear Lord, help me drive this car if it is Your will," he prayed.

He pushed the clutch pedal as far down as his leg would reach and shifted into first. No problem so far. Slowly, he pulled his leg back, allowing the clutch pedal to move. The car began to inch forward. Then he released the clutch completely, and the old Ford bucked and jolted forward like a young, unbroken colt being ridden for the first time.

Momentarily disoriented, Gerthy depressed the clutch again to keep the engine from stalling. The motor kept chugging, but the car had moved forward just enough to catch the slope of the hill, and it coasted with increasing speed toward the road. As the car continued to gain speed, Gerthy panicked. Instead of putting on the brakes, he jerked both legs backward in a sudden, involuntary reaction. The old car lurched forward with a jolt and threw Gerthy hard against the seat. Just as abruptly, the engine died, and the old Model T rolled down the slope and stopped on the edge of the road, precariously close to the ditch.

With renewed determination, he moved quickly. Standing in the ditch, he recranked the engine, this time with less sputtering. Then, back in the driver's seat, he reviewed the steps to get the car to move. *Depress the clutch pedal, and push the gear shifter forward to find reverse.* Slowly, he released the clutch, and with only one slight hiccup, he backed the old car away from the ditch to make the turn onto the road.

Then he put the car in first gear and moved forward steadily. When he shifted into second, he forgot to release the accelerator. The engine revved loudly, and the car bucked, but it continued to move forward at a steady pace. He was content to drive without shifting into third.

As the old Ford sputtered along, Gerthy smiled with self-satisfaction. His confidence grew, and he discovered an unanticipated thrill as he drove the old car. *Maybe the automobile is an improvement on my horse and buggy,* he thought.

Gerthy wanted to find Doc Beeler. Although it was unlikely that the doctor had returned in the few minutes since Gerthy had called his house, he decided to stop to check.

At a junction, Gerthy left the car in second gear and slowed down just enough to turn toward the doctor's home. *Anything to avoid having to use the clutch,* he thought. Suddenly, he shuddered and his heart rate accelerated as Dixon Hill, the steepest hill in Fulton County, loomed just ahead. He removed his foot from the accelerator and allowed the car to slow down, but in another instant, he topped the crest of the hill. Through the dirty windshield, he saw only treetops and sky. The road seemed to have disappeared beneath him.

Just over the crest of the hill, the car began to descend rapidly. Gerthy's head jolted forward, and he now saw the road again passing under him at a high rate of speed. Instinctively, he mashed the clutch pedal and stepped on the brake. The old car creaked and skidded, veering first to the right, back to the left, and then back to the right again as deep ruts in the dirt road helped steer it down the hill. Finally, as the road leveled out and the car slid to a complete stop, Gerthy knew he had survived.

With the car in first gear for the remaining quarter of a mile, he finally reached the Beeler place. He limped to the back door and knocked. When the door swung open, a tall, stately woman appeared, peering out through a screen door. She had a youngish-looking face framed by shoulder-length, prematurely gray hair. She was barefooted, and the apron that almost covered her dress was dirty—especially at her midsection.

"Yes?"

Gerthy tipped his wide-brimmed hat he wore anytime he left the house.

"Afternoon, ma'am. I'm Gerthy Jennings. I'm looking for the doctor. Are you Miz Beeler?"

"I am, indeed. But my Lee is not at home. Is there anything I can do for you, Mr. ... uh, what did you say your name is?"

"Jennings. Gerthy Jennings is my name," he answered as he removed his hat. "You may know my brother, Franklin. It's his boy, Joshua, that's lost—I don't know if you heard. He got washed away in the flood, and your husband was good enough to help us look for him until ..."

"Oh my, yes! Why, Lee did tell me about that. He thinks the world of that boy. I remember the time he sewed up the boy's head after he'd been kicked by a horse."

"Yes, ma'am. He did."

"I think some young man came by here to pick Lee up."

"That was Lonnie."

"Well, I've been out working in my flower garden all day. Can't you see how dirty I am? Please excuse the way I look! Anyway, I saw him ride off with some young man in a wagon this morning. I guess they went off looking for the boy, and I haven't heard from him since."

"Uh, yes, they did."

"I never seem to know where that husband of mine is. He goes off to see his patients, and I don't even ask where he's going anymore. Sometimes I don't even think he knows where he's going."

"Uh-huh."

"But there's one thing I can count on. He may gallivant around the whole county all day long, but one thing's for sure. Just like clockwork—unless it's a true emergency—come six o'clock in the evening, that man will be here for supper!"

"Yes, ma'am. I ..."

"If it's six o'clock in the evening and he isn't sitting at the table all washed up and ready to eat, I know somebody must be dying!"

Gerthy's endurance wore thin. Putting on his hat, he turned to leave.

"Thank you, Miz Beeler. Thank you for the information. But I'm in a hurry to find my nephew before it gets dark. If you'll excuse me, I must go."

"Oh, yes! By all means! I understand. I sure hope you find that boy soon."

Quickly, Gerthy walked back to the car, confident that he would find the doctor at the Samples' house. Gerthy looked at his pocket watch quickly before he cranked the car—this time like a seasoned driver. It bucked and jumped at the start, as his footwork on the clutch was still unsteady. He dreaded his challenge to get the old car to climb Dixon Hill.

For a new driver, Gerthy's instincts were sound. Still in first gear on the flat road at the base of the hill, he accelerated to gain speed and power for the climb. He fought against the car's loose steering to keep it from bumping against the sides of the ruts as it had done on the way down. He gave it even more gas, and the old engine revved to its limit as the car reached the steep incline. Gerthy opened the throttle all the way. Midway up the hill, the car's forward momentum slowed drastically, and the engine groaned. He pulled hard against the steering wheel and rocked forward and back repeatedly.

"Come on, baby! Come on baby!" he shouted.

Just before the crest of the hill, the engine backfired and sputtered, and Gerthy feared that the car would stall. He lunged forward mightily with his body. The engine backfired again and then regained just enough power to push the car over the crest of the hill.

Gerthy breathed heavily, removed his hat, and placed it on the seat beside him. He wiped sweat from his forehead with his sleeve, first on one side and then on the other. *Never again will I drive a car,* he thought. *Especially up and down Dixon Hill.*

16
CHAPTER

AT THE SAMPLES' HOME, Gerthy wheeled off the road and up to the side of their small, unpainted house. He parked under a pecan tree that appeared to have been struck by lightning. Branches had been stripped off on one side, and a large scar was visible in the tree trunk all the way to the ground.

As Gerthy crawled out of the car, Doc Beeler emerged from the front door. The doctor paused briefly in the doorway to say goodbye to someone inside. Lester Samples walked around from the back of the house and approached Gerthy as he stepped out of the car.

"Howdy. Can I he'p ya?"

"Hey." Gerthy extended his hand. "I'm Gerthy Jennings. I stopped by here to see Doc Beeler."

"He's on the porch talkin' to my wife. He's the finest man I know of. Saved my boy's life—matter'a fact, he's saved my boy's life mor'n oncet. He's a fine man, an' he's a fine doctor. Why d'ya need to see him? Is he doctorin' yer leg? I couldn't he'p noticin' that you got a bad gimp in yer step."

"A what?"

"You know—a gimpy leg. You walk all gimpy-legged."

"Oh, yeah. I was born with a bad leg and foot, but I manage to get around all right. Just never could run real fast, that's all. I'm happy to hear your boy's gonna be okay."

"Yeah, well, maybe one'a these days he'll quit havin' them fits altogether. Well, here comes the doctor. I'll let him an' you talk. Nice talkin' to ya."

"Yeah. It was nice to see you, too."

Dr. Robert E. Lee Beeler bounded down the steps toward Gerthy, as full of energy as he had been when Lonnie picked him up in his wagon that morning. His eyelids blinked repeatedly, and he pursed his lips back and forth as he reached out to shake hands with Gerthy.

"What brings you here, Gerthy?" He looked quizzically at Gerthy and then at the old Ford. "When did you start to drive a car? Have y'all found Joshua yet?"

"Hey, Doc. Let me explain. It's about Joshua. I needed to talk to you, and there was nobody else around. I had to drive myself—never drove a lick before today."

"What's the matter? Have you found Joshua or not?"

"Nope, we haven't found him. But I found out somethin' that may help us figure out where to look, an' I need your help. Are you through here? Are you through with the Samples' boy?"

"Yeah. He's gonna be all right for the time being. But I thought we'd lost him there for a little while. Do you need me to go with you?"

"I sure do."

"Well, okay. Lester was gonna take me home in his buggy, but I'm happy to go with you an' pass on that buggy ride. Let me tell him he won't need to take me home, and then I'll be with you. You can tell me all about it on the way. Do you want me to drive?"

"I sure do!"

Gerthy cranked the engine to save time. Sliding in on the passenger side, he watched the doctor trot back to the car from behind the house.

"Now, Gerthy, tell me what's goin' on." Doc Beeler adjusted himself in the seat. "Where are we supposed to go?"

"Just head toward the Willingham Bottom. I'm hoping you can help decide where to go to look for Joshua."

As the doctor backed up to turn toward the road, Gerthy explained his new concerns and why he had come. He described Lonnie's arrival back at the house and reviewed in detail Lonnie's insistence that he had searched thoroughly but unsuccessfully, all along Binford Road. He recounted Lonnie's hurried departure to prepare to leave early the next morning to work on a dredge.

As Doc Beeler tapped nervously on the steering wheel, Gerthy related Maggie's account of her dialogue with Lonnie. Before Gerthy had time to offer his interpretation of the conversation, the doctor waved his hand.

"You don't have to say another word! Hang on to your hat! I think I know where to look for the boy."

"I hoped you would," said Gerthy, nodding.

Doc Beeler pushed the car up to the maximum speed its old engine and the muddy road would allow. He sawed the wheel back to keep the old car in the road despite looseness in the steering linkages. His legs moved from side to side as if magnetic forces in his knees repeatedly attracted and then repelled each other.

Doc Beeler described his encounter with Lonnie. In great detail, he told how their trip had been interrupted unexpectedly by Dorothy Samples, as she had summoned him to care for her sick child. As he began to relate how he had sent Lonnie on to search alone, Gerthy grew impatient to hear the only part of the story that seemed pertinent.

"Where do you think Joshua might be?"

"Well, I was just getting to that. When I said goodbye to Lonnie and sent him on his way, I told him about a place where I go to hunt and fish. It's a lane that leads back to the edge of the swamp. It's on down toward Hickman from Binford Road—maybe half a mile. I told him to look back in there if he didn't find Joshua along Binford Road."

"I pray that's where we'll find him …" Gerthy looked heavenward to finish his prayer is silence.

"Me too. I'm worried that he's been wet an' cold for so long. I can't believe that Lonnie would find him and then intentionally lie about it. What kind'a person would do that? Who'd do that to his own stepbrother?"

"That's a long story, Doc. He's had a tough life, I guess. I just hope we find Joshua. And I hope he's …"

"Where's Franklin an' all the rest of the men? You know, you said the sheriff an' everybody had gone out lookin' an' you stayed back at the house. Where are they now?"

"Well, Franklin rode with Vernon. They were headed down to Binford Road. Tom Parker an' some other men were bringin' Tom's boat down in a wagon. They planned to look on the edge of the swamp along the levee."

"What about the sheriff? Didn't you say he showed up with a couple of his deputies?"

"Yeah. The sheriff an' his deputies, an' I think Elmer an' Joe went to put a boat in Chapman's Creek. They were gonna float down an' look along the creek to where it flows into the swamp."

"We're almost to Binford Road now, but I'm gonna keep goin'. We need to find that boy soon."

The engine sputtered and rattled its opposition to being pushed to its limit. The men squinted into the setting sun and wished for heavier clothing as shadows lengthened.

Doc Beeler turned off the road into a little clearing and parked the car in a grassy area.

"Here's the lane I was talkin' about. It's prob'ly kind'a muddy back there toward the water. We'd better walk from here."

"Yeah. Let's go. I'm a mite slow on this bad leg, so go on ahead if you want to, an' I'll come on as best I can." Gerthy's quickened gait was a combination of walking, hopping, and skipping.

"Naw," said the doctor, keeping pace. "You're movin' along pretty good, an' it's not too much farther back to the swamp, anyway."

Scant remnants of daylight illuminated the shady lane winding back through a heavy stand of hardwoods. Darkness would come quickly, especially in the thick woods. The dampness of the marsh made the chilly air even more disagreeable. The men walked in silence, encouraged by their newfound hope of finding the boy, but worried about his condition and the ominous possibility that he wasn't there.

"Come on, Gerthy. It's not much further. Just a little ways around this next bend and through those trees, we'll come to the edge of the water."

"Good!"

"If Lonnie did come here, an' if this is where he saw Joshua, we should be able to find him, too."

"I hope and pray we do."

Doc and Gerthy walked to where the lane ended and then trudged through muddy ground for the last few feet to reach the edge of the deep swamp. Gerthy looked all around at the wide expanse of water, swamp grass, and cypress trees. He had never seen the swamp, except for the part that was visible from the road. The panorama was both awesome and eerie. Chills crept up his spine.

"This is the most water I've ever seen back in here," said the doctor. "Usually, I can walk another fifty yards or more before I get to the edge of the swamp."

"Yeah," said Gerthy in a whisper. "I'm afraid we aren't gonna find Joshua in here—but I still don't understand why Lonnie said what he did. D'ya think he could have been somewhere else? Is there anywhere else besides here an' Binford Road he might have looked?"

Doc Beeler shook his head.

"I don't know of any other place to get from the road back to the edge of the swamp. An' I've pretty much covered all this area fishin' an' huntin' over the years. If there's another place he could have looked, I don't know where it is."

Gerthy turned away and sighed.

"Well, we didn't stop to see if they found him back along Binford Road. An' who knows? Maybe those guys found him somewhere along Chapman's Creek. Maybe that's where Joshua was. I sure hope somebody finds him soon. It's almost dark now."

"Well, let's don't give up on this place too soon. Why don't you stand here for a minute while I take a look around? No use comin' here an' leavin' without makin' sure he's not here."

Doc Beeler walked along the water's edge in search of any sign of the missing boy. Repeatedly, Gerthy yelled out Joshua's name. His deep voice resonated throughout the swamp as he called out.

"Jaa-shoo-aaaa! Jaa-shoo-aaaa!" His words echoed loudly throughout the marsh. Again, he yelled.

"Jaa-shoo-aaaa! Jaa-shoo-aaaa! Can yooo heeear meee?"

The men listened intently. They moved slowly in opposite directions. Then in unison, they called out again.

"Jaa-shoo-aaaa!"

They froze as the eerie silence was broken. There was a faint sound that seemed to come from beyond a clump of bushes on the edge of the swamp several yards away.

"I'm over here."

The voice was weak, but it had to be Joshua's.

"Oh, praise the Lord," shouted Gerthy.

"Joshua, is that you?"

"It's gotta be him," insisted the doctor.

Gerthy and the doctor hurried toward the sound.

"Joshua, is that you? It's your uncle Gerthy. Can you hear me?"

"I can hear you—Uncle Gerthy? Did you say it's Uncle Gerthy?"

"Yes!" shouted Gerthy. "An' Doc Beeler is here, too. We've come to get you. We've come to take you home!" Tears streamed down Gerthy's face.

"Why did it take you so long? Lonnie was here a long time ago. I didn't think anybody was comin' to get me."

"Well, we're here now! Thank God we finally found you." Gerthy chose not to mention Lonnie's lie.

"I'm hungry an' thirsty, an' I don't feel very good. What took you so long? I was …"

Joshua began to shake and cry, but he covered his face to stifle the sound.

The men fought their way through the cluster of bushes that blocked their view.

"Joshua, I can't see you. Where are you?" called Gerthy.

"I'm over here! Please get me out'a here. My ankle hurts."

Doc Beeler spread the branches of the last bush in the thicket and saw Joshua sitting on his little island. It was surrounded by deep water, clearly too far away to swim to retrieve the boy.

"We'll get you out soon," he shouted. "Did you injure your ankle?"

"Yes, sir. It's all swelled up."

Gerthy pushed his way through the bushes to join the doctor.

"What should we do?"

"This water's deep. We're gonna need a boat. Why don't you stay here an' talk to him while I drive up to Binford Road? Didn't you say they had Tom Parker's boat up there?"

"Yep. I believe that's what they said."

"Okay. I'll be back as soon as I can." The doctor turned and ran to the car.

"Doc!" Gerthy called out.

"Yeah?" answered Beeler. He slid in the mud as he stopped.

"I wouldn't tell Franklin about Lonnie an' all if I was you—no tellin' what he might do."

"Yeah, I understand."

Doc Beeler disappeared into the darkness as he ran to get help.

"What's goin' on?" shouted Joshua. "Why can't somebody come get me out'a here?"

"Doc Beeler went to get a boat. He'll be back soon. I'm gonna stay here an' wait with you."

"Get a boat! Where's he goin' to get a boat? How long is that gonna take? Why can't ya get me out'a here right now? I'm cold!"

Gerthy felt helpless, desperate to rescue Joshua and take him home. He realized the extent of his own fatigue. He was unaccustomed to so much physical exertion. His legs ached. In the falling darkness, he groped, stumbled, and found a half-rotten stump to sit on.

Joshua was quiet now. *Is that good?* Gerthy wondered. *Am I supposed to keep the boy from goin' to sleep?*

"Joshua!" he called out. The boy did not respond.

"Joshua!" he yelled. "Joshua! Answer me!"

"Huh? Oh, did you call me?"

"Yeah. I just want to talk to you a little bit."

"I'm kind'a sleepy."

"Yeah, I know. Are you on dry ground? You're not in the water, are you?"

"Uh-uh. I'm sittin' in the grass. It's kind'a wet, but it's not in the water."

Gerthy's intuition told him to keep the boy alert. He decided that in Joshua's weakened state, especially in the chilly night air, any activity would be advisable over allowing him to fall asleep.

"Do you remember the time the bees got after me at the picnic?"

"Uh-huh."

"I reckon I danced quite a jig tryin' to get away from 'em, didn't I?"

"Uh-huh."

"Would you like to sing?"

"Uh-uh."

"What would you like to sing? How about 'Trust and Obey'?"

Although his suggestion evoked no response from Joshua, Gerthy began to sing, hoping the boy would join in.

"When we walk with the Lord
In the light of His Word,
What a glory He sheds on our way.
While we do His good will,
He abides with us still;
Never fear ..."

Gerthy stopped singing. He realized that Joshua had sung only the first two or three lines.

"Don't you feel like singin', Joshua?"

"I'm tired."

"Well, usually you like to sing with me, an' I just thought it might help us pass the time. But we don't hafta sing if you don't feel like it."

After a few moments of silence, Joshua spoke in a soulful voice that made his uncle shiver.

"Is God mad at me or somethin'? I don't ..." Joshua's words trailed off into an alarming silence.

Gerthy trembled again.

"Joshua," he began, "I don't claim to know all about God. There's lots'a questions I can't answer. Why that flood came the way it did, an' why it came when it did, an' why you got caught in it—I can't say. I haven't got any good answers. But I just don't think we ought'a blame God when bad things happen to us." After a brief silence, Gerthy continued.

"I just don't picture God sittin' up there in heaven yesterday thinkin' to Himself, 'Well, let's see now—I reckon I'll just send some floodwaters rushin' down the Big Ditch to wash away that Jennings boy. An' then I'll make him float down into the swamp in the Willingham Bottom an' make him spend the night an' the next day there all alone.' Ya see, Joshua, I just can't picture God doin' somethin' like that on purpose. I ..."

"My Sunday school teacher told us God sent a flood to teach people a lesson," Joshua insisted. "What about that? Maybe He sent this one to teach me a lesson."

"Well, it's like I said before," replied Gerthy. "I don't claim to know what God thinks or how God thinks. An' I can't tell you why there are storms, an' floods, an' earthquakes, an' fires, an' plagues, an' all that. I guess God doesn't promise to give us physical blessings all the time. He doesn't promise us we'll never get hurt. An' He doesn't promise us we'll never get sick. He doesn't even promise us we'll never get lonely or scared. But what He does promise us is that He'll give us spiritual blessings."

"What d'ya mean, spiritual blessings? What are spiritual blessings? Name some."

Gerthy removed his hat, wiped his brow with his shirt sleeve, and got up from his stump to walk around.

"Well, let's see, now. What are some spiritual blessings? Well, God gives us the ability to love an' care for each other. I think that's a spiritual blessing. Remember in the Bible where it says that God is love? Well then, when we love someone else, or when someone else loves us, that love is a part of God that we can share. That's a spiritual blessing."

"Yeah, I guess so."

"An' remember. God says that if we have His love within us, then He's with us all the time. That way, we're never really alone. He's always there."

"Uncle Gerthy?"

"Yes."

"This mornin' when I woke up, I was real scared. I didn't know where I was, an' I was hungry, an' I didn't think anyone would ever find me. I was really scared—an' then I closed my eyes, an' … You're gonna think this is crazy."

"No, I won't. I promise. Tell me."

"Well, after I closed my eyes, I felt like … It seemed just like my mother was sittin' right here beside me. An' I even felt her hand on my shoulder. An' then I felt her other hand wipin' away my tears, an' I even heard her talkin' to me, tellin' me not to worry. I heard her say she was proud of me. Is it crazy for me to feel like my mother was here with me?"

"No. I don't think that's crazy at all. I think that's a spiritual blessing."

"Yeah. I guess so."

"I'm sure it is. I'm sure your mother is as proud of you as she can be. As a matter of fact, I bet that's how God feels about you, too."

For a few moments, there was a lull in the conversation, but the swamp was anything but silent. Bullfrogs near the bank beside Gerthy croaked in answer to similar calls from somewhere in the distance. Insects began their nightly ritual chants. Young, tender leaves, still growing to reach maturity by summertime, rustled quietly in the stiff breeze.

"I don't feel like talkin' any more right now," Joshua said.

"That's okay, son. Your papa and the others should be here with the boat soon. We're gonna get you out'a here. We're gonna take you home."

17

CHAPTER

Barely touching the brakes, Doc Beeler slid onto Binford Road and parked his old car behind Vernon's, alongside the sheriff's Chevy. Steam wafted from under the hood. Tom Parker's team of mules and wagon were visible a bit farther up the road. Moving as quickly as he could, he slogged through ankle-deep mud toward lantern light that flickered in the distance and the sound of men's voices that was barely audible.

Franklin sat on Tom Parker's bottom-up rowboat that had been dragged ashore. With his elbows on his knees, he rested his head in his hands. His shoulders slouched forward, and his eyes were closed. Vernon Starr sat beside him. He wondered how to console Franklin, and he wished he knew where else to look for the boy.

Sheriff Ridley paced back and forth. Waiting was not his forte under any circumstances, and now he fretted that that his crew had not yet arrived from Chapman's Creek. He, too, was devoid of a new search plan.

Always overzealous, Ducky followed him closely, step for step. The sheriff tried to ignore his eager deputy, but as he continued his short, quick strides, he glanced back at Ducky with a sneer. But Ducky continued to follow close on the sheriff's heels, jumping out of the way just in time to avoid a collision when the sheriff pivoted to change directions. Finally, Ridley had had enough. He stopped suddenly and whirled around to face

Ducky. The deputy stopped just before their noses touched. "Go find a place to park your ass, and git off'a mine!" the sheriff shouted.

Finally, Elmer, Joe, and Hambone had floated into the swamp from their trip down Chapman's Creek. They reported their lack of success in finding any sign of Joshua and waited to get medical treatment for Hambone's ugly, painful wound.

In spite of the muddy road, Doc Beeler began to trot, and then he dashed to share his good news.

"We found Joshua!" he shouted as he ran. "We found him! We found him!"

Franklin was the first to meet him. His eyes were wide, and he opened his mouth and gestured as if he were speaking, but no sound came out.

"Where'd you find him?" queried Sheriff Ridley.

"He's down in …"

"Is he all right?" interrupted Franklin. "Is my boy okay?"

Doc Beeler placed his hand on Franklin's shoulder and answered in a strong, confident, assuring tone.

"Franklin, quit worryin'! We found your boy, an' he's alive. But we need to get back to him quickly."

"What d'ya mean? Is he gonna be okay?"

"Just listen to me. Gerthy an' I found him on a little island—a small mound in the swamp—down about a half a mile from here. We're gonna need one of these boats to get to him. Come on with me in the car, an' I'll give you the details on the way."

"You heard the good doctor, boys," shouted the sheriff. "Git one'a them rowboats in Tom's wagon, an' let's git goin'."

"Doc!" yelled Elmer Dixon as the doctor walked toward the road.

"Yeah?"

"Doc, I know you're in a hurry, but Hambone got caught in a trotline, an' he needs you to take a look at his arm."

"What?"

"Yeah. Hambone got caught up in a trotline, an' a big ole catfish hook tore a plug out'a his arm. It's buggered up pretty bad."

Doc Beeler quickly examined Hambone's wound.

"It's pretty bad, but I'll see what I can do. Come on with me, Hambone. If somebody else can drive, I'll work on cleanin' up your arm while we ride. My bag is in Franklin's car."

Franklin sprinted to his car. By the time Elmer, Doc Beeler, and Hambone got there, he was ready to go. Vernon followed in his car with some of the other men. Sheriff Ridley stayed behind to supervise those who had volunteered to load the rowboats into Tom's wagon and to direct them to the right place.

In the back seat of Franklin's car, Doc Beeler cleaned Hambone's wound with iodine and bandaged it with some clean cloth he kept in his medical bag. While completing this procedure (which he often bragged he could do with his eyes closed), he also described the place where he and Gerthy had found Joshua. He related the brief conversation they had had with the boy, but he didn't divulge any details of Joshua's condition or how Gerthy had come to suspect Lonnie's deception.

Franklin was too focused on getting to his son to care about details of his discovery. At Doc's instruction, he pulled off the road and parked, with room for Vernon Starr to park directly behind him.

As Doc Beeler hurriedly escorted Franklin back along the lane into the dark woods, Vernon volunteered to stay back to direct the others when they arrived with the boat.

Franklin felt his heart palpitate with excitement in anticipation of being reunited with his son. The long hours since Joshua's disappearance had seemed more like days, and Franklin had felt trapped in an unending nightmare.

He rushed out of his car, broke into a trot, and slogged through mud along the moonlit lane. The closer he got to the edge of the swamp, the faster he ran, slinging mud on Doc Beeler only a step or two behind.

Hearing the onrushing footsteps, Gerthy rose from his resting-place on the rotten stump. "Franklin! Is that you?"

Now at Gerthy's side, Franklin panted to catch his breath.

"Where's Joshua?"

"He's over yonder behind those cypress trees, on a little island, or somethin'."

"How far away is he?"

"Not far—he can hear you if you talk loud."

"Bud, can ya hear me? It's your papa!" Franklin's voice trembled. "We're gonna get ya out'a here."

There was no response.

"Joshua! Can't you hear me?"

Again, there was silence. Panic-stricken, Franklin glanced first at his brother, then into the eerie darkness of the swamp, and then to Doc Beeler.

"I thought you said …"

"Papa! Get me out'a here!"

Joshua's words pierced the darkness like a sword.

Franklin gasped. He covered his mouth with both hands, clenched his teeth, and closed his eyes to choke back tears of relief and joy.

"Joshua, I'm right here. We're comin'! Just hang on. We're gonna get ya out'a there."

"Papa?"

"Yeah, bud. I'm right here." Franklin shook his head. Gerthy heard him mutter, "I dunno why I let him go back there in that storm."

"Papa!" yelled Joshua.

"Yeah, son. What is it?"

"Papa … Ole Dick is here with me. You gonna get him, too?"

Franklin frowned at Doc Beeler. "What …"

"Yeah, we'll get Ole Dick," interjected Doc Beeler. Then, turning to Franklin, he whispered, "We need to get him home in a hurry."

They could hear harness rings jangling and horses' hooves as they plopped and slopped through the muck.

"We're gonna get you out'a there soon," yelled Franklin uneasily.

Ducky Brown ran ahead of the pack with a lantern to light the way for the team. Tom Parker's wagon carried two rowboats and all other members of the search party, who hung onto every available space in the wagon to avoid having to wade through the mud. As soon as Parker reined his mules to a stop, the men jumped off, unloaded one of the boats, and carried it to the water.

"I'll row," Tom volunteered. "Who else is coming?"

"I'm goin'," insisted Franklin, grabbing a lantern and moving to sit in the front. "Doc, you come with us."

"There he is—over there!" shouted Franklin as Tom oared past the clump of cypress trees that had blocked their view from the bank. With a couple of strong, swift strokes, Tom steered the rowboat to the little island where Joshua lay in the marsh grass. Franklin was silent as he waited for the boat to glide over the last few yards of black water to reach his son.

As the bow nudged gently against the muddy bank, he stepped out, deftly held his lantern with one hand, and pulled the boat up onto the edge of the shore with the other. As Tom leaned to one side to allow Doc to get out, Franklin knelt to greet his son and help him to his feet.

"Hey, get away from me!" Joshua swatted at his father as he had done when gnats and mosquitoes had plagued him.

Franklin recoiled and looked at the doctor with sadness and mystery in his puffy eyes.

Moving quickly to fend off the boy's clumsy attempts to fight, Doc Beeler grabbed Joshua's arm and placed it around his shoulders. "Help me get him into the boat, Franklin," he said stiffly.

As he helped the doctor to lift Joshua to his feet, Franklin looked into his son's face. By the flickering light of Tom's lantern, he saw Joshua's red, puffy eyes and his pallid skin. His face was covered with insect bites, and his hair was matted together with partially hardened mud.

"No! No, Lonnie! Don't throw me in the swamp," screamed Joshua. "I want to go home."

"Lonnie? Lonnie's not here," said Franklin with a frown. "Why's he worried about Lonnie?" he whispered to Doc Beeler.

Motioning toward the boat with his head, the doctor replied, "I think he's a little bit delirious. He really doesn't know what he's sayin'. Let's hurry up an' get him home."

"Oh, my leg," shrieked Joshua. "You're hurting my leg."

"I think he hurt his ankle. Let's pick him up and get him into the boat," instructed the doc.

Joshua struggled slightly as the men lifted him up and carried him to the edge of the water. With his oar dug into the muddy bank, Tom swung the stern of the boat around so that they could place Joshua directly onto the seat.

With Doc Beeler in the bow holding his lantern aloft and Franklin holding Joshua, Tom rowed quickly to get back to solid ground. The boy shivered uncontrollably. As they neared, the men on the bank cheered and clapped spontaneously. Gerthy turned away to wipe tears from his cheeks, but when he turned back toward the other men, he noticed that he was not the only one who cried.

Vernon stepped forward to help Franklin get Joshua out of the boat onto the bank of the swamp. Carried quickly through the crowd of well wishers, Joshua seemed to make brief eye contact with his uncle. He appeared to return Gerthy's gentle smile, but there was no indication whether Joshua felt his uncle's touch as he passed. Gerthy wiped away more tears.

"Put the boy in the wagon an' take him to the car," said Sheriff Ridley. "We'll come back to get the boat later."

Franklin hustled ahead, climbed into the back of the wagon, and motioned for the men to lift Joshua in to lean against him. Doc Beeler climbed in too. He held Joshua's leg to elevate his injured ankle and to provide extra support for the bouncy ride through ruts and deep potholes.

Beeler shed his jacket and draped it around Joshua's shoulders. He reached under Joshua's shirt to feel his abdomen, and then he gently examined his swollen ankle. Though it was twice its normal size, there was no obvious sign of a break. *Just a bad sprain,* he thought. Time and rest would cure that.

Of more immediate concern to Doc Beeler was the boy's general condition. His listlessness had turned to drowsiness, and his breathing seemed shallow. The realization that Joshua had been without food and water and exposed to cold, wet conditions was especially worrisome—particularly in light of Joshua's previous bout with pneumonia. A more thorough examination would have to wait until they got him home.

18
CHAPTER

From the time Gerthy had driven off in the car, Maggie had found herself trying to manage a madhouse. The children had become incorrigible, and although she knew that the recent two days had been difficult for them, her patience wore thin.

In her dour mood, Maggie thought the children behaved badly to spite her. They had begun to misbehave the minute Gerthy drove off. Matt had asked to go along with his uncle, but of course, Gerthy had refused.

Matt headed out the door and toward the barn.

"I'm gonna ride Ole Kate an' find Joshua."

"You are not!" insisted Jessie in her most adamant, motherly voice. "You don't even know where to look."

"You can't even ride a horse by yourself," chided Naomi.

"I'm goin' anyway!"

Matt sprinted to the gate, climbed over, and ran into the barn.

Jessie let the screen door slam shut as she entered the kitchen. "Mama! Mama! Matt said he's goin' to ride Ole Kate. He's gone to the barn … Mama!"

Maggie rushed into the kitchen with a frown and brushed by the girls on her way out the door. In a trot and holding her skirt up out of the dirt, she crossed the yard, went through the gate, and entered the barn. She found Matt in the stall with Ole Kate. He was dragging a saddle through the dirt toward an old wooden crate he had positioned next the horse. A saddle blanket lay askew on the mare's back.

Maggie appeared in the back of the stall and stood with her hands on her hips.

"What do you think you're doin', young man?"

Matt struggled to lift the saddle off the ground as he climbed up on the crate.

"I'm puttin' a saddle on Ole Kate."

"Don't get smart with me. You know what I mean. What are you doin'?"

"I'm gonna ride Ole Kate to look for Joshua."

Matt grunted as he used both hands to lift the saddle, but he was unable to raise it high enough for the stirrups to clear the ground.

"You wanna help me with this saddle?"

"Of course not! You aren't goin' anywhere but back to the house. Now get down off'a that box. I've just about had enough'a you!"

"Aw, come on, Mama. I wanna go find Joshua."

Maggie grasped her apron into a wad, pointed her crooked finger at Matt, and moved toward him quickly. Matt dropped the saddle, jumped off the crate, and ran under Ole Kate's neck to escape on the opposite side of the stall and to avoid getting whacked by his stepmother.

"You better run! An' I better not have to put up with any more of your shenanigans."

Matt ran across the lot, crawled through the gate, and went to his cabin to be alone.

About to reenter the house, Maggie heard a wretched combination of screams and wails coming from the front room. For a moment, she considered retracing her steps to take refuge in the barn away from the bedlam, but she decided instead to face her tormentors.

"Who said you could wear my shirt?" shrieked Jessie. "Give me back my shirt, an'—an' you're gonna have to wash it, too!" Jessie began to sob.

"I'll give it back when I'm good an' ready," declared Reba. "An' I won't wash it, neither!"

"Mommie!" yelled Jessie when she heard the back door slam. "Make Reba give me my shirt. Come here! Look what she's done to my shirt."

Maggie saw Reba nonchalantly sprawled on the bed with her head propped up against the wall and her knees in the air. Indeed, she was wearing a shirt that belonged to Jessie, but it was old and it was nothing special. Jessie jumped around to the foot of the bed. She ranted and flailed her arms wildly.

"What's goin' on in here?"

"She's wearin' my shirt! An' she's got it all messed up!"

"That's no reason to be throwin' such a conniption fit, Jessie. I think you better get a hold of yourself."

"Mama," Naomi interjected. "Reba got ..."

"Take it off!" interrupted Jessie as she stomped the floor. "Take it off! Take it off an' give it back."

"You gonna make me?" taunted Reba sarcastically. "Why don't ya come over here an' try gettin' it off'a me?"

"Mama, can I say somethin'?" Naomi tried to get her mother's attention for the second time, but Maggie ignored her.

"You girls just calm down! I've just about had it with all'a you! I really don't see a reason for such a fuss."

Naomi yanked at her mother's apron.

"Mama?"

"Let me say ..."

"Just look at my shirt!" shrieked Jessie. "Look what she did to it!"

"What? I don't see ..."

"Mama!" shouted Naomi. "That's what I've been tryin' to tell ya. Reba got snot all over the front of Jessie's shirt. See? See that big spot on the front? That's a glob of snot!"

"Naomi, I told you not to use that word. Now, Reba, did you ..."

"I sneezed! I couldn't help it."

"Oh, for cryin' out loud!" Maggie threw up her arms and turned to leave. "Can't you see I've got more important things to worry about?"

Jessie glared at her stepmother.

"You're just gonna leave? You're not gonna make her wash my shirt an' give it back?"

Maggie left the parlor and walked to the kitchen without responding.

"You always take her side," bawled Jessie.

Reba rolled her eyes at Jessie and then stuck out her tongue.

"I hate you!" shouted Jessie. "You're a horse's butt!"

Naomi headed for the door.

"Come on, Jessie. Let's go outside an' leave her alone. She is a horse's butt."

For once, Maggie was glad it was time to cook supper. Earlier in the day, she had decided to prepare a meal in anticipation that someone might be there to eat it.

Lifting the lid of her black cast-iron pot, she stirred black-eyed peas that had been soaking there since midmorning. The peas were from their garden. They had been picked, shelled, and dried the previous fall and then stored in cloth bags in the cool, dry smokehouse.

She removed several pieces of oak firewood from a bin beside the cookstove and placed them in a crisscrossed stack in the stove's firebox.

On tiptoes to reach the top shelf of a sideboard beside the stove, she took down a box of matches and a can of kerosene-soaked corncobs. She removed one of the cobs, lit it and placed it under the stack of firewood. The seasoned oak caught fire readily, and Maggie knew that in a matter of only a few minutes the stove would be hot enough to cook the peas.

She wiped her mouth with her apron, grabbed a butcher knife, and walked quickly out the back of the house to the smokehouse, located only a few yards away. She pushed open its heavy door and stepped over to slabs of salt-cured pork, or "side meat," hanging from a rafter. A slice of about one half inch thick and four inches long would be plenty to season the peas. Then she grabbed a crock jar full of kraut and a mason jar of home-canned tomatoes. *Kraut, black-eyed peas, canned tomatoes, and corn bread—that will make a decent meal,* she thought.

As she walked back to the house, she remembered a jar of home-canned corn relish that she could open to supplement the meal. It was the last jar from a batch of yellow, whole-kernel corn that she had pickled with vinegar and sugar and canned in pint jars.

After she drained the excess water off the black-eyed peas, Maggie placed the slab of side meat in with them and placed the pot on the rear left-hand eye of the stove's cooktop. The stove was full-sized, with four eyes and an oven for baking. The two eyes on the left, directly above the stove's firebox, provided maximum heat.

The oven was adjacent to the firebox on the right-hand side of the stove, and the two eyes just above the oven were used for cooking at a lower temperature.

When the peas came to a rapid boil, Maggie moved the pot to one of the eyes on the right-hand side to simmer until they were done. She wiped her brow with the bottom of her apron. The cookstove had heated up more than her pot of peas.

Maggie made corn bread or biscuits, or both, every day that she cooked. This meal would definitely include corn bread. In the Jennings household, a menu that included black-eyed peas demanded corn bread. The children liked the corn bread sliced open and covered with peas ladled with pot liquor directly from the pot. Joshua was especially fond of that dish, and Maggie was reminded of him as she prepared the meal. She couldn't completely clear her mind of her fear that he would not be there to enjoy this meal, but she prayed silently that he would be found.

With a large spoon, Maggie dipped approximately one half cup of lard from a crock jar that she kept in her cupboard. She placed it in a large, black cast-iron skillet and placed the skillet on the stove to melt the lard. She went back to the cupboard to get two eggs and a pitcher of freshly churned buttermilk. After beating the eggs, she mixed in two cups of buttermilk, one teaspoon of soda, one teaspoon of salt, two teaspoons of Calumet baking powder, and two and one half cups of white cornmeal that had been milled from corn they had grown.

Next, she poured most of the melted lard into the mixture and placed the skillet back on the stovetop to heat. After adding more wood to the fire, she poured the batter into the hot skillet and placed it into the oven to bake. In twenty minutes or so, it would be golden brown and ready to eat.

Usually, she would have waited to cook the corn bread so that it would come out of the oven to be served piping hot just as everyone sat down to eat. But Maggie had no idea when the search crew would return, and she knew that the girls and Matt would be hungry at their usual suppertime. She would serve the children and store the leftovers in the warming oven located above the stovetop.

Matt bounced into the kitchen.

"I'm hungry. When can I eat?"

Matt was always hungry, it seemed, and the aromas from Maggie's kitchen were more alluring than the clanging of her dinner bell. She rang the bell only when work or play had taken the family too far away to smell the smoke of burning oak combined with the scent of freshly baked corn bread.

Maggie wiped her hands on her apron and smiled.

"You're just in time. The corn bread will be done in about twenty minutes, and everything else will be ready then, too. Did you remember to wash your hands?"

"Nope."

"What did you say?"

"No—I mean, no, ma'am."

"That's better."

Matt walked over to a small table on which there were a washbasin and a pitcher of water. A bar of Castille soap lay on a cloth beside the washbasin.

Maggie feared that Matt would drop her only pitcher.

"Here, let me pour you some water. Be sure to wash real good. Those hands'a yours look mighty dirty."

"Where's Jessie an' them?"

At that moment, the three girls walked in, now much calmer and more agreeable that when Maggie had walked out on them earlier.

Jessie gave Matt a teasing poke in his ribs.

"Were you talkin' about me?"

"Naw. I just didn't know where y'all were. Mommie, you gonna make them wash their hands too?"

Maggie turned and looked at the girls. They washed up for supper.

"Dinner will be ready real soon. Is everybody hungry?"

"I don't really feel like eatin'," said Jessie quietly.

"Can I have hers?" asked Matt. "I'm starvin'!"

Maggie felt of Jessie's forehead.

"Are you feelin' sick, Jessie? Do I need to get you some black draught?"

"No! Please, Mommie. Don't make me take any of that stuff. I'm not sick—I guess. I just don't feel like eatin' right now."

"Are you worried 'bout Joshua? Is that why you don't feel like eatin'?"

"I dunno. Maybe."

"Has Joshua drownded?" asked Matt abruptly.

"Don't say that!" Jessie shrieked. "Mommie, make him quit sayin' that. I hate it when he says things like that!"

"I'm worried 'bout Joshua, too," said Reba, in a rare expression of concern for anyone other than herself.

"Me, too," added Naomi, nodding.

"Well, I wanted to go find him, but you wouldn't let me," reminded Matt.

"I guess we're all kind'a worried," said Jessie. "I just don't understand what could'a happened to him."

Maggie untied the straps of her apron and pulled it over her head. She pulled one of the two remaining empty chairs away from the table and sat down quietly. It was rare, indeed, for the children to sit quietly—especially around the supper table. As Maggie was about to speak without really knowing what to say, Jessie interrupted the silence.

"I feel like Joshua's gonna be okay," she whispered with her head bowed.

"What'd you say, honey?" Maggie asked.

Jessie looked up with a sweet smile and spoke confidently.

"I said, 'I feel like Joshua's gonna be okay.' I've been talkin' to God about it, an' I believe He's gonna keep Joshua safe. 'Cause the Bible says that if we ask God for somethin', He'll give it to us—an' I just asked God to protect Joshua."

"You sound like my Sunday school teacher," Matt interjected.

Maggie reached across the table to pat Jessie's hand. "That's a wonderful thought."

She smiled at Jessie and squeezed her hand.

"I'm proud of you."

Nothing else was said as Maggie quietly got up from her chair to set the table and serve the food. Before every meal, a blessing was uttered aloud—most often by Gerthy. It was rare that the whole family was not gathered around the table at mealtime, and Maggie was unaccustomed to saying a blessing. Looking nervously around the table, she made eye contact with Jessie.

"D'ya want me to say the blessing, Mommie?"

"That'd be nice, honey. Let's hold hands."

Matt nervously looked back and forth at Jessie and Reba, who flanked him.

"I don't wanna hold no girl's hand."

Maggie moved around the table quietly, slipped between Reba and Matt, and grasped his hand. Jessie held his hand on the other side. She began her blessing before he could protest.

"God is great, God is good, and we thank Him for our food ... an'— an' bless Miz Starr ... an' forgive our sins ... an' bless Papa an' Uncle Gerthy, an' the sheriff ... an' dear Lord, please watch over Joshua. Amen."

Maggie reached around Matt to pat Jessie on the shoulder.

"Thank you, honey. That was a sweet blessing."

"Why did ya pray for Miz Starr?" asked Naomi.

"Well, she's been sick."

"Oh."

The children helped themselves to hearty portions. Maggie picked at small bits of food on her plate. Although her appetite was gone, she was glad to see the children eat heartily. As they took their last bites, she mixed up another batch of corn bread batter and re-stoked the fire to reheat her oven. She wanted to have plenty of hot corn bread ready just in case, and she needed to stay busy.

19
CHAPTER

Matt bounded off the porch and into the yard. "Somebody's comin'! Hey, did ya hear me? Somebody's comin'!"

Maggie pitched her dish towel onto the table and ran to the back porch. Cold sweat popped out in her hairline as she watched two cars turn from the road, one right behind the other. Yellow beams of light from the lead car flickered through the darkness. For months, Franklin had vowed to fix the loose connections in his car's headlights.

Before the old car rolled to a complete stop, the children had it surrounded. Matt jumped up on the running board on the driver's side and held on to ride the last few feet as Franklin brought it to a stop and killed the engine. Jessie peered through the darkness to look inside.

"Joshua! They found Joshua!"

Maggie held onto the crude corner support post on the porch and covered her mouth with her other hand.

"Oh, thank God!" she gasped. She hurried to meet Franklin and watched as Doc Beeler helped Joshua out of the car.

The children jumped up and down, danced in circles, and cheered.

"Yeah! Joshua's home! Joshua's home! They found him! They found Joshua!"

Hurrying to greet him, they stopped short when they saw him more clearly in the shadowy light of a full moon. He limped badly, even though Doc Beeler bore most of his weight. He was dirty and stared ahead through tired, hollow eyes. His pale skin was blotched with dried mud, and he didn't say a word.

Maggie hurried to Franklin's side.

"We found him, Maggie." Franklin' voice trembled. "But I'm afraid he's in bad shape."

Tears welled up quickly and then streamed down her face as she looked into Joshua's expressionless eyes. She covered her face and wept uncontrollably. Franklin pulled her to him to console her.

"You go on in with Joshua and the doctor," she sobbed. "I'll be all right."

Gerthy motioned for the children to join him as Franklin helped Doc Beeler get Joshua inside. Dropping to one knee to be on the children's level and to rest his tired, crippled foot, Gerthy looked at each one and spoke quietly.

"Joshua's gonna be okay. He's been through a lot, and his ankle is hurt, but the doc says he should be okay in a few days. He just needs some food an' water, an' lots'a rest."

"Where'd they find him?" Jessie asked.

"He was down in the swamp—down in the Willingham Bottom."

"Was he drownded?" asked Matt.

"Of course not, stupid!" corrected Reba loudly. "If he was …"

Gerthy patted her arm.

"It's okay, Reba. Matt is just a little confused."

Matt clenched his fist and inched toward his much larger stepsister.

"He said Joshua was in the swamp! An' you better not be callin' me …"

Gerthy pulled Matt close and spoke directly to him.

"Your brother got washed down the Big Ditch in the flood. He ended up on a little mound in the middle of the swamp, an' he stayed there 'til we found him just a little while ago."

"What's a-matter with his leg?"

"Don't reckon I know for sure. The doc's gonna give him a good goin'-over before he leaves this evenin'. Maybe he'll tell us what's wrong with it."

Jessie reached out to touch her uncle.

"Can we go in an' see Joshua now? We didn't even have a chance to say hello."

"Not right now," Gerthy replied. "We best leave him with the doctor to get checked out. Y'all come with me to my room. I'll tell you some stories or somethin'—I know, maybe we can play some games or sing some songs."

"Can we play pretty bird?" asked Matt as they followed Gerthy to his room.

Gerthy's hand rested on Matt's head. "That might get a little noisy, but we'll see," he said.

Moving quickly, Doc Beeler had escorted Joshua to the main bedroom, where Maggie had stoked the gentle fire in the stove.

"Joshua," he said with a firm tone, "we gotta get you out of those wet clothes and into bed."

"I'm too tired," muttered Joshua. "I just want to go to sleep."

Doc instructed Franklin to help him strip off all of Joshua's wet clothing and get him into a pair of long underwear. As Joshua grumbled and fought weakly to keep his clothes on, Doc Beeler calmly restrained his arms and assisted Franklin to get him into the warm, dry bed. Beeler pulled up the blanket folded at the foot of the bed and asked for a second blanket, preferably wool.

Maggie stood silently in the doorway with her hands folded, her fingers interlocked, and her thumbs pressed gently against her lips.

"Maggie, could you heat some water and make some warm cambric tea?" Doc Beeler asked. "You don't even need to put any tea in it. Just some warm water, sugar, and a tad of milk will be fine."

The doc then turned toward Franklin and gestured toward the stove. "We'll need to keep the fire goin' all night. Joshua needs to get warmed up. But don't put too much wood on the fire—I want it warm in here, but not hot."

After he rolled up his sleeves, Doc Beeler dug into his black medical bag to get his stethoscope.

"All right, young man. Let's get you checked out right quick, an' then I'm gonna get out'a here an' let you get some rest. Okay?"

Joshua nodded.

The doctor pursed his lips back and forth—his official signal that the examination had begun—and reached under the blankets to listen to

Joshua's heart and lungs. Then, after checking his pulse, the doc nodded to Franklin to relieve his anxiety and smiled at Maggie, who had come into the room with a cup of cambric tea. Doc Beeler lifted Joshua's head and encouraged him to drink. Joshua frowned at first; then he sipped for taste and then downed the warm brew with gusto.

Doc nodded his approval to Maggie. "You must make a mean pot of cambric tea," he said. "You can give him some more after I'm through checking him over."

Next, the doctor moved to the foot of the bed and pulled the covers loose just enough to expose Joshua's injured ankle. It was swollen and discolored, too, with blue and purple hues extending from his toes to his calf. Holding Joshua's foot in both hands, he moved it around slowly and gently. Joshua winced in pain, but the doctor continued to move his foot slightly, and then he felt all around the injured area with both hands, squeezing as gently as possible to minimize the pain, but as firmly as necessary to determine if there were any broken bones.

"Joshua, sorry to bother you, but did you feel a *pop* or hear a snapping sound when you hurt your ankle?"

The boy blinked and responded hoarsely, "I don't think so. But it was way under the water, an' I don't know if I could'a heard it if it did snap."

"Did it swell up immediately after you hurt it?"

"I think it was later that it swelled up, but I'm not for sure."

"Well, I don't think anything's broken. It's sprained pretty bad, though. Franklin, I'm gonna wrap it real tight with a heavy bandage, an' I want you to keep it elevated as much as possible. An' he's definitely gonna have to stay off of it for several days. Does Maggie have any old flour sacks or an old sheet layin' around? I don't have anything with me to wrap up his leg properly—an' while you're at it, ask her if she has an extra pillow or two. We're gonna need somethin' to prop up the boy's leg."

Doc Beeler shifted his attention back to Joshua's torso. He transferred his stethoscope from his neck to his ears and helped Joshua slide up to a sitting position so that he could listen to the boy's lungs. First his chest. Then his back.

Beeler remembered that Joshua had been near death from pneumonia at the same time his mother died. The fact that the boy had been wet and exposed to chilly night air with nothing to keep him warm made the doctor especially concerned. He listened very carefully for any sign of a recurrence of his prior respiratory problems.

"Take a deep breath for me, Joshua. Okay, again … okay … now one more. Good! Have you been coughing much?"

"Uh-huh. Last night I did, when I got cold."

"Did you cough up anything?"

"A couple'a times I did. I just spit it out."

"Did you cough up any blood?"

"I dunno. It was dark."

"Okay. Sorry for askin' so many questions, but I'm just tryin' to keep you well."

Doc Beeler pulled the covers down and thoroughly examined Joshua for ticks, leeches, or any other sucking insects or parasites.

"Looks like you had plenty of mosquitoes to keep you company out there in that swamp."

"Yes, sir. An' I hate mosquitoes!"

"Me, too! Tell ya what. If you start itchin' too bad, ask Miz Maggie to take some uncooked oatmeal an' add a little water to it to make a paste. An' then she can put that right on the insect bites. It'll help keep the itchin' down a little."

Doc Beeler pulled the bedcovers back up to Joshua's waist. He cupped his left hand slightly and placed it palm-down on the boy's chest. Then he tapped it firmly with the ends of his right-hand fingers. As he moved his left hand around from one location to another, he tapped rhythmically—three firm taps in each location. One, two, three—move. One, two, three—move. One, two, three—move. He kept a steady beat, tapping three times at each location as he moved his hand from Joshua's chest down to his abdomen and back to his chest again. It sounded like a combo tune without any instruments except percussion.

Joshua frowned.

"Doctor Beeler? Why did you do that?"

"What? Oh, you mean the tapping?" Doc Beeler had listened intently to the sounds he made as he played the boy's body like a tom-tom.

"I s'pose that does seem a bit strange, huh? I bet you thought the ole doc had gone nuts, huh?"

"No, sir. I—I was just wonderin'."

"Well, it's a good question. Ya see, we hafta use every possible way to find out what's goin' on in there. We're taught to use all our senses. We use our eyes to see how things look—like when I examine your throat or look at the swellin' on your ankle. An' we examine by touchin' an' feelin' around on you—like I did on your ankle. We want to find out if things feel like they're s'posed to, or if we can feel somethin' that's not s'posed to be there. If you had a broken bone, then most likely, I would'a been able to feel it. D'ya understand?"

"Yes, sir. I think so. But what about tappin' on your own hand?"

"Well, I was getting' to that—but I guess I started givin' you a long medical lecture, didn't I? Along with our sight an' feel, we use sound. We know how things are s'posed to sound—you know, when there's nothin' wrong. That's why this stethoscope here is one'a my best friends. I can hear what's goin' on way down in your lungs, an' I can tell if your heart's beatin' strong an' steady. Now, then! Let me tell you about the tappin' on my hand. Tappin' my fingers on the back of my hand is another way I use sound to know how you're doin' on the inside—where I can't see or feel."

"Oh."

"If everything is okay in there, it sounds one way, but if there's a consolidation—that's a big word, huh? A consolidation is like congestion— you know, a clump of somethin' that's not s'posed to be there. Well, if there's somethin' like that, it sounds completely different when I tap on my hand right over that spot. D'ya see now, or did I go too much into detail?"

"Yes, sir. I think I see what you mean. Maybe it's kind'a like when my papa thumps on a watermelon to see if it's ripe or not."

"That's exactly right!" said Doc Beeler, laughing loudly. "Son, you just might grow up to be a doctor someday."

"Uh-huh."

The doctor placed his stethoscope back in his black bag, unrolled his sleeves, and buttoned his cuffs.

"Thumpin' a watermelon." He laughed. "I declare, I'm gonna hafta remember that one!"

"Doc, here's those flour sacks you wanted." Franklin held a fistful of flowery print sacks Maggie had saved to cut up and use for fabric. "They've been washed, an' Maggie says you can use as many of 'em as you need."

"Oh, thanks, Franklin." Beeler put his bag back on the little table. "Goodness me, I was ready to walk out'a here without wrappin' that boy's ankle. Must be getting' old, huh?"

The doctor took one of the sacks from Franklin, examined its weave pattern, grasped it firmly in both hands, and tore it lengthwise from the opening at the top all the way to the bottom. Then, he turned it over and ripped it along the same line from the bottom to the top. Now the sack was a rectangular piece of cloth. Then he ripped it into uniform strips, each one about three inches wide.

"That wasn't somethin' they taught me in medical school. I've learned that by bein' a country doctor. I hafta use what's available."

Beeler bound Joshua's foot and ankle tightly from the base of his toes all the way to his calf. Then he propped it up with a pillow. As he picked up his bag to leave, the doctor patted Joshua on the knee.

"You're gonna be just fine, son! But I want you to stay off'a that ankle. I'll come back to check on you in a couple'a days. I know you're bound to be hungry. I'm gonna talk to your mama and papa about what to give you an' how to take good care of you 'til I come back. Maybe I'll thump on ya again like a watermelon!"

"Yes, sir."

Franklin followed Doc Beeler out of the parlor and escorted him to the kitchen, where Maggie was seated at the table sipping tea from a cup.

"Can I get ya somethin' to eat? We have some peas an' kraut an' corn bread."

"Oh, no, ma'am. Thanks, but I best be goin'. My wife's gonna think I've run out on her completely. Just let me tell you an' Franklin a couple'a things about your boy, an' then I'll be on my way. I was a little worried at first about him catchin' another case of pneumonia—him bein' out there in the elements an' all. But I'm happy to say I don't see any sign of problems right now. I'm pretty sure his ankle is sprained, but I don't think it's broken. Keep him warm and in bed 'til I say it's all right to let him up. I'll be stoppin' by to keep an eye on him."

Franklin and Maggie nodded.

"The boy is bound to be mighty hungry, but I don't want him to light in an' eat a whole passel of food right away. Feed him some of that corn bread—maybe you can crumble it up in some milk an' feed it to him that way. Just give him a little bit at a time, an' let him eat more often than normal. An' be sure he gets plenty of water an' cambric tea to drink. I'm sure he's dehydrated, so he needs plenty of water—an' speakin' of water, heat up some an' get him all cleaned up real good. He'll feel a lot better after he's had a good warm bath."

Franklin extended his hand to the doctor.

"Thank you, Doc. We're much obliged to ya for helpin' to find him, an' for doctorin' him, too."

"Thank you so much," added Maggie.

"Don't mention it. He's a good boy, an' I'm just happy I could help out. Oh yes—I almost forgot."

Beeler reached back into his bag.

"Give Joshua a couple'a these aspirin tablets every four or five hours or so. They'll help with the swellin' and pain in his ankle."

Franklin followed Doc Beeler out the back door and walked beside him through the yard. Vernon and Elmer rose from their seats on the front bumper of Vernon's Model T Ford.

"How's the boy doin', Franklin?" Vernon inquired.

"The doc here says he's gonna be okay in a few days." Again, Franklin extended his hand to each one.

"I don't know what I'd'a done without all the help y'all gave me. I 'spect I would'a never found Joshua if it hadn't been for all my good neighbors, an' the sheriff, an' everybody. I don't know how I'll ever pay y'all back."

"Don't think nothin' of it, Franklin," said Elmer. "You'd'a done the same for us if we'd needed it. We're just sorry it happened, an' glad it turned out okay."

"I want y'all to know that this fella, here, is the best doctor there ever was."

"You're mighty right about that," agreed Elmer. Then he cupped his hand beside his mouth and spoke in a fake whisper, "He's the best—but don't ever tell him I said that!"

Then, he turned toward the doctor and smiled, and all the men laughed.

Franklin shivered as he watched his friends get into Vernon's Model T and drive off. The night air was chilly, and his emotions were raw.

Seemingly, this ordeal was over, but Franklin was still edgy. He began to remember scenes from the past few hours, and he shuddered again at what could have happened to his son.

By the time Franklin returned to the house, Maggie had begun to heat water for Joshua's bath. She had given him a glass of sweet milk with corn bread crumbled in it. She sat beside Joshua's bed, where he was propped up with pillows behind his back and under his leg. His appearance had improved quickly. Some color had returned to his face, and his eyes looked less hollow and more alive.

"How can I clean this mud out'a my hair?" he asked as Franklin walked into the room.

"There's a kettle of water heating up on the stove," said Maggie. "But I don't know how you can manage to take a bath with your ankle all bandaged up like that."

"Can I just wash my hair without gettin' in the tub?"

"I don't see why not," said Franklin. "I can bring the big tub in here an' set it on the floor. Then if you can get down on your hands an' knees with your head hangin' over it, I can pour the water while your mama washes out the mud."

"Okay, if somebody can help me get out'a bed. I dunno how Uncle Gerthy gets around so good on his crippled foot."

Franklin left to get the big galvanized tub they bathed in. In the summertime, they placed it on the back porch and bathed in the open. In colder weather, they bathed in the kitchen.

Franklin retrieved the tub from its storage place on a large nail just outside the door of the cabin and put it in the parlor. Maggie brought warm water, a bar of soap, and a towel. After they helped Joshua wash his hair, they left the room for him to complete his bath in privacy. He dangled his injured leg over the side of the tub and sat in the shallow, warm water to wash away the mud and slime of the swamp. It was the best bath of his young life. He closed his eyes and thanked God that he did not have to spend even one more minute in that horrible place.

After his bath, Maggie changed the sheets on his bed, and his father helped him back in. It was the bed he had lain in when he had pneumonia, and when his mother had died. Back in the place that evoked so many memories, he would remember this night as well, but now, he was too tired.

Franklin lowered the wick to extinguish the lantern beside Joshua's bed. "We'll talk in the mornin', son."

Before his father was out of the room, Joshua was asleep.

20
CHAPTER

JOSHUA HAD NEVER SLEPT past noon in his life, except when he was gravely ill with pneumonia. When he began to wake up on the day after his rescue, he had no idea where he was, or what time of the day it was, nor was he totally sure of his own identity.

He blinked and tried to open his eyes, but afternoon sunlight that filled the room made him squint and blink, and his eyelids closed again. In a few more minutes, he forced his eyes open and tried to focus on the old wardrobe situated on the opposite wall. It was a giant cypress tree. He looked at the sooty globe of the kerosene lamp sitting on the little nightstand beside his bed. It was a swarm of gnats. *Oh, please,* he thought, closing his eyes tightly again, *won't somebody get me out of this swamp?*

Gradually, Joshua became aware of the clean sheet and soft mattress underneath his body. He rubbed his eyes, and although he was reluctant to open them, he sensed the daylight. With a few more blinks, he focused again on the dark wood of the wardrobe contrasted against the pale-blue cardboard wall covering. He knew he was in the main bedroom. *Do I have pneumonia again?* he wondered.

He had a vague recollection of his arrival there the previous evening. He recalled the sight of Doc Beeler as he hovered over his bed. Although he was unsure of how he had gotten there, he sighed deeply as he realized fully that he was now dry, warm, and safe at home.

"Hey! Is anybody here?"

There was no immediate answer.

"Hey! Hey, I'm hungry!"

He heard the back door slam, and the sound of footsteps in the back part of the house.

"Hey!"

Finally, an uneven gait suggested Maggie was coming. She limped slightly and complained from time to time about pain in her left hip.

"Well, now. Good afternoon, young man. We were beginnin' to be a little bit worried about when you'd wake up. How're you feelin'?"

"Okay, I guess. But I'm real hungry."

"Well, I guess you are! You haven't had a thing to eat for almost two days now!"

"Two days? What day is it now?"

"It's Monday."

"Oh—am I missin' school?"

"Uh-huh—but we're not worryin' about that right now. I have some biscuits left over from breakfast, an' I could scramble you up some eggs, 'cause I kind'a kept the fire goin' in the stove since dinner. An' you know there's always plenty'a molasses to go with it. Does any'a that sound good to ya?"

"I'll eat anything!"

"Okay, then. I'll go fix it right now."

"Can I have somethin' to drink?"

"Sure. I'll bring some milk. An' I'll go tell your papa to come inside. He said for me to call him just as soon as you woke up."

Joshua stared at the ceiling. He had not helped his father feed livestock and milk the cow before sunup. He had slept past noon. He was not working long division problems and studying his English lesson at school. Instead, he was about to be served breakfast in bed. *Must be a dream.*

"Hey, bud, how're ya feelin'?"

Joshua was relieved to hear his father's voice and to see a smile on his face as he entered the room and walked over to the bed.

"I'm doin' okay, I guess. But I'm starvin'!"

"Yeah, I know. Maggie's out in the kitchen fixin' somethin' for you to eat."

"How much longer d'ya think it'll be 'til …"

"She's workin' on it—shouldn't take her too much longer."

Joshua stared at the ceiling again. Words didn't always come easy between him and his father. He didn't know how to begin to describe his experience in the storm and his time in the swamp.

Franklin was equally devoid of words to express what he wanted to say to his son. Simultaneously, they began to speak, and simultaneously, they stopped abruptly, neither one wanting to butt in and each one wanting the other to break the silence.

"Go ahead, son. You were tryin' to say somethin'."

"That's okay. I—I was just gonna say I'm sorry I couldn't help with the feedin' this mornin', an' …"

"Don't be worrin' about that. There wasn't that much to do. An' besides, Doc Beeler said for me to keep you in bed 'til he says you can get up. I wouldn't'a let ya help even if you had wanted to."

After another pause, Joshua spoke, but again, with only a brief glance at his father.

"I'm really sorry for all the trouble I caused. I should'a been able to get that harrow across before the storm hit the Big Ditch."

"I don't want to hear none'a that! You got nothin' to apologize for. It's me that should be sayin' he's sorry."

Joshua looked at his father. This was the first time in his memory that his father had apologized for anything.

Franklin scooted his chair up closer to Joshua's bed.

"I don't know how many times I wanted to kick myself for lettin' you go back there to get that harrow in the storm. I dunno what I'd'a done if we hadn't found you, an' I'm just glad you're gonna be okay."

Joshua didn't know how to respond to his father's admission of guilt, and he was glad to hear Maggie's footsteps in the hallway.

"Sounds like your food is comin'. Maybe you won't starve to death after all!"

Maggie entered the parlor carrying a large tray. It was loaded down with a plate of scrambled eggs, a basket half-full of biscuits she had reheated in the warming oven, and a small metal pitcher filled to the brim with clear, sweet sorghum molasses. She put one end of the tray on the edge of the small table beside Joshua's bed, moved the kerosene lamp over to make room, and then slid the tray onto the table.

"How does that look to ya?"

"Good! Very good—I'm starvin'!"

"I'll be right back with your milk."

This was the first time in Joshua's memory that he had been served a meal in bed. When he had had pneumonia, he was too sick to eat any solid food, and by the time he had resumed his normal diet, he was out of bed.

Up to that time, Joshua had rated the quality of his stepmother's cooking far below that of his mother's. This meal, however, tasted as good as any other meal he had ever had. He sopped up the last traces of molasses on his plate with his last bite of biscuit.

"Thanks. That was very good."

"You're welcome. I'm glad to see ya feelin' like eatin' again."

Maggie rearranged the dishes on the tray to carry it back to the kitchen. She glanced back at her stepson.

"We're just glad you're back home."

"Me, too!"

After Maggie left, the room was silent again. Joshua followed the "speak respectfully, but only when spoken to" rule, and for a brief time, Franklin didn't know what to say or what question to ask first.

"How did ya get all the way down to Willingham Bottom?"

"Uh … I—I caught on to this big tree limb, an' I kind'a rode it—hangin' on the best I could."

"How'd ya get caught in the deep water to begin with? Was it deeper'n you thought when you started across?"

"Uh … uh … I dunno what ya mean. I …"

"I mean—what I'm askin' is, was the water in the Big Ditch already too deep when you started across with Ole Dick?"

"Oh—oh, no, sir! 'Course there was more'n a trickle 'cause it had already rained pretty hard. But I tested it out. I waded out in it without Ole Dick, an' I knew we could make it across."

Joshua saw his father's furrowed brow and the confused look on his face.

"See, I was standin' on the harrow, ridin' it across. An' Ole Dick wasn't afraid, even a little bit. Then, just about the time me an' Ole Dick was right in the bottom of the ditch an' makin' it fine, there was a loud noise. I heard it comin' from up the ditch. It sounded kind'a like the train when it comes through Cayce. It scared me real bad."

"You mean you an' the horse was almost across?"

"Uh-huh. But right after I heard that roarin' that sounded like a train, I looked up an' ... uh ... there was water comin' at me ... uh ... an' it was way taller'n me—even taller'n you are. That's what hit me. The water hit me an' the harrow an' Ole Dick, an' that's when I thought I would be drownded.

"Uh ... that's the last time I saw Ole Dick. Is Ole Dick dead, Papa?"

"Yep, 'fraid so. He got caught up under some roots in the bank of the ditch, an' with the weight of the harrow an' all—well, Ole Dick just didn't have much of a chance to get loose an' get out'a there."

"I'm really sorry, Papa. I know Ole Dick was your best horse."

"I told ya not to worry about it, son. There wasn't a thing you could'a done. You're okay, an' that's all that matters to me."

"The worst part was bein' stuck out there all by myself in that swamp—'specially in the dark."

"If only I'd'a known where you were ... I'd'a never let ya stay out there if I had known."

"I know, Papa."

"I was worried sick. I dunno what I'd'a done if it hadn't'a been for so many others that pitched in an' helped to find ya. I can't remember ever bein' so worried—'cept maybe when your mother was so sick."

Joshua pushed himself up in bed and tucked his pillow behind his lower back for support. It was rare for him to have an extended conversation with his father, and he had wanted to talk to Franklin about her death since the day she had died. Until now, he had had neither the opportunity nor the courage to bring it up.

Joshua looked directly into his father's eyes.

"Papa, do you still miss my mother?"

"'Course I do. What kind'a question is that?"

"I dunno—I just wonder sometimes. You never talk about her anymore, an' I ... I guess I was just wonderin' if you miss her."

Usually shy and quiet, and always respectful of his father, Joshua had never before been bold enough to ask him so personal a question. Franklin had no idea how to respond to his son, and under different circumstances, he might have walked away.

"Like I said before, I still miss Hannah a lot. I've just never seen much use in talkin' about it to you kids—or to anybody else, for that matter. I kind'a figure it's nobody's business how I feel. Why're you askin' me about your mother now, after all this time? We were talkin' about what happened to you in the flood."

"I did lots'a thinkin' about my mother while I was out there all by myself. I've quit wishin' for her to come back, like I used to, 'cause I know she can't. But when I'm in trouble, or when I'm worried about somethin', seems like I think about her. I guess I wonder what she'd tell me to do if she was here. So when I needed somebody to talk to out there in the swamp, I just started talkin' like she was sittin' beside me."

Joshua hesitated and then looked at his father, who sat staring at him.

"An' then ... then, I felt like she was there beside me. An' she sort'a told me not to worry—not in her own voice out loud, but I knew she would'a told me to say a prayer, an' somebody would come get me. So that's what I did—I said a prayer."

Joshua pulled his pillow out from behind his back, sighed, and lay back in his bed.

"An' I guess that's why she's on my mind. I guess I was just tryin' to find out if I'm the only one that misses her."

Franklin did not respond immediately. Not given to intimate conversation, he could not find a suitable reply to Joshua's words. With his elbows on the arms of his chair, he rocked back and looked at the ceiling before speaking.

"You ain't the only one that misses her. Like I told ya before, I miss her, too. I guess I just don't know much about how ta talk about it. Maybe I just didn't know you wanted me to."

"It's just—well, when you said somethin' about her, I just felt like I had to tell ya. It just came out."

"Yeah, I know. An' I do want ya to feel like talkin' to me. I don't want ya to hold nothin' back."

"No, sir."

Franklin rose from his chair and stepped over to look out the window. "I do believe you were right," he said.

"What d'ya mean?"

"When you said your mama would'a said not to worry, an' that somebody would come to find ya sooner or later. I believe that's what she would'a said, all right—an' don't ya see? She'd'a been right, too. 'Cause somebody did come an' find ya."

"Uh-huh. 'Course, I … I never expected it to be Lonnie."

"What? What'd you say? Lonnie?"

Franklin jerked his head around and then turned to stare at his son.

"Yeah, Lonnie. I said I never expected it to be Lonnie. Lonnie was the one that came first. I guess I … I never thought Lonnie'd be the one to find me."

Franklin's face was instantly flushed. For a moment, he stood slack-jawed. He stared at Joshua and hesitated to let Joshua's words sink in.

"When?" he shouted. "When did Lonnie find you?"

"I dunno, exactly. I know it was still daylight."

"Daylight? You sure?"

"Yeah. An' he said he'd hafta go to get help. An' then it took a long time 'fore y'all showed up. Didn't Lonnie tell you where I was?"

Franklin grimaced.

"Naw! He said he couldn't find you. He said you was not in Willingham Bottom!"

Franklin's face turned red, and his jaw tightened. He recalled each word Lonnie had uttered in mock despondence as he insisted that he had not seen Joshua. Finally, he pictured Lonnie's goodbye waves and heard his shouts of "Good luck!" as he stood in his wagon to drive his team away. Franklin was enraged.

"I swear—I'll kill him!"

He slammed his fist against the back of the rocker and knocked it over.

"He won't get away with it! I'll find him, an' I'll kill him!"

"Papa! Papa, please don't …"

Franklin stormed out of the room. Maggie met him in the hallway, just outside the doorway of the parlor.

"Where's Lonnie? Where is he? Where's that no-good, low-down son'a yours? Where's my gun?"

Maggie tried to block his path.

"Franklin, no! Get control'a yourself. Please don't do nothin' crazy."

"Get out'a my way, Maggie!"

Franklin moved her aside and rushed by her down the narrow hallway.

"Oh, yeah. I remember now. He said he was goin' to Hickman an' then he was gonna get a ride to Memphis to start his job workin' on the river. I'll just hafta track him down. But I'll find him one way or the other—an' when I do …"

Franklin looked for his rifle where it usually stood in the corner of the kitchen by the wood box.

"He's gone!" Maggie shouted. "Lonnie's gone to work on the river. You can't …"

"Like I said, I'll find him. Where's my gun? Who took my gun? Why can't things ever be where they're s'posed to be?"

"Please, Franklin—please. Can't we just talk about this?"

"Don't need ta talk—ain't nothin' to talk about! Where's my gun?"

Maggie muffled her words with her apron.

"Please, Franklin—please! Joshua's been found. Please don't go after Lonnie. Please …"

Maggie collapsed into a chair and sobbed.

Franklin was incredulous.

"Don't go after Lonnie? Don't go after Lonnie when—when he found Joshua an' then left him out there to die?"

Franklin slapped his hand down hard against the table. "You mean I ain't supposed ta go after a scoundrel that'd do somethin' like that?"

"It won't do any good," sobbed Maggie. "It'll just get you in trouble. Where'll that leave the rest of us? What'll Joshua an' the rest'a your kids do then?"

"It ain't right, Maggie! It ain't right for Lonnie to do somethin' like that an' get away with it—an' I don't aim to let him get away with it! I should'a known he wasn't gonna change."

Maggie tried to control her sobs.

"I—I never said … I never said what he done was the right thing. But I don't want you to shoot him, neither. He hadn't always had such a good life. You know he got beat by his daddy an all … an' …"

"Yeah … yeah. Here we go with that business 'bout him gettin' beat by his daddy when he was little. You've told me that a hunderd times! But that doesn't give him the right to take it out on Joshua. Bein' beat up by his daddy doesn't give him the right to leave Joshua down in the swamp—an' then lyin' about it to keep us from findin' him! You expect me to just forget about that 'cause he had a daddy that beat on him when he was little? Well, I ain't gonna forget about it!"

Maggie covered her face and cried quietly. "I know, Franklin. I know."

Franklin turned and left. He walked out the back door, got in his old car, and drove off.

After drying her eyes with her apron, Maggie got up from the table and started back toward the parlor to check on Joshua. Gerthy met her in the hallway.

"Are you okay?" he asked.

"I'm worried about Franklin. I'm scared he's gonna do somethin' he'll wish he didn't."

"Where'd he go?"

"Don't know. He went out the door, got in the car, an' left—didn't say nothin' about where he was goin', but I think he's goin' to find Lonnie. I just hope he …"

"He's prob'ly out tryin' to think it all through, Maggie. Maybe when he cools down a little, he'll be able to think a little clearer. Just try not to worry. He'll likely be back in time to get the feedin' an' milkin' done."

Maggie nodded.

"'Course, I'm kind'a worried about Lonnie, too. He's still my boy, an' even if he has done some mean things, I can't help it if I still care what happens to him."

"That's natural. Nobody's blamin' you for what Lonnie did. An' nobody's gonna blame you for bein' concerned like any mother would be."

Maggie sighed and shook her head.

"Maybe havin' a job will straighten him out—but I 'spect I won't see him around here again. I … I …"

Maggie lifted her apron with both hands to cover her face and wipe her tears. Gerthy put his arm around her shoulder and patted her arm.

"I don't know, Gerthy," she muttered between sobs. "How will I ever see Lonnie again?"

"You'll see Lonnie again, Maggie," assured Gerthy. "I don't know exactly how it'll happen, but you will. You just try not to worry."

"Uh-huh. I'm sorry for cryin' so much. I ... I ..."

Gerthy patted her on the arm again.

"I'll be in my room if you need anything. Oh—an' one more thing. Franklin's rifle's not exactly lost. I've got it back in my room. I'll give it back when he really needs it."

"Thanks, Gerthy."

Maggie dried her eyes again and tried to put on a more cheerful countenance as she walked on down the hallway to the parlor.

"Can I get ya anything, Joshua? Can I get ya somethin' to eat or drink?"

"No, thank you, ma'am," Joshua replied. "I think I just want to rest."

Joshua turned over in his bed, and Maggie left the room. She returned to the kitchen, sat down at the table, waited for the other children to return from school, and prayed through her tears that Franklin would not kill Lonnie.

21
CHAPTER

ALTHOUGH HE WAS STILL asleep, Joshua was aware of something aflutter around his ear. With his eyes still closed, he tried to shoo away the annoying intruder with a quick stroke of his hand. Only a moment later, there it was again, this time around his other ear. He turned onto his side and pulled his pillow around his head to cover his ear. In another instant, he felt it tickle his upper lip. He brushed at it with his hand. It didn't leave. He hit at it again, determined not to open his eyes and let this nuisance wake him up. For a moment, he thought it was gone for good, but then it was back, and now it was crawling up his nose!

"Hey!" he shouted. He slapped at his nose and bolted upright in his bed. There beside his bed was Matt. He held a feather in one hand, pointed at his brother with the other, and laughed.

"You little rat!" Joshua yelled. "I ought'a ... You better be glad I can't get out'a this bed. I'd ..."

Matt continued to roll with laughter.

"You think it's funny, huh? Well, it won't be so funny when I beat your little butt. Why'd ya hafta wake me up? Doc Beeler said for me to get lots'a rest."

"All you been doin' is sleepin'! Aren't you goin' to school?"

"Nope—not 'til the doctor says I can."

"That's not fair! Why can't I stay home too?"

"'Cause you don't have a hurt ankle."

With his devilish grin, Matt held up the feather he had used to harass his older brother.

"I could take care'a you all day."

"Matthew, get in here an' put your shoes on," Maggie called. "It's time to go to school."

"Aw, do I have to?"

"Have fun!" Joshua teased.

Matt went to join Naomi for their mile-and-a-quarter walk to Lodgeston School. The jaunt to and from school was fun for him. He would run out ahead of his stepsister and then have time to throw rocks or look for tadpoles while she caught up. He taunted her with bugs, worms, and other crawly critters to hear her scream.

Although he would not have admitted it to Matt, Joshua wished he could get out of bed and go to school. Except for his classes in American government, he enjoyed schoolwork, and he realized he would soon be bored lying there in the parlor. Since his bout with pneumonia, that was his least favorite spot in the house—it was too full of difficult memories.

Joshua turned onto his side and looked back over his shoulder to see through the window. Leaves on the two big oak trees were a dark, lustrous green. They seemed to wave invitingly for him to come outside so that he, too, could enjoy the gentle morning breeze.

This was typical weather for the middle of May. The sky was cloudless, the sunshine was warm but not yet hot, and air currents moved easily, still bearing fresh aromas of spring rains and sweet scents of jasmine and honeysuckle. *Work behind the plow might even be enjoyable on a day like this,* Joshua thought.

"Mama," he called, wanting his stepmother to know that he was awake.

She came right away, with some leftover biscuits and hominy grits.

"You hungry for some breakfast?"

"Yes, ma'am, I'm starvin'. But first …"

He hesitated, sheepishly trying to find the correct words.

"What's the matter?" inquired Maggie. "D'ya need me to get somethin' else?"

"No, I—I … d'ya think I can get out'a bed an' go to the back porch? I don't like havin' to use that thing."

He hesitated again and then pointed to the slop jar under the bed. It was the country folks' version of a chamber pot, and Joshua thought it was appropriate only for women's use.

"I can hop on one leg."

"Tell ya what I'll do. I'll get Grandpa Jennings's old walkin' cane, an' you can use it to go to the porch. Just be careful not to put any weight on that bad leg."

Joshua had been itching to get his hands on Grandpa's cane for years, but his father had put it away, fearing that he and Matt would damage or lose it. He swung his legs over the side of the bed and waited for Maggie to return with the cane.

The cane was made of ash, with multi-colored wood grain clearly revealed through its glossy finish. At first, Joshua didn't know how to use the cane, and even after trying it out for a few short steps, he was disappointed to find that it didn't help as much as he had expected.

He stood on the back porch and peed on the ground. Then he hobbled back to join Maggie in the kitchen.

"Where's Papa?"

"I don't know. He left yesterday, and I haven't seen him since."

"He got mad when I told him about Lonnie bein' the first one to find me. I didn't know …"

"That's okay. You had no way of knowin'. It's not your fault."

"I hope he comes back soon."

"Me too," answered Maggie, nodding. "Me too."

Joshua sat down at the table. He used another chair to support his leg to keep his ankle elevated, as Doc Beeler had instructed. He gobbled down a plateful of buttered grits and warm biscuits covered with honey and asked for more. He used his spoon to scrape the last bit of honey off his plate.

"You might as well just pick up that plate an' lick it," teased his uncle, who had limped into the kitchen without being noticed.

"Mornin' Uncle Gerthy."

"I'm kind'a surprised to see you sittin' out here at the table. How's that sore ankle doin'?"

"Okay, I guess. I haven't tried walkin' on it, but it doesn't hurt me too bad. Mama let me use Grandpa's walkin' cane, an' that helps me get around on it better."

"I didn't think it would hurt for him to use it," said Maggie.

"I'm sure the boy's grandpa is dancin' in heaven at the very idea of Joshua usin' his cane—not to say he's happy you got a sore ankle an' all …"

Gerthy gave Joshua's shoulder a squeeze.

"Matter of fact, it'd be all right with me to give the walkin' stick to you to keep. Seems to me like you're old enough to take care of it, huh?"

"Oh, yes, sir. I would. Can I really have it to keep?"

"Let me talk to your papa about it when he gets back. We'll see."

Gerthy turned to go back to his room.

"D'ya feel like comin' back an' spendin' some time with me? A little change of scenery might do ya a world'a good, an' I'd like to have the company."

"Can I bring Grandpa's cane?" Joshua examined it again. "I really do like this cane."

With her hands on her hips, Maggie watched as Joshua and Gerthy left the room. Gerthy limped out first, followed closely by his nephew, hopping on his good leg and using his cane. *With his sore ankle, that boy sure is the spittin' image of his uncle,* she thought.

"You get up there in my bed," instructed Gerthy as they entered his room. "That way, we can prop up your foot. Anyway, I was aimin' to sit here in my favorite chair."

Joshua sidled up to his uncle's bed and managed to turn so that he partly sat but mostly leaned against it. He discarded the cane and sprang back just enough to sit comfortably on the bed, with his feet dangling just above the floor. As Gerthy settled into his rocker, Joshua picked up a book from the small, simple table that served as a nightstand.

"What's this book you're readin'?"

"Oh, that? Yeah—that's a collection of some of the writings of Henry Wadsworth Longfellow. Do you know Longfellow's work?"

"I've heard of him. I think we had to memorize one of his poems in school."

"Was it 'By the shore of Gitche Gumee, By the shining Big-Sea-Water'?"

Joshua nodded his head and smiled, joining in to recite with his uncle, "Stood the wigwam of Nokomis, Daughter of the Moon, Nokomis …"

Joshua shrugged. "I guess that's all I can remember."

"That's fine! I'm proud of you for knowin' that much. D'ya remember what that is from?"

"I don't know what ya mean."

"That part we were sayin' together. Do you know the title of the poem that came from?"

"Uh-uh. I guess I forgot."

"It's from *The Song of Hiawatha.* Don't ya remember Minnehaha, which means Laughing Water?"

"Yeah, sort'a. But it was last year, in Miz Clement's class. I forgot most of it."

"D'ya like Longfellow's poems?"

"I never really thought about it. I guess I do. You must really like 'em if you're readin' a whole book full of 'em."

"Yes, I suppose I do."

Joshua replaced his uncle's book and lifted his feet onto the bed to lie down. His uncle used a quilt that had been folded neatly at the foot of his bed to support Joshua's ankle and foot, and then he slid back into his chair. Fresh air from an open window behind him cleared out some of the musty smell of old books and the stale odor of partially smoked pipe tobacco. Joshua tucked his hands under the back of his head and stared up at the ceiling. He liked being in his uncle's room. He was relaxed there. He felt no need to make conversation just for the sake of it, but when he did want to talk, Gerthy was an attentive listener. Since his mother's death, Joshua had felt most at home and comfortable when he was with his uncle in his uncle's room.

Gerthy sat silently, content to read from a three-month-old issue of the *New York Times* somebody had left in Lloyd Brinson's general store. Dated Wednesday, February 22, 1922, its headlines announced the crash of the *Roma,* a 410-foot army dirigible built for the United States by Italy.

Thirty-four people had perished in the wreck after the craft hit a high-tension wire, fell to the ground, and burst into flames. For many citizens, that was old news, but out in the country, news was not easily available. Gerthy read every word of the banner article with great interest, and he knew that before he placed the paper in his stack of materials to keep, he would read every other article, too. He was elated that he had been the lucky passerby to find this treasure lying on the counter of Brinson's store.

"I kind'a like Doc Beeler," said Joshua.

"He's a pretty good ole country doctor, all right—an' a good man, too," agreed Gerthy. "What do you like most about Doc?"

"I just like how he takes care of people. He's real nice. An' I like the way he'll stop an' explain things."

"That's a good quality in a doctor."

"He's kind'a funny though. Did ya ever see the way he does his lips in an' out when he's workin' on ya?"

"Yep. That'd be hard to miss. He's kind'a nervous—kind'a jittery. He's got all kinds'a tics. Did you know they used to call 'im Skeeter when he was younger?"

"Doc Beeler has ticks? Why don't he get rid of 'em? I thought ticks are bad for ya!"

Gerthy threw back his head and rocked back in his chair with laughter.

"No, no. Not that kind'a ticks—not the ticks that get on ya an' suck blood. I was talkin' about how Doc Beeler twitches an' jerks, like when he moves his lips back an' forth. That's called a tic, too, but it's referrin' to a muscle spasm, not a bug."

"Oh. I was just picturin' Doc Beeler all covered with ticks—the suckin' kind!"

They roared with laughter at the thought of ticks all over the doctor's body. Gerthy reared back in his rocker and chortled especially as Joshua imitated Doc Beeler frantically pulling ticks off of every part of his body.

"Lordy mercy! I haven't laughed like that in a blue moon! You must be feelin' better. Doc Beeler with ticks—I declare, I'd pay good money to see that!"

Gerthy wiped his eyes with a big red bandana and picked up his newspaper again. He let Joshua initiate the conversation and choose the subject matter he wanted to discuss. Besides, he was intrigued by another *New York Times* headline, "Strikers Shot Down in Pawtucket Riot," and he was anxious to read the article. Joshua didn't give him an opportunity to get past the third line.

"I'm glad it was you an' Doc Beeler that found me—'course, I'm not countin' Lonnie."

Gerthy laid his paper aside.

"Well, I'm glad we found you, too. We were gettin' mighty worried not knowin' if you were all right—or even where you were, for that matter."

"What I mean is—well, like I said, I kind'a like Doc Beeler, an' I knew he'd be able to take good care of my ankle an' all—but I was glad you were there to talk to me 'til they could come with the boat. D'ya know what I'm tryin' to say?"

"Well, I guess so. I know I wanted to get you out'a that swamp mighty bad."

"I remember what you told me about spiritual blessings, an' how me bein' able to remember my mother is one of 'em."

"Yes."

Joshua sat up in the bed.

"Well, I used to think maybe she would come back. I used to ask God to send her back to us. But now I know she can't come back, an' I don't even ask for that anymore."

Gerthy nodded, but he kept his silence. He anticipated that Joshua had more to say.

"I'm lucky she was my mother, an' I won't ever forget all the things about her that was so special."

"She was a wonderful woman," agreed Gerthy quietly. "An' you're right. You are lucky she was your mother, an' don't ever forget that."

"But Uncle Gerthy, I still can't understand why she had to die. I know she got sick an' all, but ..."

"Nobody can understand why those things happen the way they do. We just have to ..."

"Why'd my papa go away like he did? Why would he do that?"

"Well, he's kind'a upset at Lonnie for lying. He's probably thinkin' he needs to teach him a lesson, but I think ..."

"No! I don't mean now. I mean before my mother got sick."

"Oh, I see. I thought you were talkin' about ..."

"Why'd he leave her here to take care of all us kids all by herself? I can't help wonderin' if she'd'a gotten sick if my papa hadn't gone away like he did."

Gerthy knew the question deserved a serious and honest answer, but he didn't know how to respond. He, too, had wondered about the wisdom of Franklin's decision to go to Mississippi and to leave Hannah to take care of the chores and the children. On the other hand, he wanted to remain loyal to his brother, and he was mindful not to say anything that would undermine Joshua's respect for his father.

"Franklin went to Mississippi to find a better farm."

"I know, but why'd we need a better farm? We were doin' okay on this one 'til my mother died."

Gerthy pulled his chair closer to the bed, scooted to the front of it, and tilted forward. He looked directly into Joshua's eyes.

"Listen to me, Joshua. Your papa was tryin' to find a way to make life better for his family. His friend told him about the place down in Mississippi, an' Franklin was afraid it would be sold if he didn't go right away. An' he wouldn't have ever gone to Mississippi if he hadn't thought it was a good chance for him to make things better."

"But if he hadn't gone, maybe my mother wouldn't'a gotten sick."

"Maybe—maybe not. We'll never know. But remember this. Your papa had no way of knowin' Hannah would get sick. She was a strong woman. He'd'a never gone if he had the least inklin' that she was gonna get sick. Your papa loved your mother very much. Don't ever forget that."

"I know. I never thought he didn't love her. I just wish he hadn't left— an' I wish she hadn't gotten sick."

Gerthy reached out and patted Joshua's leg.

"I know, son. We all wish your mama hadn't gotten sick."

"Well, I was just thinkin' about it when I was out in the swamp waitin' for sombody to find me. I guess I couldn't help thinkin' about it—an' I needed somebody to talk to."

"Well, I'm honored you chose me. I can't say I have many answers for ya, but I'm always happy to listen."

"When do you think my papa's gonna come home?"

"I'm sure he'll be back soon," Gerthy assured. "He cares for his family more'n anything, an'—well, I think your papa just needs some time by himself to think."

"Uncle Gerthy?"

"Yeah, what is it?"

"Uh … when my papa gets back … uh … please don't tell him … I …"

"Don't you worry. This conversation is just between us—this is strictly man to man."

Joshua let out a big sigh.

"Thanks!"

"Oh, one more thing." Gerthy pointed to the table beside the bed. "That book, there—a collection of Longfellow's poems and essays …"

"Uh-huh. What about it?"

"Hand it over here to me, if you don't mind. I think I remember somethin' in there I want to read to you."

Joshua was puzzled, but he did as his uncle had requested. Gerthy quickly found the table of contents and ran his forefinger down the page.

"Ah, here it is—*Hyperion*. It's on page 321."

Just as quickly, he turned to page 321, and then he continued to flip through additional pages until he found one with its corner turned down. He sat back in his chair and adjusted his book to accommodate his farsightedness.

Gerthy was emphatic.

"Now, listen close, Joshua. I want you to hear what Mr. Longfellow had to say. This is from *Hyperion,* book four, chapter eight. Now, listen close."

Gerthy read slowly, and he paused after each phrase.

> Look not mournfully into the Past. It comes not back again. Wisely improve the Present. It is thine. Go forth to meet the shadowy Future, without fear, and with a manly heart.

After the final word of the quote, Gerthy glanced up at Joshua. He saw in Joshua's furrowed brow that his young nephew didn't fully comprehend the meaning of Longfellow's words.

"I—I guess I don't know exactly what that means. I kind'a do, but not really."

"That's okay. I've read that passage many times, an' yet I may not understand its full meaning either. But let me explain what it means to me, an' we'll see what you think about it."

"Okay."

"Longfellow starts off by sayin' that we shouldn't be sad about what's happened in the past, 'cause we can't bring it back. We can't do it over or make it come out different. D'ya see?"

"Did he mean we should forget what's happened? 'Cause I don't aim to forget about my mother."

"Oh, no! He surely didn't mean for us to forget about the past, an' especially the people we've known an' loved. I think he's just suggestin' that we shouldn't be sad about it. We ought'a remember the happy part. *Mournful* means unhappy or sad. So don't ya see? Longfellow's tellin' us not to let the past keep makin' us unhappy in the here an' now."

"I think I'm beginnin' to understand."

"Good! Now then, let's see what he says next. Ah, right here. D'ya want to read the next part?"

Joshua sat up in the bed again.

"Okay,"

Gerthy handed the book to Joshua and pointed to the place for him to begin.

"'Wisely improve the Present. It is thine. Go forth to meet ...'"

"Wait—sorry to interrupt, but let's talk about what he says about the present for a minute. Then we'll go on the rest of it."

"Okay, I see what ya mean. I'll read it again. 'Wisely improve the Present. It is thine.'"

"All right, let's see now. He's already said for us to not be sorrowful about the past. Now he's sayin' for us to make the present better. Ya'see? We don't have control of the past, but we do have control of today, an' Longfellow's tellin' us to improve it."

Gerthy hesitated. He looked at Joshua with a warm smile. Joshua nodded.

"An' when he says *thine,* who d'ya think that's referrin' to?"

"I guess if he was talkin' to me, then *thine* would mean me!"

"You're exactly right! Whoever's readin' this—I guess that's who he's talkin' to, don't ya think?"

"Uh-huh."

"An' since we're the ones readin' it right now, he must be talkin' to us. So I suppose he's tellin' us the present is ours. It's like it belongs to us—we own it. An' since we own it, we're the ones that get to decide how to use it."

"I never thought about it like that before."

"That's what I like about the way Longfellow writes. He makes you think about things in a little different way than you did before."

"Yes, sir."

"Are you getting' tired of talkin' about all this?"

"Oh, no, sir! I like talkin' about it."

"Good. 'Cause there's one more thing about ownin' the present. We get to choose how to use it, all right, but then we're at least partly responsible for how it turns out. I think that's why Longfellow says for us to make it better."

"How am I s'posed to know how to make things better?"

His uncle began to rock slowly.

"Well, that's a good question. I guess we can make things better each day by workin' hard an' doin' our best—whether it's workin' arithmetic problems or plowin' behind Ole Kate."

Gerthy hesitated for a moment and looked off into space.

"An' for me it means askin' for the Lord to help me out along the way. Ya'see, I don't always know how to improve the present, either. I need the good Lord to show me what it takes to make things better."

"Me too."

Gerthy got up from his rocker to stretch.

"I didn't mean for this discussion to go on an' on this way."

"That's okay."

Gerthy picked up the book once more.

"Well, the last part is what I 'specially want you to hear."

"What d'ya mean?"

Gerthy pointed back to the passage.

"The last part—this part right here, where Longfellow talks about the future. I think he's talkin' directly to you."

"Talkin' to me?"

"Yeah. Listen. He says 'Go forth to meet the shadowy Future without fear, and with a manly heart.'"

"What does that mean?"

"Well, first of all, he reminds us that the future isn't clear. That's what he means by a 'shadowy Future.' We can't tell for certain what's out there. But he says for us to face it without bein' afraid —in other words, for us not to worry about it just because we don't know what's goin' to happen."

"How's that talkin' to me? Seems like that's the same for everybody."

"Well, it is. I agree with ya. But it's the very last part that I think might speak 'specially to you. It says to go into the future 'with a manly heart.' Seems to me like you've done lots'a growin' up lately. I believe you're ready to start thinkin' more like a man, an' less like a boy. An' that's why I think Longfellow might be talkin' to you when he says to go into the future with a manly heart."

"Uh … how can I be a man when I don't even know what a manly heart is?"

Gerthy hip-hopped across his room to the window.

"Well, I don't know what anybody else thinks it takes to have a manly heart, but I think it takes courage, and strength, and honor—an' I think you have all those traits. On top of that, you're smart, you're a hard worker, an' you trust in the Lord."

Gerthy paused and gazed out the window. Joshua sat on the bed with his head bowed. He tried to soak in his uncle's words, but he didn't know how to respond. Gerthy limped back to the bed and held onto the footboard for stability. He waggled his forefinger in the air.

"So what I'm sayin', Joshua, is that you can go into the future with a manly heart. Even though there are things about the past you'd change if you could; an' even though you don't always know how to make the present better; an' even though you don't know exactly what the future will bring; you'll be able to face the future boldly, 'cause you've got strong character. Besides, you've got God on your side."

Gerthy walked back to his chair and sat down. Rocking slowly but steadily, he looked back into Joshua's eyes.

He stroked his chin.

"You may not know what a manly heart is right now, but I'm confident that you'll learn."

"I need to pee!" blurted Joshua.

He slid down off the bed and hopped toward the door without his cane. He almost reached the door to his uncle's room before tears welled up in his eyes. He needed to relieve himself, but mostly he didn't want his uncle to see him cry. *So much for facing the future with a manly heart,* he thought.

22
CHAPTER

"WELL, I'M SURE GLAD to see you girls are up an' at 'em." Maggie greeted Jessie, Reba, and Naomi as they walked through the back door into the kitchen.

"Let's eat some breakfast, an' then we can all get started on our Saturday chores."

Maggie was especially cheerful—just as she had been since Franklin's return in the early morning hours two and a half days after his vengeful departure.

At the small Army Corps of Engineers office in Hickman, he learned that Lonnie had been bussed with other recruits to Memphis, Tennessee, where he was to board the dredge, *Iota*. It had been commissioned in 1919, three years earlier, and it was being used to dredge out the Memphis Harbor. Lonnie had been hired as a deckhand to do grunt work during dredging operations and to assist in washing out boilers and making minor repairs when needed.

Franklin had driven all night to find him. He was still enraged over Lonnie's deceit and hateful behavior toward his son, and he vowed to mete out his own brand of punishment to set the record straight.

Barely in the outskirts of Memphis, only a few miles from the harbor where the *Iota* was docked, Franklin had an apparent change of heart. He turned around and drove his old Model T as fast as it would run back up US Highway 51 to get back home. That was all he had told Maggie when he crawled into bed beside her only minutes before dawn on Tuesday morning, and she had not asked him for any additional details. She was elated that he had returned. And she was equally happy that he had done so without doing any harm to her son.

Jessie helped her stepmother prepare their breakfast.

"When can we get out'a that stinky ole shack?"

"Yeah," agreed Reba. "We're sick of sleepin' out there. When can we have our regular beds back?"

"We've been sleepin' out there for almost a week," Naomi chimed in. "When …"

Maggie retied her apron strings.

"I can't say for sure, girls. Doc Beeler said he'd pass by here sometime today an' check on Joshua. If he says it's okay, we'll move him an' Matt back out there, an' y'all can have your beds back."

"Well, I don't see why we need a doctor to tell us where people should sleep!" insisted Jessie. "He's been walkin' around for a couple'a days—seems to me like he's fine. He doesn't hafta work, doesn't hafta go to school—an' he's been takin' up that whole big bed all by himself. Is he a king or somethin' now?"

"We'll see about it, I said!"

Matt wanted life to be normal again, too. He wanted his real brother back. He needed a playmate. He needed someone to rassle with. He even missed nights in the cabin with his big brother. He preferred the relative freedom of being out of the house—especially since Lonnie had moved out.

Franklin desperately needed Joshua's help to get his plowing done in preparation for planting summer crops of corn, sorghum, and sweet potatoes. The month of May was half gone, and like other farmers in the area, Franklin was behind schedule due to heavy spring rains and the late season flood that had kept fields too wet to plow. Once they dried sufficiently, all available hands would be required to get the work done in time.

Joshua was particularly anxious to return to his normal routine. He was tired of being confined. He was bored. He felt fine—his cough was gone, and his appetite had returned. Although his ankle was still sore, he managed to walk lightly on it within the restricted limits imposed by Doc Beeler. He saw no reason to continue to keep it elevated. He missed going to school; he even missed doing homework and his daily chores. He realized that on any other clear Saturday in May, he would be behind a plow or a harrow, or otherwise helping his father in the fields. *That would be better than standin' here lookin' out this window with nothin' else to do,* he thought.

While the morning dragged by for Joshua, Maggie and the girls were busy with household chores. Maggie watched over a big pot of soup beans she was cooking for the noon meal and supervised the girls, who were assigned housecleaning duties.

Matt had his own list of things to do: look for worms, throw clods of dirt at blackbirds, chase Ole Rover, make mud pies and put them in the sun to bake, and complete other tasks to "help" Gerthy, who worked in the garden.

Soon after daybreak, Franklin had taken a team of mules to plow an area of high ground, the only part of the field that wasn't too wet. He would come back to the house promptly at noon to eat and to rest the team.

Jessie whispered as she walked into the parlor with her broom.

"Hey, lazybones."

Joshua sat up and glared at his sister. "What did you call me?" he demanded.

"Who? Me? Why, I don't remember callin' you anything."

"You said somethin'—I heard ya. It sounded like you called me lazy."

"Now, why would I call you lazy? Look at ya! Look at how hard you're workin'!"

"Don't be makin' fun of me! You know I'd be workin' if I could."

Jessie extended the broom handle toward Joshua.

"Sure you would. I bet if I handed you this broom, you'd prove it to me,"

"I don't know what you're talkin' about."

"Uh-huh. I bet you're gonna take this broom an' show me how good you can sweep just to prove you're not a lazybones."

"I knew you called me lazybones." Joshua shoved the broom handle away and lurched toward his sister with a raised fist.

"Mama, help! Joshua's gonna hit me!"

"What's the matter?" Reba asked Jessie.

Jessie screamed to be sure Maggie would hear.

"I was in there tryin' to sweep the floor, an' Joshua threatened to hit me."

More than ever, Joshua wished to be out of the house and back to his normal life.

"Please, God," he sighed. "Please get me out'a here."

Just before noon, his prayer was answered. As he limped down the hallway, drawn to the kitchen by the aroma of hot corn bread, he heard Doc Beeler's voice at the back door.

"Where's that patient of mine?"

Joshua stepped into the kitchen.

"I'm right here."

Doc Beeler stepped forward to shake hands with Joshua.

"Well, I see you are—an' it looks to me like you're getting' along pretty good, too."

"Yes, sir. I am!"

The doctor looked first at Joshua and then at Maggie.

"Sorry I didn't get over here sooner. I swear, I've been meanin' to come for two days now, but seems like every baby in the whole county decided to be born yesterday or the day before. Honest to goodness, I've delivered three babies in the last two days—an' all of 'em are girls, too!"

"That's okay, Doctor Beeler. Would ya care to join us for some dinner? We're just havin' some soup beans an' corn bread, but you're sure welcome to sit down with us."

"Oh, no, ma'am. I'll just check out my favorite patient right quick, an' then I gotta be goin' on back to the house. My wife's got all kinds'a things lined up for me to do today. But I thank you just the same."

"You sure? Franklin's due to come in from the field shortly, and we be right pleased if you'd care to join us."

"No, I'm much obliged for the offer, an' I want you to know it's hard for me to pass up a good plate of beans an' corn bread. But I can't stay this time."

With more than a nod but not quite a bow, Doc Beeler gestured his appreciation to Maggie for her kind offer of food. Then he turned to face Joshua.

"Son, let me get you checked out real quick before the smell of those beans and that corn bread makes me just divorce my wife! Where should we go to get this done?"

Joshua led Doc Beeler back to the parlor. He listened to the boy's lungs to be sure there was no indication of fluid or congestion. Joshua tried to look away as the doctor looked into his eyes, ears, and throat. He knew that he would laugh aloud if he caught the slightest glimpse of the doctor's lips pulsating rhythmically back and forth.

Quickly satisfied with his examination of Joshua's upper torso and extremities, Doc Beeler shifted his attention to the boy's ankle.

"I see you took that fancy wrapping off."

"Well, when the swellin' went down, it dropped down onto my foot. I tried to put it back, but I couldn't keep it up."

"Well, that's a good sign. I'm glad the swelling is gone."

The doctor used his thumb and forefinger to press gently all around Joshua's ankle and down to the top of his foot.

"Does it hurt when I press on it like this?"

"It's a little sore, but it doesn't hurt too bad."

"Bet ya wouldn't tell me if it did, would ya?"

"No, sir. I mean, yes. I guess so. It really doesn't hurt."

"Good! I'm glad you're gettin' along so well. Tell ya what. I think you're gonna be just fine. I still don't want ya runnin' around too much for the next few days. You'll pretty much know by how that ankle feels when it's okay to really get on it."

"Thanks, Doc Beeler."

"Maybe you better not thank me too quick, 'cause I'm gonna tell your daddy that on Monday you'll be ready to go back to work."

"That's all right with me."

At exactly 12:00, Franklin walked onto the porch, just as the doctor was ready to leave. Although he seldom carried a watch, Franklin could tell by the position of the sun when to drive his team back to the barn with just enough time for him to reach the house exactly at noon.

After receiving Doc Beeler's report of Joshua's improved condition, he thanked the doctor and entered the house to wash up and eat dinner. He spoke softly to Maggie and nodded to the others, who were gathered to eat. He was pleasant, but much less talkative that usual. He had been quiet and reserved since his return earlier in the week. He passed it off as "having lots of work to do to get the crops in on time."

His subdued demeanor was unsettling to all members of his family, but it was particularly worrisome to Joshua. He felt a sense of responsibility for his father's unusual behavior merely because he had been at the center of the odd events of the past few days. His father had not done, nor had he said, anything to indicate that he blamed Joshua. But it was Joshua's nature to worry if he saw any signs of worry on his father's face.

Franklin laid down his knife and fork.

"Bud, the doc tells me you're doin' real good. I'm really glad to hear it."

"Me too. I feel fine."

"Why don't ya come with me as soon as you're through eatin'? I could use some help this afternoon."

"You're not gonna make him plow, are you, Franklin?" interceded Maggie. "The doctor said …"

"Naw, I don't aim to hitch him up to the plow just yet—but me an' him got some talkin' to do. There's some things we can be doin' out in the barn while we're talkin'."

Joshua rose from his chair.

"I'm through eatin' now."

"Can I come too?" asked Matt. "I got some talkin' to do too!"

"You can come talk to me," Gerthy said. "If you go out yonder with them, who'll I have to talk to?"

Joshua hurried to get his shoes to join his father in the barn. He was glad to be getting out of the house, but most of all, he was relieved that his father no longer seemed angry, and he was anxious to know what his father wanted to talk about.

Franklin had driven the team into the cool shade of the barn's middle aisle. Still hitched to the plow, the mules stood in apparent contentment, shifting their weight from one back foot to the other and swatting flies with the coarse, heavy hair of their tails.

Franklin motioned for his son to follow him.

"Let's go into this stall, here. It's pretty clean, an' we can sit down on the feed trough."

As he went with his father into the narrow stall, Joshua remembered the times he and Matt had played there. They would crawl onto the back of whichever horse they found and "ride" it bronco-bustin' style, without a saddle or bridle, but only its mane to hold on to. He shuddered to think what his father would have said or done, had he known.

Franklin coughed and cleared his throat.

"There's a lot'a things I need to say. An' there's a lot I want to say just to you. But I don't know how good of a job I'm gonna do tryin' to say it."

Joshua looked up at his papa, but he remained silent.

"I already told you how thankful I am that we found you an' that you're gonna be okay. I'd never been able to forgive myself if somethin' really bad had happened to ya. When you told me about Lonnie findin' you an' I remembered how he said he didn't know where you were, I lost my temper. That's why I went off tryin' to find him. I couldn't abide somebody doin' somethin' like that to you."

Joshua nodded. "I'm glad Lonnie's gone!" he said.

"I know you are, son—an' I am too. I hope he never comes back here, an' I hope I don't ever see him again—ever! I doubt I'll ever forgive him for what he's done."

Franklin hesitated. He stood up, walked around in a circle, and then sat down again.

"But, see, that's one thing I wanted to tell ya. I know now that Lonnie never was good to ya. When Maggie an' me married, we brought him an' his sisters in on y'all, hopin' we'd all be one big ole happy family. I thought you an' Lonnie would get to be like real brothers—really carin' for one another an' all. But now I can see that didn't happen. Havin' to live with Lonnie wasn't good—'specially for you, an' I can see that now. But I want to say to ya is that I didn't know at the time that's how it would turn out to be. I didn't know Lonnie was gonna turn out to be so mean to ya. D'ya see what I'm tryin' to say?"

"Yes, sir. I think so."

"The other thing is this—I want ya to know why I came back before I caught up to Lonnie. I don't figure Maggie told ya about me goin' all the way to Memphis tryin' to get him."

"No, sir. She didn't tell me about it. I didn't know where you'd gone, but I was worried."

"I know, an' that's part of what I'm sorry about. But there's more to it than that."

"What d'ya mean—more to it?"

"Well, I was real close to where Lonnie was stayin'. He's workin' and livin' on a dredge boat in the Memphis harbor. I had driven through the night to get there, an' finally, I was right close to where he was. Then, all of a sudden, I recalled the last time I was down that way. It was when I had gone to Mississippi to look at some land."

Joshua trembled, and the little hairs on the back of his neck bristled. *Did Uncle Gerthy tell my papa about our conversation?* he wondered.

"I remembered drivin' along that same road goin' to Mississippi an' then again comin' back," Franklin continued. "I was drivin' right along that same road through Memphis, an' I didn't know your mama was so sick. Then, I remembered when I got home an' we lost her, how many times I wished I hadn't gone down there—an' most of all, I knew it was my fault that Hannah came down with the pneumonia." Franklin removed his glasses and looked away.

Joshua remembered how his uncle had defended Franklin. "You didn't know she was gonna get sick. You couldn't'a known."

"Well, just let me finish sayin' what I want to say. There I was, drivin' along, tryin' my best to find that no-good Lonnie so I could teach him a lesson for what he'd done—Lord knows what I'd'a done if I'd got to him. What I'm tryin' to explain is, when I recalled how I left y'all the first time, an' all that happened because of it, that's when it hit me. I was doin' the same thing all over again. It was like somebody took a two-by-four an' hit me right between the eyes with it."

Franklin rose to his feet again and wiped his eyes with his dirty bandana. He sat back down, this time on the ground facing Joshua, with his back leaning against the planks.

"That's when I stopped the car an' just sat there for awhile—an' then pretty soon, I turned around an' headed back as fast as I could."

Franklin dropped his head in silence.

"I'm real glad you came back, Papa. An' I—I didn't know you had those feelin's about bein' gone the other time."

"Well, I been doin' lots'a thinkin' since I got back. When I look at all'a you kids, an' Maggie, an' when I remember my time with Hannah, I figure I'm a rich man. An' I 'spect I need to be more thankful for what the Lord has given to me."

Franklin gently grasped Joshua's forearms. He stood, pulled Joshua to his feet, and then enfolded him in his arms.

He whispered as tears fell from his eyes.

"I want you to know how proud I am to have you as my son. Don't ever forget how much I love you."

"An' I'm proud you're my papa, too."

Joshua held on tight so that his father would not let him go too soon.

23

CHAPTER

JOSHUA SPRINTED OUT OF the schoolyard of Lodgeston Elementary at the close of the third school day of the fall term. It wasn't that he was anxious to leave the two-room schoolhouse—he liked being a sixth-grader under the tutelage of Vernon Starr. Mr. Starr was an excellent educator, his neighbor, and his friend. School was not a problem. It was just a good day for running.

In the summer months subsequent to his experience in Willingham Bottom, there had been many good days for running, and whistling, and singing. Even as he sweated behind the plow, he whistled. As he helped his father cultivate fields of sorghum, sweet potatoes, and corn, he sang. Without Lonnie around, he and Matt enjoyed evenings in the cabin, which now had become their refuge.

The trip from school to home covered a mile and a quarter of hilly dirt roads and two wooden bridges—one that spanned a creek and the other a slough. When he walked, the jaunt took about twenty minutes, but at a trot, he would make it in half that time.

With his burlap schoolbag swung over his shoulder, Joshua passed by the Starrs' house and sprinted down the hill to his home. He jumped a small ditch, raced across the front yard, and slowed to a walk as he turned up the dirt lane leading to the back of the house.

There he saw Doc Beeler's car, two buggies with their horses tied up in the shade, and a wagon with a team of horses that he did not recognize. Just off the back porch, Franklin and Maggie were talking to Doc Beeler and three other men who were strangers to Joshua.

"Hey!" he shouted. "What's goin' on?"

Immediately, Franklin and Doc Beeler left the group to greet him in somber tones and usher him over to a crude wooden bench in the shade of a large maple tree beside the house.

"What's the matter, Papa?"

"Sit down here with me, bud," his father said. "I have somethin' I gotta tell ya."

Doc Beeler stood beside the bench as Franklin and Joshua sat down.

"What is it, Papa? You're scarin' me."

"I don't aim to scare ya, son, but I gotta tell ya somethin' that I wish I didn't. It's your Uncle Gerthy. Your Uncle Gerthy has been havin' a problem, an'—an' last night, he passed away in his sleep. I wish I didn't have to tell you that."

"No! No, Papa! Please don't tell me that ..."

Joshua lowered his head into his hands and began to sob. His father pulled him close and patted his arm.

"What happened? I didn't even know he was sick—why didn't he say he was havin' problems? Why did he ...?"

Tears continued to stream down Joshua's face as he sat shaking his head.

At the sound of the other children, who had walked from school, Maggie hurried out to escort them away from the strangers and onto the front porch.

"I gotta go tell the other kids," said Franklin. "Doc Beeler will stay here with you, an' I'll be back in just a few minutes."

"Where's Uncle Gerthy now?" whispered Joshua. "An' I didn't even get to tell him goodbye. I still don't understand why ..."

Doc Beeler took Franklin's place on the bench beside Joshua.

"Your uncle's body is still inside—in his bed where Franklin found him. We had to wait for the man from the funeral home to come get him. They'll be takin' him shortly."

Joshua stood and wiped his face with his sleeve.

"What happened to him? What made him die?'

"Well, son, a couple'a months ago I came to see your uncle. He was short of breath an' feelin' tired all the time ..."

"Where was I?" interrupted Joshua. "Where was I when you came to see him?"

"I believe Maggie said you were helpin' your daddy with the plowin'. Gerthy didn't want any of you kids to know, 'cause he didn't want you to worry."

"How would feelin' tired cause him to die?"

"Well, the feelin' tired didn't cause him to pass away, but it was a sign that he had a problem with his heart. He was havin' heart failure, an' there wasn't anything we could do for him. We pretty well knew it was just a matter of time."

Joshua picked up a small stick and snapped it in two.

"I just wish he didn't hafta die. I wish you could'a done something to make him well, an'—an' I just wish I could'a told him goodbye."

Doc Beeler stood and placed his arm around his young friend's shoulder.

"I know, Joshua. I know. I wish I could'a done something too."

Franklin and Matt left the girls with Maggie to join Joshua and Doc Beeler.

"Come on with me, boys," said their father. "Let's us go to the cabin. I'll talk to you a little later Doc. Thanks for comin'."

After the boys were tucked away in the cabin with Franklin, Fred Rhodes, the undertaker from Fulton, and his two assistants loaded Gerthy's body onto their wagon and left to prepare it for burial.

Gerthy's funeral was held at the Mount of Olives Baptist Church in the morning on the third day following his death. There were no clouds to hide the azure sky, and a light breeze was a precursor to crisp, fall weather.

Most of the well-wishers arrived early to pay their respects prior to the service. The Jennings children stood quietly on the front lawn with Franklin and Maggie and other family members as they accepted condolences and words of comfort and friendship.

A few minutes before the service was to begin, a hearse drawn by a single black horse with gleaming gear turned off the road and into the graveyard. It stopped only a few paces from the front steps, in full view of Joshua and his siblings. It was the first hearse any of them had ever seen.

The hearse was made of wood, painted black and polished to a glistening sheen. The driver, a young man dressed in a black suit with a white shirt and a gray tie, sat on a padded bench behind the splashboard, which had a stylish curve at the top.

Behind the driver, the hearse looked like a wagon that had been fully enclosed with beveled glass windows on each side, a roof, and doors on the back to allow the casket to be placed in and removed. Rollers built into the floor of the enclosure facilitated entry and removal of the casket. The windows were adorned with gray velvet drapes. The wheels with polished black spokes were tall and thin.

At the appointed time, the church was jam-packed with family and church members and friends from throughout the county who had come to pay their respects to a man who was held in high esteem by all who knew him.

Joshua shifted in his seat on the family pew at the front of the small church. He was troubled to think that his uncle was closed up in the pine box atop a table in the front of the church.

He listened to the prayers, but he didn't hear the words. Thoughts of times spent in his uncle's room occupied his mind. He sang along with the hymns—"In the Garden," "In the Sweet By and By," and "Leaning on the Everlasting Arms," one of Gerthy's favorites—but they didn't sound the same without Gerthy leading the congregation as they sang.

The pastor's words were intended to comfort the grieving, and they were well-spoken. But Joshua was especially touched that his words turned the funeral service into a celebration of his uncle's life. *That's the way he would have wanted it to be,* he thought.

After the service and brief graveside remarks, food brought by church members and other friends was served on the church grounds. Mount of Olives Baptist Church was well known for their "dinner on the ground" events, and this was another sumptuous feast. It was another celebration that was carried out just as Gerthy would have wanted.

Back at home, Franklin motioned for Joshua to follow him down the narrow hallway to Gerthy's room. Joshua hesitated, unsure about entering the place where his uncle had died, but dutifully, he followed his father's silent command.

Franklin stepped over to the table beside Gerthy's bed and pointed to a fabric-covered box sitting beside the kerosene lamp.

"Here's something your uncle wanted you to have. He knew he wouldn't be around too much longer, so he got some things together and put 'em in this box. He asked me to give it to you after he was gone."

Joshua hesitated but then took off the lid and looked inside. Lying on top of a book was a piece of paper folded once in the middle. He opened it and read his uncle's note, obviously written with an unsteady hand. It said:

To Joshua, my nephew and my friend,
Here are two gifts I want you to have.
I hope they will bring you joy,
Just as you have been a joy to me.

Gerthy Jennings.

Joshua laid the paper down beside the box and saw that the book his uncle had given him was entitled *Selected Works of Henry Wadsworth Longfellow.*

Joshua shivered. He picked up the book to discover that a marker had been placed in it about two-thirds of the way to the end. He opened it to see the words from *Hyperion* that his uncle had underlined: "Look not mournfully into the past, it comes not back again. Wisely improve the present, it is thine. Go forth to meet the shadowy future without fear and with a manly heart."

Joshua's hand shook. He glanced up at his father; then he closed the book and laid it on top of Gerthy's note.

Still shaken, he reached into the box to take out the remaining article, another, smaller box. After he removed the lid, he stared wide-eyed at the contents and then gently pulled out Gerthy's gold pocket watch attached to a gold chain. He examined its white face with gold hands and gold Roman numerals to mark the hours. It was more handsome than the watches he had seen on display in Brinson's store.

"Look on the back," his father suggested.

Joshua flipped it over and read the engraved words:

Joshua Jennings
With a Manly Heart

Joshua stared at the inscription, unable to say a word. After examining it repeatedly, he returned it to its box and placed the small box, together with the book and the note, back in the box on Gerthy's table.

Again, he glanced up at his father.

"Do ya think it would be okay if I sat here in Uncle Gerthy's room for a while?"

Franklin turned and headed to the door.

"I think Gerthy would like to have you sit here for as long as you like. I think that'd be nice."

After about half an hour, Joshua got up from his uncle's rocking chair and left the room through the side entrance. He went to the red oak tree beside the fence close to Vernon Starr's field and sat down in the rope swing that hung from a large limb.

The air was cooler now, and the breeze had picked up. He swung gently, listening to the sound of the ropes rubbing on the limb above and the call of a Kentucky cardinal in another tree nearby.

In a few moments, Matt strolled across the backyard and joined his brother at the swing. He grabbed one of the ropes that held the swing and began to pull Joshua from side to side.

"Why did Uncle Gerthy hafta die?" he asked.

"I don't know for sure," Joshua answered. "I've been wonderin' that myself."

"An' why did Brother Davis say God has called him home? Why would he say that?"

Joshua shifted his weight on the wooden swing.

"I reckon that he meant that Uncle Gerthy has gone to be with God in heaven. Maybe heaven is like God's home, an' when Uncle Gerthy died, God asked him to come live with Him. I ..."

Matt frowned and kicked at the dirt.

"Yeah, I guess so, but I'm gonna miss Uncle Gerthy. I still don't know why he had to die."

"Maybe he's not really dead."

"Huh? What d'ya mean? They said he's dead—an' they put him in that box, an' they're gonna cover him with dirt!"

Joshua stopped swinging and looked directly at his brother.

"Yeah, I know. But what I mean is that he's still alive, just like Mother is."

"Our mother? Well, she's dead, too."

"Do you remember her?" asked Joshua.

"'Course I do."

"Do you remember how she looked, an' how she smelled, an' how she sounded when she talked an' sang?"

"Yep, I liked it when she sang."

"Well, if you remember her, she's alive in your mind."

"I guess so."

"Yeah, she is—an' in mine, too—an' in Jessie's, an' Papa's, an' lots'a people. She'll never die in my mind!"

"Mine neither!" agreed Matt.

"An' it's gonna be the same with Uncle Gerthy. He'll keep on livin' in our minds, too."

Matt turned and walked around the tree and started to leave. He paused and looked back at Joshua.

"Do ya want me to go get the girls an' play a game of pretty bird, or somethin'?"

"No," said Joshua. "Not now. You go ahead. I kind'a want to go to take these things Uncle Gerthy gave me to the cabin."

24
CHAPTER

IN JOSHUA'S MIND, ALL that was objectionable about the cabin had been removed when Lonnie left with his meager possessions. The musty odors of old bags of rotting seed and rusty hand tools and the stench of unseen rat droppings were still present, but Joshua paid them no mind. The cabin he had once abhorred was now his retreat.

The screen door squeaked as he entered and then clapped loudly against the jamb as he let it slam behind him. The room that had been Lonnie's was now a place to sleep and escape for Joshua and Matt. Moved down from the loft, their small beds now faced out from the back wall with room for only a crude table between. A small kerosene lamp sat on the table.

For the first time since his bed had been moved to the ground floor, Joshua felt the urge to climb the ladder to the loft. Skipping a rung with each step, he scaled the ladder quickly. The bed frame Lonnie had used had been taken apart and stored there. It leaned against the wall with the moldy old feather mattress draped over it. The smell of it made Joshua wish momentarily that he had stayed below, but he sat down on the floor, leaning against the lower railing of the banister, with his feet dangling over the edge. He shuddered as he recalled his dread of waking up to the sight of Lonnie sleeping below.

As he inched back to pull his feet up to stand, Joshua was startled by a rustling sound behind him. Feeling a sinister presence, he turned to look, but instantly, he was engulfed by a burly arm around his torso and a calloused hand over his mouth. He flailed his arms and twisted his body in an effort to escape, but he quickly relented, as his captor was bigger and much too strong to fight.

Joshua's attempts to yell and get his breath were stifled by the meaty paw that now covered both his mouth and nose.

"Don't try to scream. Don't even make a sound!" demanded the man.

The sound of his voice and the smell of his hot breath were unmistakable. It was Lonnie. *Lonnie has come back to torment me or even worse,* Joshua feared.

"I ain't gonna hurt ya as long as you don't yell," Lonnie said. "You gonna yell if I let ya go?" he asked.

Joshua shook his head, and then he uttered a muffled "Uh-uh."

Gradually, Lonnie released his grip over Joshua's mouth to test his truthfulness, but he maintained his hold around Joshua's chest.

"Why did you come back?" asked Joshua. "I thought you went to work on the river. Do you know what my papa will do if he finds you here?"

"Yeah, I reckon I do. That's why I didn't want you to yell for help." Lonnie loosened his grasp, allowing Joshua to turn to face him.

"Why are you here?" Joshua asked boldly.

"I came to say hello to my mama," insisted Lonnie. "An' matter'a fact, I wanted to talk to you. I didn't come to hurt you or nothin', if that's what you're worr'in' about."

"Why shouldn't I worry?" Joshua yelled. "You never cared anything about me before, so why should I trust you now? Besides, I can't hardly forget that you left me out in the swamp. Why'd ya do that anyway? Did ya really want me to die?"

"That's what I came to tell ya. I came to say I'm sorry for the way I treated ya, and mostly I'm sorry that I didn't tell yer daddy where you was. I was more mad at your daddy that at you."

"Well, why are you sayin' you're sorry now? Why do you think I'll believe you?"

"Lots'a stuff has happened to me since I went to work on the river," Lonnie replied. "I ain't the same as I used to be."

Lonnie told Joshua that when he first went to work, he didn't take it seriously. He was a constant source of discord, both with his superiors and his fellow deckhands. On the verge of being fired, he had slipped and fallen overboard and almost drowned. One of the men who had plucked him out of the capricious river currents and helped to resuscitate him was a man he called Mr. Willie.

Mr. Willie befriended him and became his mentor and father figure. As Lonnie related to Joshua, "Mr. Willie kept me from drownding, an' then he taught me 'bout livin'. So because of him, I just ain't the same as I used to be."

Joshua listened to Lonnie's story in disbelief. Lonnie was different. His angry mood had vanished. His menacing demeanor had diminished. And at times in the telling of his renewal, he almost seemed kind.

Joshua stood to stretch his legs. "I'm glad you came back," he said. "I always wanted us to get along. I just wish ..."

The screen door flew open with such force that it slammed against the cabin wall. Armed with his rifle, Franklin burst through the door and shouted, "Lonnie, I know you're in ..." Then, spotting Lonnie and Joshua standing in the loft, he raised his gun, took another step into the room, and yelled, "Son, get away from Lonnie! Get away from him now. This is between me an' him."

As Joshua refused to move away from Lonnie's side, Franklin drew a bead on Lonnie and moved closer. "Get away from him now!" he demanded.

Lonnie stood frozen without attempting to restrain Joshua.

"I told you to never come around here again," screamed Franklin. "I should'a never come home from Memphis when I had a chance to settle this. If I'd known you would come back here, I would'a shot you there."

Franklin motioned with the rifle barrel for Joshua to move away. Instead, Joshua stepped over in front of Lonnie and held up his hands toward his father. "Don't shoot him, Papa. Please put the gun down."

"Don't talk back to me, boy," he bellowed. "Don't ever talk back to me. You just do as I say."

Joshua didn't move.

"Papa, you don't understand," he said firmly. "Put the gun down an' let me explain. Lonnie's not here to hurt anybody. He—he just wants to say 'hey' to his mama."

Slowly, Franklin lowered his rifle and moved to the side to allow Joshua and Lonnie to come down the ladder. When Joshua was down and out of the way, Franklin again aimed at Lonnie as he descended.

"You make one wrong move, an' I'll shoot ya!" he exclaimed.

Lonnie turned to face Franklin with his hands raised in the air. "I don't want to do nothin' to nobody," he insisted. "I just came back to see my mama, an' to tell Joshua that I'm sorry for what I done. I was tryin' to sneak in an' sneak out again, 'cause I didn't want you to shoot me. Please, just let me see my mama. I have some things to tell 'er."

Franklin hesitated but then motioned with the rifle for Lonnie to go. "Okay," he conceded. "You can go on in an' talk to Maggie—but I still don't want you comin' around here."

Lonnie nodded and left the cabin to visit with his mother. Seated on his bed, Joshua related Lonnie's story to Franklin, who remained silent but attentive. When he was finished, Franklin shook his head, patted his son on the shoulder, and walked out.

Joshua lifted the box he had received from his uncle to his lap. Still amazed at the gifts left to him by his beloved uncle, heopened the box to re-examine its contents. First, he took out the watch and rubbed it against his shirt to restore its sheen. Turning it over, he reread the inscription:

Joshua Jennings
With a Manly Heart

Joshua lay down and stared up at the ceiling. His thoughts raced through a collage of images, first of times he had spent with his uncle and then shifting to remembrances of his mother. Her voice; her gentle touch; her laughter; her cooking; her patience, and her glee as she played games with her children—especially pretty bird. Her presence with him on his little island in Willingham Bottom, and his sense of her presence with him there in the cabin at that moment.

He reached back into the box and took out the book. Opening it at random, he saw a poem entitled "Footsteps of Angels." Scanning through the first few stanzas of this work by Longfellow, his eyes fixed on these words:

> With a slow and noiseless footstep
> Comes that messenger divine,
> Takes the vacant chair beside me,
> Lays her gentle hand in mine.

Then, sensing his mother's hand, he read the remaining stanzas:

> And she sits and gazes at me
> With those deep and tender eyes,
> Like the stars, so still and saint-like,
> Looking downward from the skies.

> Uttered not, yet comprehended,
> Is the spirit's voiceless prayer,
> Soft rebukes, in blessings ended,
> Breathing from her lips of air.

> Oh, though oft depressed and lonely,
> All my fears are laid aside,
> If I but remember only
> Such as these have lived and died!

Joshua closed the book and laid it on the table. He rested his head in his hands on his pillow, sighed deeply, closed his eyes, and smiled.

ACKNOWLEDGEMENTS

A PERSONAL THANK YOU IS extended to my wife, Susanne, and to other family members and friends who kindly read earlier versions of my manuscript. Your useful comments and support are greatly appreciated. A special thank you goes to Don White for his undying encouragement and reassurance throughout this project.

This book is dedicated in loving memory to my father, Papa Jeff, for sharing memories of his boyhood that inspired this novel.